THE DELAWARE VENTURE

THE DELAWARE VENTURE

a fiction novel

Richard Mark Ebert

iUniverse, Inc.
New York Lincoln Shanghai

THE DELAWARE VENTURE
a fiction novel

iUniverse books may be ordered through booksellers or by contacting:

iUniverse
2021 Pine Lake Road, Suite 100
Lincoln, NE 68512
www.iuniverse.com
1-800-Authors (1-800-288-4677)

This is a fiction novel with fictional characters. Any similarity between actual individuals and those fictional characters portrayed in *The Delaware Venture* are purely coincidental.

ISBN-13: 978-0-595-38462-4 (pbk)
ISBN-13: 978-0-595-67621-7 (cloth)
ISBN-13: 978-0-595-82843-2 (ebk)
ISBN-10: 0-595-38462-5 (pbk)
ISBN-10: 0-595-67621-9 (cloth)
ISBN-10: 0-595-82843-4 (ebk)

Printed in the United States of America

Acknowledgments

While writing this book, I had contacted the following individuals to ensure its technical accuracy. I cannot overemphasize the professionalism, expertise and hospitality that I had encountered. These experiences were some of the high points during my writing of *The Delaware Venture*.

I would like to thank Master Sergeant R. Darrel Lewis of the Dover Air Force Base Public Affairs Office and the men and women of the 436th Airlift Wing for their help with information on the C-5B Galaxy cargo plane.

I would also like to thank Mr. John Taylor, of Summit Aviation, for sharing his wealth of aviation experience and knowledge of the Douglas DC-3 aircraft.

Visit The Delaware Venture website at **www.thedelawareventure.com.**

CHAPTER 1

Caesar Rodney Rides Again

The Year: 1992
Dover, Delaware 19903

Douglas Oliver was an ambitious man who was articulate in speech, meticulous in dress and manipulative in wealth. Enslaved by his ego, he sought all but the important things and even those things he sought for the wrong reasons. Predictably, it was his ego that brought Oliver to Delaware's Old Statehouse on a chilly fall evening to confront his lifelong adversary.

A couple of state troopers were leading the two men through the corridors of the Old Statehouse when they came upon a cluster of inquisitive, note scribbling and bleached teeth members of the media.

With all of the tact and fervor of Captain Ahab, they began thrusting their questions as if harpooning a great white whale.

"Congressman, are you ready for the debate?" asked a woman sporting a press pass.

"How do you think you'll do, Congressman?" barked a man wielding a microphone.

Leaving no time for the congressman to reply to the questions already posed to him, yet another reporter inquired, "Do you have any surprises for the governor?"

Congressman Douglas Oliver spun around on his heels at the end of the hall and with a slight raise of an eyebrow responded, "All of your questions are about to be answered."

"Please be patient," interrupted Oliver's press aide, "the congressman will answer your questions after the debate."

With a hand clasped on Oliver's shoulder, Gil Hickman steered his candidate toward a door, "What did I tell you about that eyebrow?" reprimanded Hickman in a whisper.

Throughout Oliver's life he had an uncontrollable eyebrow raise. When Oliver spoke his eyebrow raise was much like a note being held in music. Then, the eyebrow would lower much as a receding tide leaves an inlet of water. This was one thing that Gil Hickman constantly harped on and by doing so he probably exacerbated Oliver's problem.

"Despite all of your political polish," Hickman pointed to the eyebrow, "that is one of the most annoying…" He didn't bother finishing the sentence. He simply shook his head in frustration, "Keep that thing under control."

"It's subconscious," countered Oliver raising his eyebrow once again. "I thought you said that I was ahead in the latest polls?" The congressman challenged.

"You're ahead by an eyelash and if you don't listen to me, tomorrow morning you'll be behind by an eyebrow."

Gathering his composure, Hickman touched on some final points, "Doug, remember the things that we had practiced, a pause to think your answer over is better than a stupid answer. Better yet, a non-answer is even better than an actual answer. Get through this debate and you'll be sitting in the governor's office come January."

The two men shook hands, "Good Luck congressman."

"Thank you Gil," Congressman Oliver gave his advisor a pat on the shoulder.

One of the State Troopers opened the door and after giving a thumbs-up, the congressman stepped through the opening, onto a riser at the front of the assembly area. His opponent simultaneously entered from a door on the other side of the riser.

The candidates were roughly the same height, about 5'9"; but the governor, while not heavy, appeared a bit stockier in physique.

A crowd of lawmakers, family members, and constituents filled the room. Amidst applause the congressman and the governor approached center stage shaking hands and then talking to each other under their breath, all the while smiling for the television cameras.

"Quite a handshake you've got there, Bob," the congressman said, surprised at the strength of the governor's grip." The governor, a farmer before entering politics, clasped the congressman's hand like a vice.

"It comes from a thing called manual labor Douglas. Something that you wouldn't be familiar with at that shell game you call a business."

"You leave my business to me and I'll leave the hair pieces to you," quipped Oliver. Subconsciously, the governor's hand moved to his head.

"All right gentlemen if you're through exchanging pleasantries," a man seated center stage interrupted, "please take your places behind the podiums."

The moderator looked directly into one of the television cameras, "Welcome to the Old Statehouse in Dover, Delaware, the site of the Gubernatorial Debates between the incumbent, Governor Robert Collins and his challenger, U.S. Congressman Douglas Denton Oliver.

"My name is Ron Mathews and I'll be moderating what will certainly be the premiere event of this election year. This race is unique because these two men have been fierce rivals ever since grade school. I should know, I was a classmate of both candidates during the little league tryouts, the spelling bees, the school plays, the science fairs, and the class elections. Now I'm moderating the second run at the governor's mansion for each of these men.

If you remember, four years ago in this same historic building, these very same candidates debated for the office that Governor Collins won as an outcome of that meeting. Will the governor maintain his grip on the helm of our nation's first state or will Congressman Oliver unseat the incumbent? Whatever the outcome, tonight we will be witnessing the Super Bowl of Delaware politics. I'll now explain the procedures for the debate. Are you ready gentlemen?"

"Ron, I can't speak for his worship the governor," Oliver's sarcasm sparked both laughter from his supporters and gasps from his adversaries, "but I say let the fireworks begin."

"Governor?" The moderator addressed the red-faced incumbent.

"Yes, of course...let's hear the rules for the benefit of the used snake oil salesman." The governor nodded toward Oliver. The remark was followed by a few snickers from the crowd.

"I object," responded Oliver, "it's obvious that the governor is trying, in his inept way, to belittle me and my business and I resent it."

"Gentlemen, let's get on with the debating rules," interjected the moderator once again.

"We don't need rules and we certainly don't need a moderator," the congressman looked sternly at Ron Mathews then looked questioningly at the incumbent.

"Agree, Governor?" asked Oliver tersely.

What to do, on one question the governor had become vulnerable. To agree with Oliver may show weakness and to disagree would make the governor appear to be childish and to hint at an uncooperative and inflexible spirit.

After a moments hesitation the governor responded, "I see that your handlers have done well in preparing you for this debate and I will agree to your premeditated forum under one condition...that I ask the first question of you."

"Why certainly, Governor," Oliver agreed with a smile. "You know, I wouldn't want you to forget your question before this debate got rolling."

"If the congressman is finished with his theatrics," Collins rebuked with a brusque wave of his hand, "then I'll proceed with the questioning."

"Why you make this sound like a court of law, Governor, but I'm prepared to answer your question at any rate."

"Very well, Congressman. Is it true that you cashed in on real estate located in the path of new road projects prior to selling it back to the state in a sweetheart deal?"

Anticipating the question, Oliver remained cool and in control, "Governor, I'm aware of previous accusations that you've made. Subsequently, I took time to have my secretary research this matter.

It turns out that the real estate transactions that you speak of were made through a subsidiary and without my prior knowledge. There is an interesting side note though. During my research, I had found that your interest in some of the properties, located at key upcoming road project intersections, was sparked by your fathers desire to find new sites for his chain of, *Blue Hen Provision Den,* convenience stores."

The governor was furious and motioned toward an attractive leggy brunette seated in the front row with Gil Hickman and Oliver's wife, "I don't know if your secretary compiled this fictitious garbage that you call research, but you should not only teach her what accurate research is; but you should also get her some typing lessons while you're at it."

The governor's alluding to Oliver's rumored affair, with his secretary, provoked both an eyebrow raise; and an uncharacteristic lame response from the congressman, "Well, Governor, perhaps you should get your chauffeur some driving lessons."

"Like I said, if you get that secretary educated, I'll get my niece driving lessons and that's a...," Before the governor could finish his counterattack on the congressman, he was abruptly interrupted, "Stop!"

Like a tremendous thunder clap focused at the candidates, a broad, sudden, and powerful command shattered the argument with all of the intensity of a bugle blast on a battlefield. It was a single word, but it was spoken with such power and authority, that it both demanded and received undivided and immediate respect.

Even more, with one collective flinch the crowd had ducked as if avoiding a projectile in combat. They sat obediently, having been startled into silence.

Then, after what seemed several seconds, the surreal and faceless baritone continued in a controlled tone, "You are representatives. Is this the way that your constituents act?" The voice paused until it was obvious that there would be no response.

Without revealing its form or location, the voice then asked, "Do your constituents attack one another by tearing each other down? If they do, then you should continue because then you would truly be representative of them and their actions."

Just as a tuning fork oscillates with each musical tone, the words resonated through the beams, rafters, ceiling and walls of the 18th century structure. The building even appeared to amplify the voice.

Even more remarkable, whether a phenomenon of acoustics; or not, the voice had no apparent source, it simply was and a person couldn't point and say, "There, there it's coming from that direction!" It seemed uniformly powerful throughout the building.

Incredibly, the oldest statehouse in the United States, *Delaware's Old Statehouse...circa 1791,* had taken on a voice and was giving a fatherly reprimand.

It seemed only fitting that the red brick statehouse sat on a square that had been designed by William Penn. Could the voice belong to the spirit of William Penn?

"All that I've heard is petty bickering," exclaimed the voice.

As the voice continued, the crowd scanned the auditorium to locate its origin.

"If I were the governor of Delaware, I'd try to set a good example for the rest of the country and what you two are doing isn't that."

There was a pause before the voice addressed the two candidates, "Will either of you develop Delaware into a model for the rest of the country? I think not. I believe that you'll look out for your own interests and the interests of your buddies, before you look out for the state's needs."

"You have no right to talk to us this way!" objected Congressman Oliver. Unable to pinpoint the origin of the voice, his eyes searched in strained frustration.

"Where are you?" shouted the governor. "Identify yourself!"

"Look around, I'm here in this hall. I build your homes…I wait on your tables in restaurants…I defend your country…I educate your children and even more, I pay your salaries. I am your constituency and I expect leadership coupled with civility and responsibility," the voice demanded.

In utter quiet, eyes slowly moved upward along the back wall of the hall, gradually leaving the safety of the dimly lit fixtures on the stage. Then, they ascended further to the dark shadows of the hall's upper gallery, where a wisp of moonlight suddenly beamed through a glass pane in the building's rooftop cupola.

Passing clouds filtered the moonlight which gradually revealed a shadowy figure. The silhouette appeared to be that of a tall being who was clutching a staff in its left hand; and the continued succession of clouds generated a kaleidoscope of light that refracted around its head much like a halo. It gave the specter both an angelic and powerful presence.

There was a collective gasp as the onlookers caught sight of the ghostly apparition and the faint sound of a woman reciting Hail Mary's while she palmed her rosary beads. As anxious spectators sat in awe and anticipation, chills moved along their spines; and hair tingled on the back of their necks.

It was one of those rare moments when a person feels alone, yet they're in a crowd. It was a moment when each individual had to rely on his, or her, own intelligence, experience, and imagination, to rationalize this vision that defied reasoning.

As the moon continued along its trajectory, its light shone brighter about the figure. Its rays seemed to emanate from the specter, rotating slowly as if they were the pulsating spokes of a wheel.

Then suddenly, as if the time of full disclosure had been preordained, the figure amongst the rafters came into full focus.

"It's a man!" gasped one of the onlookers in a trembling voice."
"Yes, it is a man," observed another in relief.

"A man holding a mop," confirmed a dumbfounded gentleman in the back of the auditorium.

Then, with the same enthusiasm that's reserved for shouting, "BINGO!" at a fire hall, a woman announced triumphantly, "It's the janitor!"

"Who did you think I was?" boomed the voice from high atop the gallery.

"Ron, get that man out of here!" the governor ordered in complete disgust. "He's disrupted this debate long enough."

"Governor, I've been stripped of my responsibilities, remember?" responded an amused Ron Mathews who didn't even attempt to restrain a chuckle.

"He's delirious! Escort him out of here before he wastes any more of our time," urged an impatient Congressman Oliver.

"No!" a dissenting shout cracked like a whip from the back of the crowd.

"Let him speak!" with some assistance from a Boy Scout, an elderly woman with silver hair stood up on her chair at the back of the hall.

"I know that I've always told you kids to never stand on furniture but sometimes you just have to press the outer envelope," the woman declared defiantly.

"Miss Higgins," the words trembled off of the governor's lips into a microphone, "I thought you were…"

"Well I'm not! It seems that the good lord has kept me around to keep you and Douglas in line. I've been sitting back here keeping my mouth shut but it's gotten so deep that I've had to stand up and give my say. You two gave me more problems in my classes than all of the other students combined.

Fortunately, those were the good ol' days, before the school shootings that you have today, when a teacher could still take a paddle to the likes of you two. That's exactly what I'd like to do to you now, take a paddle to you."

The sight of the able educator had dredged up some painful memories for Congressman Oliver and Governor Collins.

During Douglas and Robert's youth, a strange educational anomaly had both Miss Higgins' career and the boys' education simultaneously advance from grade to grade. Yes, from their ABC's, to dissecting frogs, to drivers education Douglas and Robert had seen Miss Higgins school-day-in and school-day-out for twelve consecutive and excruciating years.

Decades earlier, the experience had so adversely affected these two high school seniors, that before committing to a college they had each inquired as to whether Miss Higgins was to be a new addition to its faculty. To their mutual relief, she wasn't.

The aging school teacher steadied her balance by clutching the Boy Scouts shoulder, "Nowadays, the schools reward you ornery devils with a day off when you get into mischief and you grow up to be a couple of buffoons like you two have become. It's apparent that neither notoriety, nor wealth, has provided either of you with character.

Miss Higgins gestured to the gallery, "With one simple word, *Stop,* this janitor made more sense than both of your sheepskins put together." Now why don't you both park it while the man finishes his say?"

Now a bystander, Ron Mathews sat quietly observing the reaction of the crowd. With very few exceptions, the murmurs and reactions were supportive of Miss Higgins and her urging the janitor to continue. Resigned to Miss Higgins and the public's will, the two gubernatorial candidates sat obediently.

"The floor is yours Mr...what is your name?" Miss Higgins directed her comment to the mezzanine where someone had since turned the upper gallery lights on.

"Bontrager...Karl Bontrager," he removed a pipe from the shirt pocket of his work uniform as he approached the mezzanine's railing and the crowd finally had its first good look at the man. They could see that he was a trim, tall man whose full head of graying hair placed him in his late fifties. Even in his work clothes, Bontrager's presence and clean-shaven appearance seemed to encompass the character, demeanor and integrity of a Thomas Jefferson.

As murmurs flowed amongst the crowd below, Karl patted some *Half-and-Half* tobacco into the pipe's bowl and lit it. He then scanned the gathering as he periodically puffed on the pipe.

"Thank you Miss," he nodded toward the aging school teacher. "I'm not a doctor, lawyer, or politician and I didn't attend an Ivy League school, or any other university, for that matter. I'm a janitor, a janitor that cracks a book occasionally.

As far as my ideas go, they aren't very fancy, but then they don't involve special interests, or political parties, or hidden agendas either. Instead, my ideas are based upon things like common decency and common sense.

I know that these may be foreign concepts in the present political climate because they don't rely upon expensive studies or polls to steer them in one direction or another.

So I ask you, whatever happened to common civility? With all of the issues facing the people of this state, we have to get past petty arguments."

The crowd sat entranced with words that seemingly flowed throughout the Old Statehouse. Each word was spoken with an ingrained, unchallengable authority that left the constituents, politicians, media and other onlookers paralyzed with attentiveness.

For Karl to have said that he occasionally cracked a book was ironic, because from an early age, he had been an avid reader. Karl's father, Hank Bontrager, grew up working on his family's farm outside of Georgetown, Delaware and Hank always looked forward to going to the local farmer's market. Beyond selling his father's produce and crops, it was a chance for young Hank to talk of current events and socialize. In 1925, during one of the trips to the farmer's market, Hank struck up a conversation with an immigrant girl who worked at a produce stand. Her name was Catherine and her family had left Germany, a country in turmoil in the aftermath of World War I.

During subsequent visits to the farmer's market, Hank familiarized Catherine with his knowledge of America; while Catherine described Europe to Hank. The contrast in the two regions seemed great, Hank's limited experience in America consisting of a flat, narrow Delaware that was a mere 96 miles in length; while Catherine's description of Europe consisted of the expanse of the Swiss Alps, the wonder of Paris' Eiffel Tower, and the ancient ruins of Rome.

In time, the farmer's son and the immigrant girl spoke of traveling the world someday. In 1927 they were married. Hank, accompanied by his new bride, continued working for a future stake in the family farm. It was demanding work for the couple, but it was accompanied by *Bontrager optimism* and a light-hearted family atmosphere; a characteristic greatly lost amidst Catherine's war weary family.

Then in 1929 the couple's secure life, and dreams of travel and adventure, were suddenly undermined by the crash on Wall Street and the Great Depression. As an outcome, the Bontrager farm was lost. Compared to others, who had no steady income, Hank and Catherine were fortunate. They still had each other and despite the financial devastation that had seized the world; their positive outlook remained in tact. The friendships that they had accumulated during the prosperous times had ensured them at least a meager income during the depression and they continued to work in agriculture; not so much for their future, but for their existence.

Although they no longer had the financial means to pursue their dream of travel, they frequented the local library in Georgetown. Through reading, they found some relief from the greatest economic crisis in American history.

Books, taking the place of railroad cars and ships, transported the Bontrager's to any destination or period in history that they desired; and in the process it helped to keep their spirits elevated during those extremely lean times.

By the time Karl came along, in 1932, the Bontrager outings to the library were an entrenched family ritual. Although Catherine lacked any advanced education, she was a natural educator and barely waited for Karl to get out of diapers before she started reading to him. As a pre-schooler Karl was very inquisitive and he wanted to know where he, his parents and just about anyone else had come from. So his mother would not only tell him about his own family history, but she would read to him about noteworthy history making people and events, as well. A book that Karl repeatedly asked his mother to read was about a Delaware patriot by the name of Caesar Rodney, a Revolutionary War hero and signer of the Declaration of Independence.

The literary seeds that the Bontragers had planted in Karl's young soul continued to take him on incredible journeys. For Karl, stepping through the library door was like stepping through an incredible access to the world.

Like many people trying to get by during the depression, Hank Bontrager had to be creative. He tried to use the few opportunities that he had to give Karl new experiences and to spark his son's imagination. So early one summer day, when he had to drive a truckload of corn to upstate Delaware; he asked his boss, Mr. Helm, whether he could take Karl along for the experience. For some people the Depression brought out the worst, but Mr. Helm's Christian upbringing gave him a genuine compassion for people regardless of the circumstances. He not only told Hank to take Karl along on the seventy mile trip north, but he also instructed him to take the boy on a side trip on the way back home.

Karl was seven-years-old at the time and it was his first time traveling more than thirty miles from his parents home in southern Delaware. As his father drove northward on the Dupont Highway they passed through the towns of Dover and Smyrna. Karl noticed that the further north that they went the more populated it seemed to get. As they neared the end of their journey there seemed to be more cars, people, and buildings than Karl had ever seen.

Then, a cluster of steel-reinforced buildings rose suddenly into view. They were nearing Wilmington. With its population of around 80,000, it was the largest city in Delaware. It wasn't New York or Chicago, but through a child's eyes it might as well have been. That day with his father was one of the single most impressionable days of Karl's childhood. He saw a mass of people like he had never seen before and large oceangoing ships sailing up the Delaware River that he never knew existed. After offloading his cargo of corn at a market in downtown Wilmington, Hank led his son to Rodney Square; a large open area adjacent to the impressive façade of the Hotel du Pont.

That's when Karl's eyes lit up and a gasp of elation exited his lungs. At one end of the square stood an immense statue of an impressive looking man upon a galloping horse. The man was in Revolutionary War attire and topped by a tri-cornered hat. Without a word, Karl moved instinctively toward the massive base of the statue and read an inscription.

With a smile of wonderment upon his face he turned to his father, "It's Caesar Rodney, from the book mom use to read to me."

Hank nodded a silent affirmation and let his son stand in reverence to Delaware's Revolutionary War hero and signer of the Declaration of Independence. It was a moment that would never leave Karl or his father.

On the way home Hank complied with Mr. Helm's wishes and referred to some directions that his boss had scribbled on a sheet of paper. To Karl's surprise, just a few miles south of Wilmington Hank steered the truck from the Dupont Highway onto an easterly side road. They traveled a very short distance when they came upon several buildings and aircraft hangars, and a sign that read Bellanca Field; it was the home of the Bellanca Aircraft Corporation. It was a significant company in aviation history because, at this very location, Bellanca had built the first aircraft to fly nonstop across the Pacific Ocean.

It was 1939 and aviation was still looked upon by the public with curiosity. Amazed, Karl scanned the variety of bi-planes and single-wing monoplanes that were parked around the airfield.

While he waited in the truck his father entered a hangar with Mr. Helm's note in hand. A few minutes later Karl's father returned to the truck with a friendly gentleman from the Bellanca Aircraft Corporation. The man spent part of the afternoon taking the two on a tour of the factory.

He introduced them to designers which drew up plans or modifications for different aircraft; then he took them to the manufacturing facility itself. There were plenty of men working on the aircraft, from assembling wing sections to installing instruments and controls. At times, Karl became distracted by the sound of aircraft being tested or moving outside of the hangar.

Their last stop was at an airplane called the Pathfinder; it was one of the monoplane designs. It was the first time Karl had seen an airplane up close and he was extremely excited by the experience. While Karl and his father watched from the safety of the field, a pilot got in the plane and took off for a test flight.

The exhilaration that Karl had felt at the airfield on that August day was the beginning of his interest in aviation. Then, one month later, Hitler's invasion of Poland began to fuel Karl's interest in history.

As Europe was experiencing the prelude to a second world war, the Bontragers listened to the horrifying news on their bulky RCA Victor radio. Karl supplemented the broadcasts by reading the newspaper and learned of terrifying events such as Germany's air war against the British.

He knew that despite Hitler's firebombing of Great Britain, many Americans wanted to stay out of the conflict. Then, when Japan bombed Pearl Harbor, Karl realized what a grave mistake it had been for the United States to respond to Germany and Japan's aggression with words, rather than actions.

The four years during the war saw a maturity and formulation of Karl's outlook on the world. While the wartime situation was intense, Karl's *Bontrager optimism* told him that the allies would triumph and sure enough, they did. He was thirteen when Japan finally surrendered and he sometimes wondered how many millions of lives could have been saved had the United States acted at the outset of Germany's hostilities.

Ready to set out on his own, the love that Karl had acquired for aviation at Bellanca Field had stayed with him. As a young man it led him into the newly established U.S. Air Force. As a flight engineer on cargo aircraft, Karl traveled throughout the United States and around the world; it afforded him an opportunity to visit many of the people and places that he had read about.

His happiest experience in the military was when he and his new wife, Elizabeth, surprised his hardworking parents with Eurail Passes; so they could finally experience the adventure of traveling throughout Europe by train. They not only hit the major tourist attractions of Europe; Paris, Salzburg, Vienna, Rome, and Munich, but visited his mother's scenic hometown of Pirmasens, Germany, along the French border.

Once retired from the Air Force, Karl had time to reflect. Through all of his reading, travels and experiences Karl realized just how unique the little state of Delaware was; concluding that few places in the world had so much to offer in such a small area. He believed that Delaware's rural and metropolitan areas, along with its history, innovation, and citizens from around the globe, made it a microcosm of the United States.

Karl always had that *Bontrager optimism*, but when his wife passed away in 1986, she had left him with something else for his arsenal; a legacy of faith that helped him put life into proper perspective. It gave him something that was unique in a modern world of excess; a genuine contentment that did not require certificates of accomplishment, nor perks of notoriety, nor the approval of others. Later, when his orphaned granddaughter had decided to attend the university, in Newark; Karl didn't think twice about taking a janitorial position at the Old Statehouse to help with the tuition costs.

Now, Karl stood at ease, as a common man overlooking the gathering at the Old Statehouse. Seemingly, his path of practical experiences, travel and *Bontrager optimism*, had groomed him just as effectively to address the citizens of Delaware; as did that alternative path taken by the governor and congressman.

"For over two hundred years, this country has survived wars, depression and tragedy. Its strengths have carried it through its weaknesses. As both Delawareans and Americans we have to remember that. Our sitting down like human beings for a few hours and working productively through the issues will not destroy our opinions or our right to express them.

Furthermore, in a world where there's an attitude that proclaims, *it's all about me*, there is something to be said for putting the country ahead of ourselves.

It was President Kennedy who once said, *'Ask not what your country can do for you, ask what you can do for your country,'* but now we often have just the opposite attitude of, *Ask not what you can do for your country, but what your country can do for you.*

It seems like everyone from the Wall Street Broker to the Statehouse Janitor has his or her hand out instead of pitching in a hand.

From their reaction, Karl had struck a positive cord throughout the crowd who began applauding as Karl went from topic to topic.

"Throughout Delaware's history it has been an innovative state that has been responsible for technological advancements. Think about it, it's 1992, the cold War is pretty much over and we're at a crossroads in history. We have an opportunity to be innovative with problems that were put on the backburner during the Cold War. Wouldn't it be a waste not to utilize Delaware's innovative spirit to tackle some of these problems?

While large scale pork barrel budgets are the norm in Washington, Delaware's small size is an advantage that could be used to identify, target and attack obstacles innovatively; in more effective and efficient ways."

Many in the crowd nodded and whispered approvingly.

"As Delawareans we're in a unique position, our state is small in size. On a football field, small often translates into a faster reaction time and the ability to adjust quickly to changing situations. Our small size means that we can try things that the larger wasteful states don't have the flexibility, or courage to attempt. Then, if the solutions work here in Delaware; they may work in other states.

These are the same states that wouldn't give Delaware the time of day. States that don't know of or ignore our very existence, and states that have never recognized the important role that Delaware has played throughout our nation's history.

Tell me, how many people outside of Delaware know that Caesar Rodney rode frantically for eighty miles on horseback to Philadelphia; casting the vote that made Delaware the first state to sign the Declaration of Independence?"

Karl raised his right hand in the air, "If Delaware is the state that started a nation; Caesar Rodney is the man that represented the state that started a nation.

It seems unfair that Caesar Rodney is a mere footnote in American history, while Paul Revere gets all of the notoriety and fame just because he had better *spin doctors*. To add insult to injury Paul Revere has a ship named after him, the U.S.S. Paul Revere. I ask you, where is our U.S.S. Caesar Rodney?"

Karl Bontrager was on a roll and he puffed on his pipe as he waited for the applause to die down before continuing his oratory.

"How many Americans outside of Delaware know that all of the astronauts that walked on the moon wore space suits made at the Latex Plant in Frederica? And how many realize that massive cargo planes from Dover Air Force Base, located right here in Delaware, airlifted over 25 percent of the cargo for the Persian Gulf War. Before that, these same cargo planes flew humanitarian assistance to places ranging from Alaska to Armenia. If that wasn't enough, in this morning's paper it stated that Dover Air Force Base is presently flying missions of mercy to our former adversaries in the Soviet Republics.

Are our fellow Americans aware that Wilmington, Delaware is one of the major banking centers in the United States, or that the DuPont Company…the largest chemical company in the world was founded and is headquartered in Delaware?

If the country as a whole doesn't know these things, then they probably don't know where our Washington lawmakers and their workforce vacation during the summer. The answer is Delaware. In fact, so many Washingtonians' vacation here that it's earned our oceanfront resorts the nickname, *the Nation's Summer Capitol.*

Yes, while California school children believe that Delaware is an amusement park in eastern Pennsylvania, with a big roller coaster called the Brandywined; we continue to make our silent but substantial contribution to the United States and the world."

The crowd was riveted to Karl's every word. He was a Delawarean speaking to the hearts of his fellow Delawareans and he was saying things that they had long yearned to hear. During a period of heavy applause, Karl paused for a moment to enjoy a glass of water that someone had brought to the balcony for him.

"So you're probably wondering what is it going to take Karl; what is it going to take to get the recognition that our state deserves?"

Many onlookers were eager to hear Karl's answer.

"It will take courage," Karl insisted, "to set out and do these things."

Yes, to gain Delaware's long overdue notoriety we may have to go as far as tackling some problems facing both our state and the world. With the exception of those dictators and groups that are bent on destroying our world, the people are looking for solutions; someone to show them the way and that someone can be us, if we so desire.

We can even show them the ways of educating our children so that they will become productive in society. I believe kids often go to class in their school, do their work and have no clue as to its connection with the real world.

Got some kids that don't like math or science? Then find something that they're interested in and show them the connection, how it applies in that area.

Maybe they're interested in aviation. Instead of just showing them a math book, take them to an airport and show them some practical applications for math and science as it pertains to actual aircraft. Have them calculate lift, or show them first hand how to use geometry to determine an aircraft's course, for instance. I believe that if more kids were shown the practical purpose behind the subjects that they take, rather than just giving them a series of homework problems, they would become self motivated."

From the gallery, Karl scanned the crowd of eager listeners who applauded his various ideas and points.

"Now, despite the good intentions that many of them may have, these changes will not come through legislation passed by politicians. These changes and the possibilities that they may bring will only occur as a result of our changed attitudes and priorities."

Karl held up the glass of water, "This is just the sort of thing that I'm talking about. A CIA study recently concluded that, in the near future, the scarcity of water in some areas of the world will spark wars. At the same time, some of you are complaining about not having enough jobs in *the First State*.

As we all seek gainful employment to take care of our families, I believe that this advancing water shortage problem is just one, of many, opportunities.

The problem is that we don't see it that way.

If we could efficiently developing solutions to problems that confront us here in Delaware, on a small scale; then we may be able to help our neighbors around the world, deal with the challenges that we all face.

Using new technologies we could work to develop innovative ways of increasing new business opportunities while still respecting the environment. What would happen if we could come up with a vastly more efficient and cost effective means to desalinate sea water?

Such innovations could supply a real human need, possibly lesson the likelihood of wars, and could result in state-of-the-art industries that could generate more jobs for Delaware.

Yes, though we are small we can make a difference. We can research, we can test and we can become a good example for other states, and yes, we may even be able to make a difference elsewhere in the world. It would be a great experience to know that our lives had made a difference not just for our wallets, but for mankind, too. Thank you and on your way home please consider what I've said."

From his lofty perch, Karl toasted the crowd with the glass of water.

Still clutching his mop like a staff, the janitor looked down upon the elated crowd which stood to their feet and chanted, "Karl! Karl! Karl! Karl!"

In disbelief Karl thought to himself, "Huh, reading that '*Power through Public Speaking*' book really worked!"

CHAPTER 2

The Battle of Woodcrest Drive

Dover, Delaware 19904

"When I was your age I believe that the month of October was colder than it is nowadays," Karl adjusted his sweater. "I wonder if it's those Chlorofluorocarbons in the ozone layer," Karl directed his observation at a brown haired little girl as he walked down Walker Road on his way to work. Amanda lived next door to Karl and waited for him each morning in front of his house.

"Whatsa ozone?" asked Amanda, lugging a plaid book pouch which made a continuous noise as it was dragged along the sidewalk.

"It's part of the upper atmosphere. Do you know what the atmosphere is?"

Amanda shook her head no.

"The atmosphere is what we breath...the air, it's all around us. Understand?"

"I think so."

"The atmosphere is necessary for plants, animals and people to live on the earth," Karl pointed to the row of maple trees along the sidewalk.

"I think Mrs. Miles told us about this in school," Amanda interjected. She stumbled with her pronunciation, "We made a te...mar...a...rum with frogs and weeds. Ben held one of the frogs in his hands and it didn't wake up. I guess it didn't get enough of that ozone stuff."

"That's it...you understand Amanda," Karl said with a smile. They stopped at the intersection on Pear Street to let some cars pass by. Once across the street Amanda looked at Karl several times out of the corner of her eye without saying a word. Eventually, Karl became curious and asked, "What is it Amanda? Why are you looking at me funny?"

Amanda hesitated, "I can't tell you."

"What do you mean you can't tell me? What is it? If you have something on your mind, tell me," insisted Karl.

"Mom said I shouldn't say anything."

This got Karl's curiosity up, "Say anything about what?"

"I can't tell you unless you promise not to tell my mother that I said anything."

This really got Karl thinking, *What in the world?* "I promise, now what are you talking about?"

"No! Promise on this," she held out her little mermaid lunch box. Karl felt silly putting his left hand on top of what appeared to be a lobster caricature but went along with it any way.

"Now what's your mother talking about?"

"Why do you hate the governor?"

"Hate the governor, what are you talking about? I don't hate the governor."

"Mom said that you were on TV last night and that you got mad at the governor."

"Oh that," Karl had written off the previous night's event as the innocent act of a private citizen voicing his opinion; he hadn't realized that the cameras continued to roll throughout his lecture.

"Amanda, I don't hate the governor. I merely had a disagreement with him and the congressman."

"Mom said that you looked like you were disappointed in him, like when I get a tuna fish sandwich for lunch."

"No, no, she's mistaken the entire thing. Politics does funny things to people and when the governor and Congressman Oliver get around each other they start throwing wild accusations around. Those two are pretty competitive to begin with, ever since grade school, apparently."

Karl looked down at the confused little girl. No, you tell your mother that I just reacted out of frustration over their squabbling and that I think that they could accomplish a lot more if they'd stop this constant bickering."

"What's squabbling?" asked Amanda, not understanding much of what Karl rambled on about.

"Never mind, there's your school," Karl pointed across the street. "You can ask your teacher what squabbling is."

Karl had a sinking feeling as he made sure that Amanda made it across the street safely. He then stopped at the corner of State Street and looked out over Silver Lake. A large flock of Canadian Geese squawked as they flew closer. The magnificent birds systematically changed leaders of the V-formation that they were flying in. He waited for them to pass overhead. *Probably just came from Bombay Hook,* he thought. The geese stopped at the wildlife refuge outside of Smyrna each year as they migrated south for the winter. An avid hunter, Karl always enjoyed the sight of animals in the wild.

He looked at his watch, *7:30…better be on my way.* He walked down tree lined State Street passing the cemetery overlooking the lake, the large Victorian homes with American flags hanging from their porch posts, the broad brick buildings that comprised the campus of Wesley College and people jogging, or walking their dogs, much of it seemingly suitable for a Norman Rockwell rendering. Then, he crossed Loockerman Street and continued down State Street; it was cobblestone and it led to Dover's historic area.

On either side of the street were law offices. Many had wooden shingles that hung out front with a short list of names; each followed by the letters, esq.

Beyond the law offices, the street broke into a large circular green that was encircled by multi-storied brick buildings of colonial architecture. They were the older state buildings and some of them dated back to the 1700's and the very birth of the nation. Karl took a leftward track around the green's perimeter toward the Old Statehouse.

He hesitated on the steps of the Statehouse while he checked his watch. It was 7:45. *Enough time to get a cup of coffee,* he concluded. Passing through the front doors, he greeted Heather, the receptionist, "Good morning."

Karl thought it was uncharacteristic for Heather to respond with a sheepish smile; then duck into a document room where some secretaries had gathered.

Before Karl could think much about it, a short, round and gruff man in a suit, stuck his graying head out of an office at the far end of the hall, "Karl, is that you?"

"Yes Lou, it's me," Karl said reluctantly.

Lou may have been Karl's supervisor, but he never made Karl's Christmas card list. You see, Lou had a proclivity for backstabbing, favoritism, brownnosing and string pulling. In addition, he was quite a hobnobber.

Unfortunately, these attempts by Lou at ladder climbing usually came at the expense, as well as upon the backs, of Karl and his fellow janitors. The janitors couldn't help but think of Lou as a custodial dictator. In fact, Lou's nickname around the Old Statehouse was Loussolini, taken from the late and ruthless Italian Dictator, Mussolini.

"I need to talk to you!" the man coughed the words between drags on a cigarette.

That guy should take a long walk on a short pier, Karl thought, as he helped himself at the coffee mess. *Let me see I'll have one cream.*

"Karl!" the custodial dictator demanded.

That sugar sure looks good but maybe I should use some of that artificial sweetener instead. He poured a packet into his coffee. *Now, where are those little wooden stirrers?*

"I want to talk to you," once again Lou appeared to be irritated by something. "Where are you?"

Karl opened the cabinet doors and found an open pack of stirrers. "Lou were you calling me?" Karl stepped into Lou's office leaving the door open behind him. The little tyrant was red-faced and his blood vessels bulged from his forehead.

"You've ruined everything, everything I've worked for!" it was typical for Lou to take all of the credit for the hard work that the janitorial staff did. At the same time, nothing was ever done well enough or fast enough to suit him. He was a tyrant that was long on complaints and when it came to praise it was non-existent.

"Political pressure," Lou stated succinctly, "you're fired."

Karl was taken aback, "Fired, what for?"

"You know what for! That three ring circus you pulled last night on television."

Karl knew that arguing with Lou was useless and he couldn't see continuing the conversation, "Don't bother, I've got a pension from the Air Force, I quit!" Karl had been tempted to leave his job on many occasions before, but held on to put his granddaughter through college.

Just then, the sound of the telephone interrupted Lou's tirade. He picked up the phone and listened for a minute.

"I don't care, you've got to come in Ernest…Karl just quit and I promised Senator Fedders that I'd have his office in top shape for when he meets that Japanese delegation today."

"You'll find the mop and dust rags next to the deep sink, Lou, and don't forget to change the water frequently," Karl stated cavalierly, finding a bit of humor in the moment.

When the shouting reached its crescendo, Karl took a sip of his coffee, grinned at the new custodian and walked out of the office whistling the theme to the John Wayne flying film, *The High and the Mighty.*

In addition, from the sound of chattering secretaries, he determined that they had gotten their earful of gossip for the week.

On the way out Karl stopped in the foyer of the Old Statehouse and looked to the spot from which he had addressed the crowd the night before. It seemed like a dream. He had given a variety of speeches at his weekly Toastmasters meetings, but that was always done among a small group of encouraging friends. This was different, it was in front of the entire state of Delaware and it had been an event in his life that he would never forget.

As a janitor he was often taken for granted and rarely appreciated; seemingly, his opinion didn't count. He didn't have the credentials, the influence or the three piece suits. On the other hand, he did have a senior citizen discount, memories of his late wife and his pension from the Air Force.

On the night of the gubernatorial debates, the suits, the influence, the arrogance and the sheepskins gave way to a janitor named Karl Bontrager and his wonderful vision of what Delaware could be.

Karl hadn't been gone but five minutes when Heather was suddenly barraged by one call after another.

Ring…Ring…Ring!
"Hello, this is the Old Statehouse may I help you? I'm sorry, but Mr. Bontrager has been terminated…yes I'm sure…I heard it myself."

Ring…Ring!
"Hello…he's no longer a state employee. Yes, I have your number and if I hear from him I'll have him call your newspaper."

Ring…Ring!
"Public Broadcasting? Oh yes, I'll pass the word onto Mr. Bontrager, should I see him."

Ring!
"Sherry, its Willard Scott, he wants Karl to appear on Good Morning America. What should I tell him?"

"What's going on out there Heather?" asked a secretary who had heard the heightened phone activity from her office.

"It's Karl," Heather blurted intently as she cupped her hand over the phone, "everyone wants to know about Karl Bontrager, newspapers, radio, television…they all want to talk to him."

Ring…Ring!

"Now answer that phone for me," Heather pointed across her desk.

Ring…Ring…Ring!

"Mr. Letterman, I have no idea whether he has a dog or whether it does any stupid pet tricks."

Ring…Ring!

"Yes, Senator Fedders…you need a coffee spill cleaned up, I'll call Lou immediately."

Karl was completely unaware of the inquiries being made to the Old State-house and the walk back to Woodcrest Drive was a chance for him to reflect on the events of the last several hours.

He had succeeded in bringing the wrath of the politicians and his boss upon himself by exercising the *First Amendment.* Was he right? Did he have a good point, or was he just an aging eccentric who was spouting out a four-course serving of pipe dreams to an eager audience? Was it only acceptable for politicians to give their vision of the role of government, or was it also the job of their constituency to contribute and even challenge those elected. Karl believed that the constitution demanded the latter but that didn't ease the pain of losing his job any.

"Karl! Karl Bontrager! Over here."

Karl was awakened from his daydream. Walking across the Dover Green toward him was a man holding a newspaper. It was Warren Brookes, a native Delawarean, retired postal employee; a fellow coffee drinker and frequenter of the Blue Hen Diner.

"Have you seen this?" Warren held up the daily newspaper:

The Goobernatorial Debates…Janitor Sweeps Crowd off Feet while Candidates End Up in Dumpster

Once an awestruck Karl had finished the headline, Warren opened the newspaper to the editorial section:

Ghost of Caesar Rodney Rides off with Debate

Janitor Urges Delaware to Solve Problems

"You're a hero Karl," Warren said enthusiastically.

"One man's hero is another man's fool," Karl shot back. "I've quit my job."

"Why did you do that?" asked Warren.

"I've never been fired during 45 years of work and I wasn't going to let them change that, so I quit."

Warren became animated, "Don't tell me…those pompous bloodsucking leeches. They ought to throw all of 'em out of office, every last one!…What's the saying? Power corrupts and that's what our system has become, a corrupted system."

"That may be the case in some instances, but I believe that it's the exception to the rule," responded Karl.

"Yes, there's some corruption…always has been and always will be, but our system has stood the test of time…at least until now. Tell me, could the Soviets have said that? Sir Winston Churchill said that Democracy is the worst form of government with the exception of all others and I believe it," Karl said with a half grin. "Last night, maybe I went too far Warren…but it sure felt good."

"Too far…that's cow manure," Warren pointed to the headlines to drive his point home. "I saw the whole thing on TV, if anything you didn't go far enough. You were right on the money. Delaware has been taken for granted.

Last night you spoke of some of the things that Delaware has done for national defense, the moon landing, chemical research and business law.

These were giant contributions; when you consider our relatively small size and population.

I don't think it can be matched. Not by California, not by Texas and not by New York. Nope, you did good Karl and don't let anyone tell you any different. Not the politicians, not the media, not the so-called experts, and certainly not the Monday Morning Quarterbacks. You did what is foreign to them; you spoke from the heart, with sincerity."

"Thanks Warren. Well, I'll be getting home."

The two men shook hands and Karl continued on his way home cutting across the Green toward Loockerman Street. As Karl waited to cross the intersection at the corner of Loockerman and State Streets he noticed some people standing on the opposite corner pointing his way and giggling. The light changed and they began walking toward each other. Karl overheard part of their conversation as they approached him at mid-intersection.

"It's him. I recognize him from television," said one lady. "He's a nut," said another, "a loon."

It was unexpected, pointed, and it struck at his very soul; Karl felt disappointed that it even angered him. When he got to the other corner he looked back at the people walking off in the distance and wondered, *Would they have the guts to stand up and voice their opinion in a public forum?*

From obscurity, to hero, to lunacy in one night, Karl pondered it all. *Now I know why some people stay out of the public spotlight. I just hope my skin is thick enough,* he told himself and he began walking down the street again.

Twenty minutes later, Karl rounded the bend at Woodcrest Drive and witnessed a great deal of activity around his house. It appeared that his house was under assault by the media. Their weapons were van-like personnel carriers that were outfitted with satellite dishes, bayonet-like boom microphones, and mini-surveillance-cams. They were also cloaked in a camouflage of neatly sculpted hair, manicures, high heels, and battle-tested perfumes and aftershave lotions.

Their battle cries included terms such as; uplink, zoom in and pan out; and their fighting units were identified by acronyms such as WDND and WDMT that they proudly displayed on their equipment and combat fatigues.

Hesitating, Karl stopped short at his neighbor's hedge row contemplating the scene and what was about to unfold. While one group of reporters continued to assail the front door with a volley of knocking and bell ringing another performed a text book *Hail Mary* play, enveloping the perimeter of his house with vehicles and personnel. Now Karl knew that there was an untold story out there; the *behind-the-scenes* story of how Gulf War General, Norman Swarzkopf, had actually become a master military strategist by observing the news media in the trenches.

Suddenly, a shout rang out, "It's him, behind the hedge."

Like a fox being pursued by ravenous hounds, Karl searched for cover.

"In here," screamed a familiar voice!

Karl turned to spot an attractive blonde motioning to him. It was Amanda's mother and Karl's neighbor, Kate Webster. "Hurry you can hide in the basement!" She held the screen door open while Karl spun away from the hedge and began his race across the leaf-covered lawn. As each of the units made a dash to acquire an exclusive interview, they tangled with adjacent units and tried to impede each other's progress toward Kate's front door.

Then in an attempt to destroy the competition's ability to cover the story, microphone to mini-cam combat broke out. This was the hottest story since Caesar Rodney made his famous horseback ride up Route 13, and no news organization worth its ratings was going to concede. It was all-out media warfare and you could throw the rule book out the window. Fist fights broke out between the different anchors and cameramen! Satellite dishes were torn from the roofs of vans which were then overturned or set afire in Karl's front yard and it was all being recorded on celluloid.

"Hurry!" Kate shouted repeatedly.

Within arms reach of Miss Webster's front step Karl was tackled by a newswoman, but undaunted, Kate risked life and limb. Leaving the safety of her foyer she threw the screen door open and applied a half nelson to the anchorwoman's neck.

"Hurry inside before the others get here," she instructed Karl. Then, after realizing that Karl must have been knocked unconscious from the fall, Kate grabbed him by his jacket and struggled to drag his limp body to safety. Acting quickly, she then closed the screen and interior doors; then bolted them shut.

Seconds later the knocking and door bell ringing began at Kate's front door. She looked out her front window across the field of battle and saw journalists in tattered-suits, pressing their smudged faces against her picture window glass; and her front lawn strewn with burning debris.

"Look what they've done to my hedge!" she drew the curtains in disgust.

"Thank you Kate, you should get the Congressional Medal of Honor for that act of heroism," it was Karl, he had regained consciousness. He pointed to the fireplace, "Ever see the movie *The Birds?* Well, you'd better close the damper."

Kate Webster did so immediately.

"Do you hear that Karl," Kate asked in disbelief. The sound of police and fire sirens could be heard coming up the street.

CHAPTER 3

Damage Control

Seaford, Delaware 19973

"Who are you trying to kid Gil?" Congressman Douglas Oliver leaned forward in his chair to emphasize the point to his press aide Gil Hickman. "It was disastrous! I had hoped that it was a bad dream but when I turned on the television this morning, there was that janitor looking down from the gallery and Miss Higgins standing on that chair in the back of the hall scolding the governor and me. We looked like a couple of school boys."

"Doug, I know it looks bad but remember that the governor's campaign was just as badly affected. We were ahead in the polls before the debate and with both of you damaged equally last night, you'll still be ahead."

"How can you say that? The newspapers are about to make the man into a king. You've read this morning's commentaries," the congressman picked a newspaper off of his desk, opened it up and read some bylines, *"Custodian takes out the Political Trash…Janitor Stands up for Delaware…and…Janitor sets out to Clean up the Governor's office."*

"Yes, but what about this one, 'Deranged man interrupts debates.'"

"Where's that one?" eagerly inquired the congressman.

"It's not there, but I overheard people talking this morning at the donut shop and many are divided. Some look at him as a kind of hero while others thought he came across as a crackpot. All we have to do is make him appear as the latter." Gil Hickman moved his finger next to his head in a circular motion.

"Crazy, isn't that what his ideas sound like? I mean really Doug, think about it. Gain respect for Delaware by solving problems…be innovative…use common sense and decency…it's crazy. I'm telling you, we can paint this guy as a real basket case." The congressman listened attentively as Hickman's eyes glowed with excitement.

"I see your point but I don't know. It sounds risky."

"Risky! What's so risky? He's a horse waiting to be put out of his misery. I've checked on his background already. He was raised on a small farm outside of Georgetown. He's a widower who lives off of an air force pension and his only living relative is his granddaughter that he's putting through school at U of D. This morning I instructed Lou Swetman to terminate him from his janitorial position at the Old Statehouse."

"You did what?" objected the congressman jumping halfway out of his chair.

"Don't worry, as soon as Lou told him that he was fired, Bontrager quit."

Congressman Oliver sat back down in his chair, "I don't know…character assassination of a veteran who's supporting his only heir through college. It's ruthless and it's immoral."

"We didn't ask him to put his two cents in last night, did we? If he hadn't been running off at the mouth we wouldn't be in this predicament and he'd be back to his job sweeping floors in the State House," insisted Hickman.

"You may be right, but I still believe we're taking a risk," the congressman rubbed his chin while in deep thought.

"What is this risk thing? There is no real risk as long as our hands don't get dirty."

"Haven't you ever heard of a thing called Watergate?" the congressman pointedly replied.

"What's that got to do with it?"

"A great deal, if we ever get caught."

"Leave it to me Doug, I'll make it quick and clean."

The two men were interrupted by Alan Bean, an assistant campaign manager who had a good reason to push for Oliver's election. The youngest in a line of accountants, the CPA was a volunteer standout at party headquarters when Gil Hickman first took notice of him. Exercising some political savvy, Bean didn't just fall in line when Hickman came around looking for an assistant. Before the twenty-eight year old would take a hiatus from his father's accounting firm, he wanted and got assurances from Congressman Oliver that he would be appointed to head Delaware's *Office of the Budget*.

To many, Delaware's *Office of the Budget* was an important, yet obscure and boring branch of the state government. While state legislators had the occasional opportunity to stand at a podium and address a myriad of exciting subjects, the *Office of the Budget* was perceived very differently.

For the average taxpayer the state's budget was presumed to be derived by a group of bespectacled, number crunching, and abacus-fixated individuals who were chained to their candle lit desks; deep within the revenue digesting bowels of the state government, and preferably, next to a coal burning boiler in a damp basement. In reality, it was a necessary part of state government that was staffed by professionals who analyzed many aspects of the actual and proposed state budgets. Its biggest responsibility was preparing the governor's proposed budgets.

Nevertheless, this is what motivated Alan Bean. Armed with Oliver's assurances, Bean put forward a maximum effort in coordinating Hickman's planned events and campaign appearances. He also managed to get the grassroots supporters energized during voter registration drives. For his efforts, Alan Bean got little thanks, but he always carried with him the thought of being the first in his family to head Delaware's *Office of the Budget*.

Bean rushed into the congressman's office, "Good news!"

"What's going on Alan?" a startled Gil Hickman asked.

"Hurry, turn on the TV!" the advisor was frantic.

"What channel?" Hickman asked.

"Any channel, it's on every station."

Gil Hickman picked the remote off of the bookshelf and clicked on the television. A disheveled Ron Mathews sporting a black eye and torn sport coat appeared on the screen. Ron held a microphone in one hand as he stood in front of the City of Dover police station. The three men listened intently.

"To repeat, former custodian Karl Bontrager has just been taken inside the City of Dover police station on charges of disturbing the peace and inciting a riot."

"Great!" Gil Hickman could not restrain his joy.

"Be quiet Gil!" the congressman snapped as he listened for more information.

"The charges stem from an incident at Mr. Bontrager's residence on Woodcrest Drive, in which several news crews had an altercation with each other. In the aftermath of last night's gubernatorial debates, news teams had sought interviews with Mr. Bontrager." As Ron Mathews continued, footage of burning vehicles and flying debris were shown.

"Also charged was Mr. Bontrager's neighbor Miss Katherine Webster." The footage showed Miss Webster being led from her house by city police. "She's being charged as an accomplice," Ron Mathews reappeared on the television screen as an off-screen voice interrupted.

"Cut it short Ron the judge is waiting," an off camera voice demanded.

"In addition, several news people who were caught up in the mishap have been taken into custody for their participation in the disturbance."

The camera panned back to show Ron's hand cuffed to an impatient police officer.

"That's it, this interview is over," a police officer put his free hand over the camera lens blocking out the picture; but Ron's voice could still be heard in the background.

"As you can see, we go to great lengths to bring you those breaking news stories…even going so far as fighting for them."

The police officer cuts in again, "If you don't sign off, a news story won't be the only thing that's breaking."

"Ron Mathews signing o…," abruptly, the television screen went blank.

"I guess that's what they call pulling the plug," Alan chuckled.

Congressman Oliver took the remote from Gil Hickman and clicked the television off. Oliver then pointed to the door, "Alan, out of the room!"

The low level advisor scurried out of the room closing the door behind him.

"That was your work Gil!" Congressman Oliver pointed the remote control at his press aide, "You set that up. You just couldn't wait for my okay!"

"So what? It's effective Doug. It discredits the janitor and it's to our advantage."

"Don't you try to sweet talk me you Ivy League know it all. This is illegal and if we get caug…," the congressman didn't have a chance to finish his sentence.

The press aid cut the congressman off, "Don't you get on your high horse with me. Remember, I know all about your dirty transactions, and more."

Congressman Oliver turned his back toward the press aide.

"So what, if I had some timely information and acted upon it? Anyone would have bought that property under the same circumstances," Congressman Oliver faced Hickman again.

"Oh no! You don't get off that easy congressman. What about skimming the lottery commission or how about the strings you pulled to get your cousin's construction company a contract on the bypass. I'm sure your old high school buddy Ron Mathews would love to fight for that exclusive."

"All right, you've made your point Gil, but remember you've been there every step of the way. If I hang, we'll both be trying to walk on air."

"Okay then, we agree on one thing. We don't want to become giraffes," Hickman made a motion as if he was being hung from a rope. "We just want to be elected," Gil's voice became more conciliatory.

"Agreed, but with me being the point man; from here on in I want to okay everything. Got it, Gil?" The congressman said trying to sound in control.

"Got it," Gil gave a nod.

Woodburn, the Governor's Mansion
Dover, Delaware 19903

For two decades Sarah Watkins had told Governor Collins what he needed to hear rather than what he wanted to hear. She was also a political advisor who could read the electorate as well as anyone in Delaware politics. Most importantly, she had become more of a friend than an advisor to the governor. When the governor seemed to stray from better judgment she had a way of steering him back on track in such a way that he usually came to a sensible conclusion.

"We were blind sided, Governor, no one could have predicted what happened last night," Sarah Watkins stood up from her chair in the governor's office.

"I agree, but what to do about it? Bontrager is being portrayed as everything from a hero to a zero," the governor leaned back in his leather chair evaluating his dilemma.

"Well, what do you think he is?" asked Sarah.

"What do you mean?"

"Which one is he, a patriot, a visionary, a senile old man? What do you think?"

"Well I don't believe that he's the latter. He's too eloquent and well read to be that. Besides it's not a comforting thought to think that a senile old man could make a horse's *you know what* out of me so easily," The governor cracked a half smile.

"Agreed, he's no crazy. Okay then, that leaves the patriot and the visionary. Which one is it, Governor?"

"Both. He obviously has great pride in Delaware's history and believes in standing on it. That would make him a patriot." Sarah nodded in agreement with the governor. "He also has some fresh ideas. You might even say some good ideas. I don't know how practical they are though," Governor Collins picked up a globe that was on his desk.

"Here we are," his index finger landed between Maryland, Pennsylvania, the Atlantic Ocean and the Delaware Bay, blotting out the second smallest state in the nation, "Delaware, and he wants us to solve some of the world's problems." He grasped the globe between his two hands and let out a snicker. "Maybe he is a senile old man and I'm just easy to make a fool out of."

"Nonsense, Governor," Sarah stepped from the window, "I think we have great possibilities before us and I think that you've come to realize it."

"I've been in state politics for twenty-three years, Sarah. Even made that run at the White House remember?" Sarah grinned as the governor reminisced. "Might have won too, if only more people had known that Delaware was one of the fifty states. I did a lot of thinking after I got home from the debate last night." Governor Collins paused for a moment selecting his words. "I don't want to be remembered as a governor whose greatest achievement was attracting more shopping malls to the state than all of his predecessors; I want to make a difference."

"That janitor had quite an impact on you. I would have never known it from listening to you last night. I distinctly remember you telling Ron Mathews to have that delirious man escorted out of the building," Sarah laughed loudly.

"Like I said, I had plenty of time to think last night. To think about the past when I was in my first race for Sussex County Sheriff. I ran because I thought that I could make a difference, a good difference. Over time I guess things became muddled. They became various shades of gray, special interest and political alliances, you know. Tell me Sarah. When did I cross over that line? It seems that I didn't even see it. There should be a bell or an alarm or something to warn you when it's near."

"I think that's why each of us was given a conscience, Governor," Sarah liked to plant key words to heighten the governor's sense of responsibility to the public. One of the things that she liked about the governor was the fact that he didn't have a deaf ear to such suggestions.

"Have I allowed common sense and decency to take a back seat to blind political ambition? Even more, have I let my long-standing feud with Oliver detract from the purpose that I was sent to Woodburn for?" The governor appeared deeply concerned, "And is it too late for me to read this janitor's handwriting on the wall?"

"I haven't heard you talk this way in some time, Governor."

"Well you better get used to it Sarah," The governor caught his reflection in a mirror on the opposing wall. "It's time for a change," the governor reached to his head, removed his hair piece and threw it into the burning fireplace, "Watch closely Sarah, Delaware's Governor has turned a new leaf and a new scalp in the same day," They both laughed.

A knock on the door announced a State Trooper. He held his wide brimmed trooper's hat in his hand, "Sorry to interrupt, Governor, but your wife says there's a breaking news story and that you should come to the living room."

University of Delaware
Newark, Delaware 19716

"Kim!" Isn't that your grandfather?" Anne sat crossed legged on the bed which doubled as a dirty laundry hamper.

"Where?" Kimberly Bontrager's voice was heard from the bathroom.

"On TV, you'd better come quickly, it looks serious."

"Oh no! What's happened to him this time? First the debate, now what?" Kimberly stepped from the bathroom with rollers in her hair, a mud pack on her face, and a toothbrush in her mouth. Worried, she watched the news story on the portable television in her room. "He's handcuffed!" Kimberly said in disbelief.

Anne began updating Kim on the news that she had missed. "They said that he's wanted for inciting a riot."

"A riot!" Kimberly took the toothbrush out of her mouth as Anne was interrupted by a knock at the door. It was Kimberly and Anne's boyfriends, Eric and Dan.

"What are you guys doing here?" asked Kimberly.

"We were just watching the TV in the student lounge; when they interrupted *The Price is Right* with a news flash," Eric spoke excitedly. "It was about your grandfather. Oh, I see you've got it on already."

"Your grandfather started a riot," Dan teased.

"What's this about a riot?" Kimberly did not appreciate his humor.

"It was in his neighborhood. There it is now," Eric pointed to the TV, "Look at all of those burned out news vans and the fighting. Hey, there's Ron Mathews getting beaten by that newswoman with the boom microphone."

"This is better than the WWF," laughed Dan.

"What are you talking about? My grandfather's been arrested! I knew it. I knew it. Ever since his doctor put him on that high fiber diet he's been acting funny. I knew he should have gotten a second opinion."

"Maybe he shouldn't have started the riot," Dan suggested.

"He didn't start a riot!" protested Kimberly. It's a mistake; my grandfather would never start a riot!" Kimberly shook her toothbrush at Dan.

"Kim is right; this is no time for kidding around. Her grandfather is in jail," reprimanded Eric.

"Sorry but levity is a great stress reducer," responded Dan. "Besides what can you do? He's in jail."

"I don't know but I can't leave him in jail for the night, not with those animalistic reporters." Kimberly shook her head, her frown deepening.

"Call and see if they've set bail," Eric suggested.

"Yeah, you can use the pay phone in the student's lounge," said Anne.

The foursome took the short walk down the hall to the student lounge. Kimberly still wearing her curlers, bath robe and mud pack and Anne wearing her worn jeans and rabbit slippers.

Students watching *The Price is Right* stopped to watch Kim and her entourage as it made its way to the pay phone then fumbled around for some change.

Korf, a chemical engineering major who also played offensive guard on the football team got out of his chair and walked over to the group.

"Hey Dan, what's going on?" the massive young man spoke in a whisper as the other students looked on from their couches and chairs.

"It's Kim, her grandfather's in jail. The guy who was on the debates the other night and who was on TV a few minutes ago, he started the riot."

"He didn't start a riot," protested Kim under her breath as she dialed the number.

"She's calling to see if she can get him out," added Dan.

"Serious stuff," Korf said in a whisper, "thanks for the info Dan." Korf slowly turned around so as not to disturb Kim on the phone, then shouted to the onlooking students seated around the television, "Kim's grandfather is in jail, she's trying to spring him."

"Big mouth," a flinching Anne smacked Korf on the shoulder.

"Awesome," a couple of girls drew closer to learn more.

"Power to the People!" hollered a young man using a '70's cliché.

"That's radical man," commented another.

"This is better than *The Price is Right!*" observed a distracted student who had been watching Bob Barker explain *Plinko* to a contestant.

By the time Kim had gotten the number for the City of Dover police station an interested crowd had formed and started exchanging views about Kim's grandfather.

"He's the guy that told the governor and Congressman Oliver a thing or two the other night during the debate."

"I remember that. He's right; Delaware does get overlooked by the rest of the country."

"If more people thought like him, maybe we could solve some problems."

"I agree with him. Delaware could be a research state to test approaches to problems on a small scale before being used by the rest of the country."

"Hush!" Kim blurted, "I've got the police station. Yes I'd like to talk to the Chief of Police...Well maybe you can help me then. I would like to know whether Mr. Bontrager has been released yet...I'm his granddaughter, Kimberly Bontrager...How much is it? When can I see him?" Kimberly hung up the phone, "They've set bail at $25,000."

"What!" said Eric. "Who do they think they have, Ivan Bosky?"

"That's not right," said Korf, "they're trying to get him back for interrupting the debate the other night."

"What are you going to do?" asked Anne. "You don't have $25,000. If it wasn't for your grandfather you wouldn't even have tuition."

"I don't know but I can't leave him in jail over night."

"Let's break him out. I've got some chemicals back at the lab that will vaporize any bars you'll find in that jail," volunteered Korf eagerly.

"Your courage is commendable Korf, but now is a time for cool heads," Eric spoke patronizingly, "we may not be able to bail him out but we can make our presence felt, am I right?"

The gathering of students voiced their agreement.

"You're right Eric and we're not going to let him stay in jail long if we can help it," Dan added. "What are we going to do Eric?"

Eric stood up on a table top, "They don't call us the University of Delaware fightin' Blue Hens for nothing?"

The crowd shouted its affirmation.

"Well then, that means that we don't give up easily; even when things look insurmountable."

"That's right!" shouted one of the students.

"Aren't we some of the world's future problem solvers?" shouted Eric.

The crowd responded with an enthusiastic, "Yes!"

"Then this is just another problem to solve."

Another loud, "Yes," spurred him on.

"This is what Karl was talking about," Eric directed his enthusiasm toward the crowd, "and it's time for us to own up to the challenge. It's time for the struggle to begin. It's time to stop talking about the problems and time to start solving them."

The crowd cheered.

"It may get ugly out there so all of you slackers or those who are faint of heart can get off now if you want," continued Eric.

But there were no takers.

"Alright then, it's time to start paying back those student loans people. First we need to get Kimberly's grandfather out of jail, then, we need to get to work."

"Karl! Karl! Karl!" the students were in a frenzy.

Dan jumped up onto the table with Eric, "I'd like to add that no fire arms, incendiary devices, or explosives are desired for this trip."

"That's right Dan, we're setting out to free Karl, not blow him up. We meet in the parking lot in front of Christiana Towers in thirty minutes."

"Eric!" Kimberly pointed to her muddy face.

"Make that thirty five minutes," Eric corrected.

The crowd quickly dispersed, going back to their dorms to prepare for the exodus south.

CHAPTER 4

The Struggle Begins

City of Dover Police Station
Dover, Delaware 19904

"I don't care who you are, if you're not on the list you don't get in, Doctor."

The police officer's patience was growing thin with the physician.

"Serious questions have been raised about Mr. Bontrager's mental health and I've been sent to give my diagnoses," insisted the relentless doctor.

"You still haven't told me who sent you and without the paperwork I can't admit you."

"The corrections department sent me over, now will you let me see Mr. Bontrager?"

The door to the lobby of the Dover city jail opened and Judge Stortz approached the desk.

"What's the problem officer?" asked the Judge.

"Judge, this is Doctor Hoffman, he says that corrections sent him over to evaluate Mr. Bontrager."

"Oh yes, I know Doctor Hoffman and I've been told of his appointment, Officer Brown. Let Doctor Hoffman in to see Mr. Bontrager."

"Yes sir, Judge," Officer Brown picked up a phone and spoke to someone for a few seconds. "An officer will be right out to escort you to his cell, Doctor."

"It's about time," huffed the psychiatrist.

"If you'll please sign the register in the meantime," the doctor signed the log.

"Sorry for the inconvenience, Albert, but you know how these young rookie officers are," the judge shrugged his shoulders.

"Yes indeed," agreed the doctor as he gave Officer Brown a scowling look. Another officer came in from a back room.

"This is Officer Jennings. He'll escort you to Mr. Bontrager's cell, Doctor."

Officer Brown pressed a button under his desk and the door lock made a buzzing sound. Officer Jennings pushed the door open and led the psychiatrist toward the cells at the back of the police station.

"Officer Brown," Judge Stortz spoke admonishingly.

"Yes sir, Judge?"

"From now on I expect you to show our community's professionals more courtesy, understand?"

The greenhorn officer turned red, "Yes sir, Judge."

"Now start processing the news people out of here, immediately. We don't have enough cells, as it is."

"Yes sir, what about Miss Webster should I process her too?"

"No, she may have helped to organize this thing with Bontrager. Better wait until we've got some answers from Doctor Hoffman."

"Yes sir, Judge."

University of Delaware
Newark, Delaware 19716

"What's this, Korf?" asked Kimberly after she, Eric, Anne and Dan stepped onto the parking lot in front of Christiana Towers.

"It's the football team; they didn't want to miss out on all of the excitement. They've even got their own bus and cheerleaders."

A cheer let out from the bus, which had *Free Karl* banners hanging from either side.

As the foursome walked around the bus to Eric's jeep, they noticed that quite a gathering had formed. Sororities, fraternities, the ROTC, and other campus organizations were ready to roll in vehicles that sported slogans in support of Karl and his ideas. There were friends and supporters from each of their respective schools; fellow students from Anne's College of Education, Eric's College of Engineering, from Dan's College of Agricultural Sciences, and from Kimberly's College of Art's and Sciences.

"Professor Ross, are you going with us?" shouted Kimberly.

"Yes, I and my political science class if you don't mind. I want to show my students the democratic system in action."

"Sure! Glad to have you along," Kim said joyfully as she followed Anne and Dan into Eric's jeep.

"All right, this is for Karl!" Eric shouted as he jumped behind the wheel. It was 11:30 A.M. when Eric's jeep led the procession of vehicles onto the southbound lane of New London Road. The column turned slowly onto East Main Street, then onto South College Avenue passing through a campus that was founded a few decades before the birth of the nation.

Students, oblivious to Karl's plight, walked or rode bicycles to their classes along the tree lined sidewalks that crossed the campus.

Some were headed to the top ranked chemical engineering school on the East Coast, while others made their way to the Marine Studies lab with its research into sea life in the Atlantic Ocean and Delaware Bay. Others were en route to the university's Ice Arena which had been used by Olympic figure skaters to hone their performances before the winter games. The list of schools went on; from one of the strongest agricultural programs in the east to the College of Arts and Sciences whose faculty members included a Pulitzer Prize winner.

Now it was time for a group of its students to take matters into their own hands and to right a wrong. Now was the time for University of Delaware Blue Hen intervention.

City of Dover Police Station
Dover, Delaware 19904

"This is Ron Mathews reporting live from the steps of the City of Dover Police Station where my journalist colleagues and I have just been released from detention. I can tell you first hand that incarceration is an experience that no one should ever have to endure. The process of being finger printed, booked, then jailed is a humiliating experience that drives a man to the very brink of frustration and sometimes violence. During my four hour long ordeal behind bars, I found myself pacing in a cramped cell while thinking about the fate that may be awaiting me. Things like the prison violence, ravenous guard dogs and poor food. Fortunately, I survived and was released.

Hopefully, in time I'll be able to pick up the pieces of my life and return to society emotionally unscarred," Ron Mathews still in tattered sport jacket and black eye, jutted his jaw forward as a sign of determination that he would overcome the experience.

"Still inside are Karl Bontrager and his neighbor Katherine Webster. They continue to be held on charges of inciting a riot and disturbing the peace," Ron Mathews stopped to accept a note from off camera which he promptly read.

"I've just received word that we have Blanche Duncan, Kate Webster's neighbor, and Kate Webster's six year old daughter Amanda with us." Ron coaxed the little girl to the microphone, "Hi, Amanda, how are you?"

"My mom told me never to talk to strangers," popped Amanda, "especially ones with black eyes."

"I'm not a stranger; I'm Ron Mathews the reporter from TV. You must have seen me on the *Channel Five News*."

"My mom doesn't watch *Channel Five News*. She says you're too much of an egg-o-maniac."

An embarrassed Ron Mathews interrupted Amanda, "Did you come here to see your mother?"

"Yes, I want my mother," still holding Blanche Duncan's hand, the little girl began to cry.

A gray-haired and bespectacled Blanche interrupted, "I've lived next to Kate Webster for eight years. This must be a mistake, she's a wonderful person."

"I just want my mom," Amanda tugged at Ron Mathew's sport coat, "I want her released from jail."

Other reporters and cameramen began to gather around the interview.

"We'll do everything we can to do just that Amanda," Ron Mathews reassured the little girl.

Meanwhile, everyday citizens who had interest in the unfolding story had been gathering around the police station. There was even a group of farmers who had driven up from Sussex County, "We're here to show our support for Mr. Bontrager," one of the farmers announced. We want to see him released."

"I agree, it's unjust for this man to be imprisoned for speaking his mind," volunteered a woman who held a young child in her arms.

"Mr. Bontrager spoke for Delawareans who want to make a positive impact, insisted another woman.

"What's going on?" an angry Judge Stortz flanked by city Policemen came down the police station steps and was making his way toward the crowd. "This is a city police station, not a park to conduct protests."

Ron Mathews shoved a microphone in front of the red faced judge, "Are you going to release Miss Webster and Mr. Bontrager, Judge?"

"That is no concern of yours!" fired back the judge.

"I think it's her concern!" Ron Mathews picked Amanda up in his arms, "Let me introduce you to Miss Webster's six year old daughter!"

The judge stood speechless.

"And some concerned citizens who came up from Sussex County to show their support for Mr. Bontrager," Ron Mathews pointed toward the onlookers.

"The city of Dover does not respond to citizens outside of its jurisdiction," snapped Stortz.

In a commotion, Eric's jeep led the caravan of Bontrager supporters to a parking lot across the street from the police station. Horns blared as students cheered, "Karl! Karl! Karl!"

The news cameras took in the spectacle as Kimberly and Eric's entourage crossed the street toward the police station and Judge Stortz.

"Stop right there!" Judge Stortz ordered the approaching mob, "This has gotten out of hand. There will be no more protests. Mr. Bontrager and Miss Webster are considered felons and will continue to be incarcerated until deemed otherwise."

"My grandfather is not a felon!" countered Kimberly forcefully.

"Young lady I will have you and your fellow law breakers arrested," the judge raised his head high while yelling to the large group. "You all must disband immediately. You do not have a permit to protest and I will take action against all of you if necessary."

The down wash was loud, sudden and forceful. Hats were blown through the air and heads turned upward to catch sight of the rotor blades whirling in a circular motion above the hovering state police helicopter.

"They're going to encircle us!" yelled a man.

The crowd began to disperse from underneath of the helicopter.

"Don't let them take us," screamed a woman. "I have a PTA meeting at 6:00.

"They'll never take me alive hollered a defiant student who waved his fist at the landing chopper."

Shouts of, "Free Karl," were heard in an undercurrent of mob determination.

The crowd had moved to the perimeter of the parking lot in anticipation of a run in with the airborne law enforcers while the judge and the city police officers had retreated to the steps of the police station. Everyone watched as the side door opened and a bald man in a suit stepped out. He was hunched over as he raced away from the slowing rotor blades, which came to a complete stop before the crowd recognized the man as Delaware's chief executive.

Governor Collins waved for the crowd to join him at the steps of the police station and they quickly gathered around him and Judge Stortz.

"I know you are all very angry about the jailing of Mr. Bontrager and Miss Webster and I was shocked to see the entire thing on television." Governor Collins turned to a nervous Judge Stortz, "As governor and chief law official of the state of Delaware, I hereby order you, Judge Stortz, to release both Karl Bontrager and Katherine Webster! Immediately!" Governor Collins quickly added.

Smiles appeared on the faces of the Dover Police officers, who were secretly sympathetic to Karl and Kate's plight.

The crowd cheered wildly, "Karl! Karl! Karl!" Then there was a pause as the crowd waited for Judge Stortz's response.

Judge Stortz hesitated for several seconds, visibly agitated by the governor's order, "I can't release them, Governor."

"What do you mean you can't release them? Didn't you hear me, Judge? I just gave you an executive order and I expect you to carry it out, pronto. Got it?"

"I can't, Governor, they're not here," mumbled Stortz.

CHAPTER 5

Stalag 202

New Castle County, Delaware

"If anyone should be under observation, it should be you, Doc!" An enraged Karl Bontrager directed his comments to Doctor Albert Hoffman, who sat on the opposite side of the table. Karl, along with Kate Webster, was seated between two emotionless hospital orderlies.

"You had no right to drug us," Kate shouted, "or to bring us to this place. I still have a headache," Kate rubbed her brow.

"Kate is absolutely right," protested Karl, "I demand to know where we are and to contact an attorney."

"Patients under observation are not afforded the same rights as inmates. I will give you no information on our location and you will not contact an attorney."

"This is insane. I speak my mind in a public forum; and subsequently lose my job, have my property ransacked, get arrested and then my neighbor and I are placed under psychiatric observation by someone who's probably wanted for war crimes. Haven't you people ever read the U.S. Constitution? Whatever happened to the *First Amendment* and due process of law?"

"Thank you for the history lesson Mr. Bontrager but I believe I'm detecting anxiety and rage from you," stated Doctor Hoffman in his best bedside manner.

"You're going to detect my foot embedded in your hind parts if you detain us any longer," Karl threatened.

The orderly sitting to Karl's right gave him a look of warning but said nothing.

"This is exactly the reason why this observation was ordered. You both have displayed anger toward authority and a penchant for violent acts leaving me no choice but to curb such rage by administering a modest prescription. We're doing this for your own good."

"What do you mean, we? Do you mean that someone put you up to this?" asked Karl suspiciously.

"This isn't Nazi Germany," Kate Webster scolded Hoffman.

"You're right Kate," agreed Karl. "But you've got to admit, the doc does look a lot like Lawrence Olivier in the movie the *Marathon Man*. Don't let him get near your teeth," Karl warned.

"The best way to keep me away from your teeth is to keep your mouth shut Mr. Bontrager," mimicking a closing mouth, Doctor Hoffman clapped his hands together.

"I'm glad to see that you have a sense of humor, Doctor," Karl quipped.

"Now let's see whether you can recognize your own mistake and release us so we can carry on with our lives."

"That's not possible," retorted Doctor Hoffman who paced the small room.

"You've committed a crime, you've incited a riot."

"That's bull and you know it," argued Karl.

"At the least you can release Kate so that she can be reunited with her young daughter," appealed Karl.

"She's your accomplice, I cannot release her."

"I have a right to see my daughter," Kate demanded.

"Enough of this bickering; open the door!" the stubborn psychiatrist demanded. A square-jawed man with a crew cut could be seen through the barred opening at the top of the cell door. He disengaged the lock and held the door open for Doctor Hoffman and the other two orderlies while ensuring that the new patients didn't escape. Karl and Kate then overheard Doctor Hoffman whispering instructions to the orderly in the hallway.

"Their rooms won't be ready until six o'clock, but I want you to start them on 10 milligrams of xylazene every 2 hours beginning immediately. That will calm them down," Hoffman left in a fit and the sound of his footsteps grew faint as he departed down the hall.

"What now?" asked Kate in a whisper?

"I know I won't be eating any food that they may bring us," Karl sighed wearily.

"We need to figure out where we are and how to get out of here before they separate us at six o'clock."

Karl stepped to the window and peered through its steel bars. They were being held on what appeared to be the third floor of the institution. An open and rolling grassy area extended out from the brick building for approximately seventy yards before it stopped at the foot of a wooded area.

"New Castle County, it's not flat enough to be Kent or Sussex Counties. We're probably north of Wilmington, it looks like the topography."

Kate joined Karl at the window, "It'll be dark soon." The wistful sound of her voice hinted tears.

"Amanda is fine Kate," reassured Karl. "She often told me during our walks to her school, that she enjoyed going to the Duncan's house when you were working late. She'd say, 'Mrs. Duncan makes the best chocolate chip cookies in the whole wide world.'"

"Blanche and Joe Duncan," Kate gave a deep sigh. "The best hearted people that I've ever known. After Harold took up with that nurse I worked at the shirt factory and didn't make enough to get by. I didn't even have a car. Joe used to take me to work and Blanche would surprise me, from time to time, with cakes or pies and even groceries. If it wasn't for the Duncans, I would have never gone back to school and I wouldn't be a computer programmer now. I'll never be able to repay them."

"They're an unusual pair, the Duncans," agreed Karl. "They do things for people without expecting any thanks in return. Yet, I've seen them help friends and strangers time and time again. It makes you angry when you think of people like Saddam Hussein and Ivan Bosky, who feel that they never have enough. Power and greed are two addictive drugs," Karl shook his head. We need more people like Joe and Blanche."

"Who do you think is behind this?" asked Kate amidst the stark surroundings.

"Who do you think?" Karl remarked sarcastically. "Governor Collins or Congressman Oliver would be my best guess. I'm sure that you've concluded that already."

"What's that suppose to mean?" asked Kate.

"I can't tell you, I swore not to divulge my sources."

"Sources, what sources?" shocked, Kate stepped back.

"Look I'd tell you, but I'd risk being harpooned by the Little Mermaid," Karl smiled.

"Oh, so Amanda told you about our little talk the other night during the debate!" Kate had reckoned.

"I didn't say that. Who said Amanda?" Karl shrugged. "You know it was quite a popular film, from what I heard, Ebert & Siskel even gave it two thumbs up. I feel sure that there are thousands of Little Mermaids swimming their way into America's lunch rooms every day."

"Is that right?"

"Yes it is, and do you know what the worst part of it is Kate? And this part is most tragic."

Kate thought for a moment, "No, what's the worst part, Karl?"

"I'll tell you what the worst part is, Kate. Many of the Mermaids are packing a lunch of tuna fish sandwiches." Karl hung his head as his elbows rested on the window ledge and his hands grasped at the bars.

Kate laughed, "You do a wonderful Glenn Ford impression."

"Thank you Kate, but if I had my choice I'd rather be doing my imitation of Steve McQueen in *The Great Escape*," Karl exclaimed.

"Sorry Karl," Kate looked around the padded cell, "but I don't see any motorcycles."

"You Steve, Steve McQueen," a commanding voice came through the barred opening at the top of the cell door.

A Living room in
Selbyville, Delaware 19975

"Give me the remote Ellen. The national news should be on." Ned Potter eased back in his La-Z-Boy after a long day of work on his dairy farm.

"How many times do I have to tell you to take your shoes off before coming into the house, Ned? Look, you've gotten the floor dirty."

"Sorry honey, I'll try to remember next time," apologized Ned.

"I've been telling you for twenty five years Ned. I would have thought that you'd learn by now," Ellen threw her hands into the air. "It's just like Oprah says, 'You can't change them once the honeymoon is over.'"

"Please Ellen, I told you that I'm sorry. Now do you think that you might have some apple pie in the kitchen for your hard-working husband?"

"I guess I'd better go get it or you'll track mud onto my clean kitchen floor."

A frustrated Ellen picked up the remote from the top of the television and handed it to a semi-reclining Ned before she went into the kitchen.

"Dag-gum thing, I need to get some new batteries for this gadget," Ned smacked the remote with his free hand and aimed it at the television. After pressing the on button several times, the set finally came to life and NBS anchor, Patrick Browker appeared on the screen.

"The president also said and I quote, "I am extremely concerned about the possible proliferation of nuclear technology from the former Soviet Republics to hostile groups or nations. To demonstrate our concerns, I have sent Secretary of State Canfield to conduct talks with the Republics to ensure the sufficient control of, and eventual destruction of these weapons."

The president had no other insight as to what negotiations may be going on with the former Soviet Republics. Up next after a commercial break, our *Down Home* segment will take us to Dover, Delaware for the story of Karl Bontrager.

"Ellen! Ellen! Come quick," Ned called from his recliner. He quickly pushed the wooden handle on the right side of his La-Z-Boy forward.

"What's all the commotion about," Ellen called out from the kitchen, while closing the refrigerator door."

Ned smacked the intermittent remote with his hand to turn the volume down, "It's Delaware! Delaware is going to be on the National News after this commercial break. You don't want to miss it," Ned sputtered excitedly.

"Delaware? You must be mistaken, Ned. Delaware's never been on the national news!"

"I'm sure he said Delaware, now get in here Ellen…and please don't forget that apple pie!"

A moment later an excited Ellen walked into the living room, "The last time Delaware was even mentioned on national TV was when they had that question on Jeopardy. Remember Ned?" Ellen inquired as she handed a piece of pie to her husband. Oblivious to the tantalizing fragrance, Ned was sitting upright, his attention frozen to the screen.

"How can I forget, it was in all of the local papers. The headlines read *Jeopardy Contestant snubs first state by misspelling D-E-L-A-W-H-E-R-E*," Ned recalled their sharp disappointment.

"Maybe we shouldn't watch this segment Ned. It may be another slap in the face for the *Diamond State*. You know, I still wake up in a cold sweat stemming from nightmares that I continue to have about the *Jeopardy* incident," Ellen patted her brow with her apron.

"Get a grip on yourself Ellen. For good or bad; we as Delawareans have a responsibility to our state. Remember Caesar Rodney, Ellen," ordered a statriotic Ned.

"Remember Caesar Rodney," Ellen responded, standing in silent homage of the state's foremost hero."

"Here it is Ellen," A silent Patrick Browker was once again on the tube and Ned smacked the misbehaving remote several times until the volume returned."

"And in tonight's *Down Home* segment our affiliate in Dover, Delaware, WDND, and correspondent Ron Mathews, will have the story of Karl Bontrager."

Ron Mathews stood on the steps of the Old Statehouse, "Thank you, Patrick. Few people inside or outside of the state of Delaware had probably ever heard of the name Karl Bontrager. That is before last night's Gubernatorial Debates here at the Old Statehouse." Ron pointed to the building behind him, "When this janitor and retired Air Force Sergeant exploded onto the scene of Delaware politics as a ghostly specter bearing words of wisdom."

Several excerpts from the Gubernatorial Debates were aired, and Karl was seen standing in the gallery addressing the gathering.

If I were the Governor of Delaware, I believe I'd try to set a good example for the rest of the country.

As far as my ideas go they aren't very fancy, but then they don't involve special interests, or political parties, or hidden agendas either. Instead, my ideas are based upon things like common decency and common sense.

I know that Common Decency and Common Sense are foreign concepts in the present political climate because they don't rely upon expensive studies or polls to steer them in one direction or another.

An excited Ellen leaned forward in her chair to observe the speaker more closely and Ned placed his apple pie on the coffee table and listened intently to capture every word from this man Karl Bontrager, who Ned now believed was the wisest of all Delawareans.

California school children believe that Delaware is an amusement park in eastern Pennsylvania that has a big roller coaster called the Brandywined.

Ron Mathews reappeared on the television screen, "As you can see Karl Bontrager is a man of vision. A man who is quickly capturing the heart and soul of his fellow Delawareans and a man who may quickly gain the respect for his state that its citizens have long sought from the rest of the country and the world.

Unfortunately a turn of events, which many people describe as a setup and that occurred this morning at Mr. Bontrager's home, has landed him and his neighbor Kate Webster, in a City of Dover prison cell. Now the latest word is that the two are being held in an upstate institution where they are presently undergoing psychiatric observation. Patrick, after sharing a prison cell earlier today with Mr. Bontrager, I've concluded that the order for a psychiatric observation is groundless. Furthermore, Mr. Bontrager's arrest was so in question that the governor, who was at odds with Mr. Bontrager just last night at the Old Statehouse, has intervened on behalf of both Mr. Bontrager's and Kate Webster's release. Unfortunately, so far the governor has not been able to gain the release of the two."

"Ron Mathews, this is Patrick Browker back at the Washington Bureau."

"Yes Patrick, what's your question?" instantaneously, both Ron Mathews and Patrick Browker appear on a split television screen.

"Are Mr. Bontrager's suggestions being taken seriously?"

"Most definitely, Patrick, with the exception of a few detractors, you know, arm chair quarterbacks; I've heard many a Delawarean talk in terms of what they can do to fulfill Karl Bontrager's vision. I even understand, through sources, that a student coalition involving the educational institutions throughout Delaware is being discussed to tackle not only the state's needs but to address national needs as well, just as Mr. Bontrager had suggested. Also, good Samaritans and clubs from around the state, such as the 4-H, Lions, Scouts, VFW, and others are interested in pulling their resources and getting more involved. I tell you Patrick, the state of Delaware has a growing spirit that is eager to tackle its problems. The question is: Where is the man responsible for this great event? Where is Karl Bontrager?"

For WDND, I'm Ron Mathews, a Delawarean and proud of it."

The screen returns to a full head shot of Patrick Browker sitting in the Washington D.C. studio. "That is truly an inspiring story from Ron Mathews at the Old Statehouse in Dover, Delaware. I hope for a safe and speedy return of Mr. Bontrager and his neighbor, Kate Webster. For NBS news, this is Patrick Browker wishing you a pleasant evening."

Ned clicked the television off after striking the remote several times, "Ellen that was the greatest event in Delaware television history. It far exceeds the Jeopardy mishap and that moron who couldn't have spelled cat if you had spotted him the *c* and the *t*.

Elated, Ellen nodded in agreement.

CHAPTER 6

Reactor Scram

Psychiatric Hospital
New Castle County, Delaware

"The door Karl," Kate pointed at the barred opening at the top of the cell door and Karl recognized the square-jawed orderly who was assigned to the hallway.

"You're the guy who was on television last night during the debate," the orderly's deep voice was confident as he addressed Karl.

"That's right, that was me," Karl answered, "I'm Karl Bontrager."

"Well who's the cute blonde then?" the orderly then asked.

Not knowing what this stranger was up to Karl moved his tall frame in front of Kate to protect her, "Leave her alone."

"Relax," urged the orderly, "I may be the only friend you two can count on right now."

Kate stepped from behind Karl, "I'm Karl's neighbor Kate."

The orderly nodded to Kate in acknowledgement.

"What do you want?" still wary, Karl continued to study the orderly.

"Did you mean all of that stuff that you said last night?" the orderly asked cautiously.

"I wouldn't have said it otherwise," confirmed Karl.

"So you want to try new ways of attacking problems and helping people?" continued the orderly.

"Yes, most definitely."

"Well, I overheard you just now," the orderly warned, "and you'll never get out of here without being caught."

"Well I had thought about digging my way out but if you have another idea I'm open to suggestions," Karl replied.

"Let's hear what the man has to say, Karl," Kate urged.

"I started here as a way to help people, but the longer that I've been at the hospital, the more that I've come to realize that it isn't for me. For the most part it seems that we have doctors who care, but over time they get frustrated from not being able to help all of the patients put their lives back together. Then many of them get into a routine and perform a rubber stamp procedure on patients, prescribing the same type and amount of medication and exercising the patients the same amount of time with the same routines. Then you get a bad egg like Hoffman who doesn't do anything unless he benefits in some way.

When he sees a patient, he sees a new set of golf clubs, a summer home at Rehoboth Beach, or a Mercedes in the driveway. He's the kind of shrink that gives the mental health profession a bad name. He keeps patients in the hospital until his latest toy is paid off; then miraculously, the patient gets better whether they need additional treatment or not."

"He didn't strike me as psychiatry's answer to Mother Theresa," Karl commented.

"I don't know you or the lady; that is, except what I saw on TV and what Hoffman told me about you. You both seem to be okay to me though and I've seen all types in this place; Schizophrenics, multiple personality disorders, paranoia, you name it. Sometimes they receive care from one of the better doctors and they get their lives back together and eventually walk out of this place. Unfortunately, sometimes they don't. I just don't see where you fit into the picture," the orderly frowned, his face reflecting a question disturbingly unresolved.

"Believe me, we don't!" Kate insisted. "Neither of us has ever experienced anything like this until Karl spoke his mind the other night. This is obviously some kind of an attempt to discredit Karl and me and it reeks of the same type of system that put Soviet dissidents behind bars."

"What Kate says is the truth, she's my neighbor. She has absolutely nothing to do with what I said the other night at the debate; she was merely in the wrong place at the wrong time. At the very least she should be released."

There was no reaction from the orderly for several seconds.

"What do you intend to do when you're released?"

"I've got my life to live; I have a granddaughter who is counting on me. I'd also like to see some of my ideas become reality, but as long as I'm in here it will remain on the back burner."

"Well I think it's time to place them on the front burner," the orderly swung the door open. "The name's Brock and I'd like to shake your hand Mr. Bontrager."

Vrodkutsk Nuclear Research Center
Commonwealth of Independent States

In the summer of 1987 in the divided city of Berlin, West Germany, U.S. President Ronald Reagan demanded, "Mr. Gorbachev, tear down this wall!" He was referring to the Berlin Wall that had divided the U.S. led Democratic countries of Western Europe from the Soviet led Communist countries of Eastern Europe since 1961. In 1989 President Reagan's demand was met when the Berlin Wall was finally torn down. It marked the beginning of the end for the Soviet Union and its domination of Eastern Europe.

At the end of World War II, Vrodkutsk along with many other countries was subjugated, against its will, by the Soviet Union; and during the seceding decades they all suffered under Moscow's oppressive Communist rule.

Prior to the Soviet takeover, the country of Vrodkutsk was small, landlocked, and bordered the northwestern region of Russia. While Vrodkutsk had primarily been an agricultural economy prior to the Communist takeover in 1945, afterward it became a center for Soviet research. Sections of its secluded woodlands and rolling terrain were cleared for the construction of Cold War research facilities and apartment buildings for the scientists, technicians and their families. While it was technically termed the Vrodkutsk Nuclear Research Center, it had actually been tasked with the development of both nuclear and non-nuclear related research. Some of its successes had ranged from satellite navigation systems, to innovative materials for shielding nuclear reactor personnel from radiation, to deep space nuclear propulsion systems, among a multitude of others.

Then in 1991, the Union of Soviet Socialist Republics had dissolved and Russia's former satellite states had gained their independence. As a result, these newly freed countries formed a coalition called the Commonwealth of Independent States, an effort to help each other transition from client states of the former Soviet Union to independent democratic countries.

Under the old communist regime, Direktor Gaslov was one of the lucky ones; instead of him, it was his predecessor who was charged with spying for the West and subsequently purged at gunpoint from the direktorship of the Vrodkutsk Nuclear Research Center. For professionals in the Soviet controlled Eastern Block, it was all about political connections and power.

Mykola Androgov, a young, politically connected adversary of the former direktor, had made the spying accusations but Gaslov knew that the charges were baseless. After the fact, when the truth had finally come to light, the Communists couldn't admit their mistake; but soon after, Mykola Androgov died when he was struck by a bus.

Even before Direktor Gaslov learned of the death of Mykola Androgov, he somehow kept an upbeat attitude; but inside, before Vrodkutsk gained its independence, Gaslov often wondered who the Communists were going to purge next. Unfortunately, it was a stressful existence for the Direktor. Even so, he found that the best way to keep such a possibility from dominating his mind was to concentrate on his work, his grandchildren and his wife Tatya who kept him happy with a steady diet of sausages, potatoes, cabbage, and his favorite, Pelmeni…a Russian meat pie. While it wasn't the healthiest diet, it was one of those few pleasures that helped Gaslov maintain his sanity in an insane Communist world.

Mercifully, when Vrodkutsk gained its independence, so did the charismatic direktor, who was finally freed from any thought of ever being purged.

A disheveled Direktor Gaslov looked troubled as he discussed a recent incident with one of his engineers.

"I tell you comrade, the men have been getting lax since Vrodkutsk regained its independence," In an effort to relieve the stress on his bad leg, Direktor Gaslov propped his left foot on the base of one of the massive turbine generators as he spoke to Engineer Viktor Belenko.

"Yes, Direktor, I know. Our cooking stove is down for repairs and just yesterday I saw a group of men warming their lunches by placing them next to the access door of the reactor compartment. Fortunately, Number Three steam generator was down and the plant was operating at low power."

"That's not all!" interrupted Direktor Gaslov as he led Engineer Belenko through the plant. "I heard that Engineer Semyonov fell asleep while supervising the night shift and the reactor operators decided to have some fun with him. While he slept at the observation podium, the three operators hid in the control room and arranged for other operators throughout the plant to sound any alarms that they could at precisely the same moment. Word has it that upon hearing the alarms, Semyonov was startled awake and leapt to his feet. Thinking that a meltdown was taking place he cried out, 'Chernobyl! Chernobyl! Where are my operators?'"

Engineer Belenko tried to restrain a smile, "Yes I believe I heard of the incident."

"It's not funny Viktor!" scolded Gaslov.

"Yes, of course, Direktor, it's not," Belenko's slight grin was replaced with the look of a dedicated nuclear engineer.

"I would have placed the operators responsible on administrative leave, but as it is we have been short handed and the rumors are flying around the plant that lucrative nuclear research positions await those men willing to work in Africa or the Middle East. Punishing those men could very well spark a mass exodus of our people to other countries," Direktor Gaslov continued to talk as the men walked pass the main condensate pumps.

"I understand," nodded engineer Belenko.

"I've received word from the higher-ups that we're to encourage the men to stay on here. They want us to play to the men's patriotism by using a theme of rebuilding an independent Vrodkutsk. They don't want hundreds of nuclear engineers and technicians roaming the world; developing nuclear programs for potentially hostile states. Lastly, they don't want to offend the Americans and jeopardize the aid that they've been flying into Vrodkutsk."

"That's easier said than done. Patriotism is not our problem. Our men have been hoping for an independent Vrodkutsk since childhood and would normally do anything to assure its growth and success. The problem is that in today's Vrodkutsk, food and clothing are scarce; prices are high; and incomes are low.

How can we fault a man for doing what is best for his family? It's hard for us to compete with foreign programs that offer good wages, housing and medical care. Tell me, Direktor, how can we compete with that?"

"Realistically, we can't Viktor, but we must try. As of yet our men haven't been gripped with the temptation of greed that is so common in the West, but soon they may be. In the mean time we must make conditions as comfortable as possible for them and their families with the limited resources that we have. Hopefully, change in Vrodkutsk will occur fast enough that we will be able to keep the majority of them from leaving."

"Direktor, I don't want to be a pessimist, but for change to occur fast enough to keep those men from leaving Vrodkutsk, it will take a miracle."

"Reactor Scram! Reactor Scram!" The two men flinched from the sound of the plant intercom system and the sound of alarms.

"Let's get to the control room," shouted Gaslov. "It better not be a prank again. Mass exodus or not those operators will pay if it's another practical joke."

"Yes sir," added Belenko who quickly followed the direktor toward the metal stairway that led to the Control Room.

Direktor Gaslov threw open the control room door and ran toward the reactor control panels which were being monitored by three operators and the shift supervisor.

"What's going on?" yelled Gaslov looking at the reactor status boards.

The duty shift supervisor continued to eyeball the plant gauges while responding to Gaslov, "During a bus shift power was interrupted. It caused the electromagnets to release the control rods which shutdown the reactor."

"I didn't know what to think," a winded and relieved Direktor Gaslov stumbled over his words, "I thought that it might have been another practical joke."

"Check the primary coolant temperature and pressure just to be sure and compare them to the auxiliary gauges," ordered Belenko.

"Doing that now, sir," responded the shift supervisor.

"Primary coolant temperature and pressure checked and verified and ready for reactor start-up." called out the operator who stood in front of the reactor plant control panel.

"Primary coolant temperature and pressure checked and verified and ready for reactor start-up," repeated the shift supervisor, adding, "very well, RPCP."

The shift supervisor turned to Direktor Gaslov and Engineer Belenko, "Sir, primary temperature and pressure are normal, request permission to perform a 1A1 reactor plant start up."

"Permission granted to perform a 1A1 reactor plant start-up," acknowledged Gaslov, watching the supervisor as he gave orders to the electrical, steam, and reactor plant operators.

"The plant operated as designed, Direktor," the engineer consoled a gasping Gaslov. "It was a reactor scram, not a melt down. The rods did what they were supposed to do."

"Nevertheless, I want those electromagnets and the bus breakers checked out. We can't be having a plant shut down every time someone throws a light switch, Viktor," insisted Gaslov.

"Yes sir," answered Belenko. The engineer reached for the phone on the shift supervisor's desk, "Aleksei, we need some men up here to check out the rod controls and the bus breakers…that's right…very well Aleksei. Belenko turned to Direktor Gaslov, "The plant electricians are on their way, Direktor."

A pale Gaslov was now leaning against a panel while watching the shift supervisor and operators complete the last steps of the plant line up, "Good."

"Are you feeling okay, Direktor?" Belenko asked in a concerned voice.

Gaslov drew out the word slowly, looking at the control rods rising slowly from the large diagram of the reactor vessel on the operator's panel. His breathing appeared to be labored.

"The reactor is critical," The Shift Supervisor passed the word over the plant intercom.

"Its beauty is in it's…simplicity, Viktor," the direktor calling his most trusted engineer by his first name began to stammer. "I'm always amazed…at our ability…to make great technological achievements…and even more amazed at our inability…to properly care for our peop…" Direktor Gaslov never finished his sentence; clutching his chest as his legs buckled. Engineer Belenko just managed to catch the direktor as he fell.

Somewhere over Route 202
Newcastle County, Delaware

"There it is Governor Collins," The pilot pointed to a large brick building on the crest of a wooded hill.

The governor swung his head around to address the four passengers that were squeezed into the rear seat of the helicopter. "Your grandfather will be freed shortly, Miss Bontrager," Governor Collins promised with a smile.

Kim could barely hear the governor but nodded anyway.

"Find a good place to set her down," Governor Collins ordered.

The pilot craned his neck so he could look out of the cockpits port and starboard windows. "That clearing in front of the hospital will do."

The governor twisted around in his seat again giving Kim, Anne, Eric and Dan a thumbs-up.

On the Hospital Grounds

"Look!" Brock pointed to the approaching helicopter over the tree line.

"They know we're missing and they're searching for us," said Karl.

"Man this is just like Nam," Brock said excitedly, "quick into those trees."

"You don't have to ask me twice," Kate followed as they hid behind some large oaks. The chopper passed directly overhead of the three escapees and flew over the hospital before dropping out of sight on its far side.

"Good they didn't see us," said a relieved Brock, "we need to make tracks and fast."

"The parking lot, how about that?" Kate asked.

"No," Brock shook his head, "even if we made it to my car, they've probably barricaded the roads. We wouldn't have a chance."

"He's right," agreed Karl, "we better move now if we don't want to spend the rest of our lives in Stalag 202."

"Come on, I know this area," Brock motioned his hand forward and Karl and Kate followed him deeper into the woods.

Inside the Psychiatric Hospital

"I wish that you had notified us of your coming, Governor," Doctor Hoffman reluctantly led the governor, Kim and her friends down the first floor hall.

"We could have better prepared for your visit, sir," continued the nervous psychiatrist.

"I'm neither here on a social, nor a media visit doctor. I'm here to have two innocent people released," the governor insisted with authority.

"I think you'll find that Mr. Bontrager and Miss Webster display violent tendencies, Governor, and they should really be evaluated for a longer period of time."

"Listen you pompous fool," Governor Collins was glaring, "if you want to see violent tendencies look into the eyes of Mr. Bontrager's granddaughter and her friends. If so much as a cuticle has been harmed on either Mr. Bontrager or Miss Webster, I'm sure that their friends will be more than happy to accommodate your zeal for violent tendencies." The governor didn't finish his sentence.

The group crowded into the elevator and nervous Doctor Hoffman pushed the appropriate button. Not a word was said during the trip to the third floor.

"This is our floor," the doctor held his hand out waiting for everyone else to leave the elevator before stepping out of it himself. Right this way, Governor." Doctor Hoffman led the group to a room at the end of the hall.

"Why where's Brock? I told him to stay here should Mr. Bontrager, or Miss Webster need anything." Doctor Hoffman looked up and down the hall.

"The door's unlocked!" Kim said pushing it open.

"Unlocked!" stammered the doctor.

"There's no one here!" shouted Kimberly. "What did you do with them you butcher?" she screamed at Doctor Hoffman.

"Well, Doctor Hoffman?" the governor demanded sternly.

In the Woods outside of the Psychiatric Hospital

"It looks like we've lost them," said a heavily breathing Karl. The trio came to a stop on the crest of a hill.

"Where are we?" Kate glanced around.

"Northern Delaware…the Brandywine Valley," answered Brock.

"It's beautiful," Kate sank down on the grass as she viewed the landscape of peaceful rolling hills, stone fences, and luxurious hilltop estates that dotted the countryside.

"Well, the du Ponts don't seem to have any complaints; their family has been making this area their home since the early 1800's."

"We'd better find a place to stay soon, we've only got a few more hours of daylight," Karl urged.

"And it's getting cooler," Kate shivered, with crossed arms.

"Here Kate," Karl removed his jacket and draped it over Kate's shoulders.

"Thank you," Kate smiled.

"I've got a place in mind," Brock interrupted confidently, "a place where they shouldn't look. It's a couple of clicks south of here," Brock pointed in the general direction. Are you ready?" he asked.

Kate and Karl followed Brock as he moved effortlessly down the south side of the hill. At the bottom, Brock separated some strands of barbed-wire that were strung along a lush green pasture so his new friends could slip through. Then grazing mares with their colts became startled at the sight of the three intruders and Brock had to fend off a stallion while Kate and Karl ran for the safety of a stone fence on the far side of the pasture.

"That's Winterthur," Brock pointed down from his hilltop vantage point. "We're lucky; it looks like it's closed for the day."

Kate looked down upon the large buildings, the wooded surroundings and the pond occupied by water fowl, "The ducks, there are so many."

"They're geese, Canadian Geese," Karl corrected. "I used to bring my grand-daughter up here to feed them when she was just a little girl. They migrate through here every year."

"What did you call this place?" she asked.

"It's called Winterthur," Karl volunteered. "It was the home of one of the du Ponts, but I can never remember which one," Karl admitted. "There were so many."

"The late Henry Francis du Pont," Brock filled Karl and Kate in on the history while they caught their breaths. "It's been renovated as a museum and contains American artifacts from as far back as the 1600's. After this mess blows over, you kids should really visit it."

Kate was impressed, "How do you know so much about it?"

"I was a tour guide in this area after I got out of the navy."

"Apparently an excellent one," complimented Kate, who seemed to be taking a new found interest in her escort.

Having caught his breath, Karl was chewing on a piece of straw that he had plucked from the pasture.

Finished with the small talk, Brock constantly scanned the surrounding area for any unwelcome visitors while he led the pair through the museum grounds. They had trod over several small hills and through several meadows before Brock came to a stop, "This is the Brandywine River," he exclaimed.

Kate's eyes grew large, "It's very tranquil."

"Fortunately, it's getting late in the day and season…and there is no one around," Brock exclaimed, following the path of the waterway. "This is where the DuPont Company legacy began, the Hagley museum, but as you can see it's much more than that. It's a step back in time, a walk into the early 1800's."

The three fugitives walked along the tree-lined road that ran beside the rippling waters of the Brandywine River. It was flanked by wooded hills on either side and it meandered through a series of natural falls that spilled across jagged rocks. Mallards and Canadian geese took advantage of the Shangri-La, diving for fish in the translucent pools and at the foot of the foaming rapids.

Magnificent stone structures and buildings, some dating back nearly two centuries dotted the rocky river bank. Brock's calming comments and the serenity of the surroundings dampened the apprehension that Kate and Karl had felt about being apprehended.

As they walked along, Brock enjoyed filling the two escapees in on the history of the area, "Although the du Pont family is originally from France, this is the birthplace of what we know as the DuPont Company. After the French Revolution, Pierre du Pont who was an economist and statesman came to the United States.

Pierre's son, Eleuthere, was a friend of President Thomas Jefferson and in 1802 Eleuthere negotiated with the president for the site of a gun powder mill that he planned to build."

As they walked by, Brock pointed to various locations along the river, "This is the site that he selected for his powder works. The stone structures that you see along the river used water power to process the ingredients that became gun powder. It was extremely dangerous work to make gun powder and during the powder mill's history over two hundred men died in explosions."

Karl's reaction was one of surprise.

"See that mansion up on the hill?" Brock asked.

"That's the original du Pont estate. Mr. du Pont believed that he should not subject his workers to any dangers that he and his family were not willing to be subjected to; therefore, he had his home built so it overlooked the operation. As a consequence, one of the du Ponts died when the house was damaged by an explosion at the powder mill."

It was getting late in the day and with Brock in the lead the three had walked along the wooded Brandywine for some time. Finally, leaving the banks of the river, Brock cautiously directed Kate and Karl to the edge of the woods. Brock slowly moved forward, checking for unwanted company, before waving Kate and Karl forward.

He had brought them to a road, it was route 141. On the far side of the road was what had to have been a ten foot high stone wall. It was an unusual wall because embedded in the top of it were pieces of broken glass.

"Here we are," exclaimed Brock, motioning for his two companions to look through a section of wrought iron gate located in the middle of the wall. "Didn't I tell you I had a place in mind?" he said with a big grin.

Karl and Kate approached the gate and their jaws simultaneously dropped as they viewed what was on the other side.

CHAPTER 7

Home Sweet Home

The Nemours Estate
Wilmington, Delaware 19899

Beyond the wrought iron gate, statues, colonnades, and formal French gardens with a reflecting pool, stood an immense Louis XVI chateau.

Kate stood open-mouth in admiration of the graceful estate.

Awed, Karl stepped back, "You've got to be kidding."

"No I'm not kidding, I know for a fact that the owner is out of town and he's not going to mind us crashing here for the night."

"And whom might that be?" asked Karl.

"The late Alfred I. du Pont," Brock placed his hand over his heart.

"Wouldn't that be breaking and entering?" Karl asked with concern.

"Look, I told you that I was a tour guide. Well, this was one of the places that I worked at and I know it inside and out. We can stay one night and leave without anyone being the wiser. Besides, it's getting late and the cops will never look here. Believe me, it's the only thing to do."

Karl looked at the top of the wall, "It's got to be ten feet if not more and what's the deal with the broken glass?"

"Alfred didn't like his relatives dropping in unexpectedly," Brock grinned.

"Nice touch," Karl pointed to the broken glass that was embedded in the top of the wall, "but I don't want to get carved up just to get a night's sleep."

"You don't have to," Brock waved a set of keys. "I thought that they might come in handy some day. There's a servant's entrance around the back."

"Kate, Kate," called Karl. "Are you coming with us?"

An enthralled Kate finally pried her eyes away from the picturesque chateau. "Where?" she asked, still lost in the experience.

"Inside the mansion, Brock has keys," Karl motioned for her to come along.

"Take me to your interior decorator," commanded Kate.

"You know the good thing about this?" asked Brock.

"No, what's the good thing about this?" Karl was still looking at the glass in the top of the wall.

"Well, if we get caught they think that you two are crazy anyway, so you'll be able to plead insanity. You'd probably get off with a light sentence."

"Somehow, I fail to see that as an advantage."

"Hey, I'm not getting any warmer standing out here," pleaded Kate.

Vrodkutsk Medical Center
Commonwealth of Independent States

"I am sorry Comrade Belenko, but there is nothing that we can do here; except wait." Doktor Kormolov said regretfully to the young nuclear engineer.

"We haven't had the medicines or equipment to treat Direktor Gaslov's condition in months. Our resources have been stretched well beyond their limits and most of the equipment is in disrepair. Look," Doktor Kormolov pointed to the window of Direktor Gaslov's room. An unconscious Direktor Gaslov lay in a hospital bed under an oxygen tent.

"That room was designed to hold two patients." There were five patients that had been crowded into the small room, "Your friend is lucky, many needy patients are going without oxygen. I had to contact the tractor plant to get that oxygen bottle." Doktor Kormolov pointed to the rusty cylinder that stood beside Direktor Gaslov's bed supplying his oxygen tent.

"What about Moscow or St. Petersburg?" implored Belenko. "Certainly they have the facilities to take care of the direktor."

"I'm afraid not," the doctor shook his head gloomily. "They have no bed space and they have been even less receptive to our sending patients to them since the breakup of the republics and word from all of the republics is the same 'no medicine—no bed space—no equipment.'"

"You don't realize the importance of Direktor Gaslov! He is the catalyst that keeps the Vrodkutsk plant operational. Without the power from that plant your hospital doesn't operate—understand?" Viktor became more animated. "Are you telling me that the doktors have not kept a stash of drugs in reserve for their families and friends?" Viktor alluded to the practice which was commonplace under the old Communist regime.

"Oh we had a stash," Doktor Kormolov admitted unashamedly. "We were instructed to keep such a reserve for high party officials, who might be in need of the specialty pharmaceuticals, but once again we haven't been resupplied since the breakup and those drugs that we did have in reserve were depleted months ago."

From his vantage point at the window, a concerned Viktor looked at the motionless Direktor Gaslov. The direktor's wife wept at his bedside. "How long will he last, Doktor?"

"With the proper medication, years possibly. Without it, perhaps a few days."

Viktor searched his mind for an answer, "There's got to be a way. There's got to be a miracle."

The Sub Shack
Kenton, Delaware 19955

"Hi Carol!" a man wearing a flannel shirt and a day old growth of beard greeted the cashier as he entered the combination sub shop and country store. A little bell hanging from the top of the door rang momentarily as he pushed it shut.

"Hi Mr. Kendall, how's that new grandson of yours?" the smiling cashier inquired.

"He's strong, smart and handsome. Apparently, he takes after me," laughed the spirited man.

"Oh is that so, have they named him yet?"

"Not yet, Steve and Alice weren't prepared for a boy. It turned out that the doctor had gotten Alice's sonogram mixed up with another expectant mother's sonogram. So they only had girls names picked out."

"I've never heard that one before," said Carol. "Maybe they could have a boy named Sue," she said chuckling to Mr. Kendall's dismay.

"My goodness, I certainly hope not," laughed Mr. Kendall.

"So what can I do for you today?" asked Carol.

"Is the grill still on? That hospital food is murder. No cholesterol. No salt. No sugar. What's the use in living if you're eating the equivalent of cardboard?"

"You'll have to ask Sandy," she pointed to a woman who was sweeping the floor at the back of the shop while humming along to a gospel song on the radio.

"Sandy, customer," called out the cashier.

Startled, Sandy looked up from her broom, "Oh, hi Mr. Kendall. How's that grandson?"

"He's doing fine; I just came from a visit at the hospital."

"That's just great," the cheerful lady said while she stepped behind the deli counter. "Have you started spoiling him yet?"

"Not yet; but I've talked to Lowell Clark about buying one of his Shetland ponies when the little guy gets old enough."

"That won't take long," Sandy raised her hand above her head," the older I get the faster my kids seem to grow up."

Mr. Kendall was obviously pleased with the idea of having a grandson.

"So, what can I do for you?" Sandy asked as she picked up a spatula.

Mr. Kendall removed a soda from a cooler, "How about one of your delicious cheese steaks?"

"Well, we normally shut off the grill at 7:45; but in honor of the birth of your new grandson, I'll make an exception."

Mr. Kendall noted the time on the clock behind the counter. It was 7:57. "No need to put yourself out Sandy, I can get something else; like a cold sub."

"Nonsense, anyone who is at least partly responsible for increasing the population of little Kenton deserves four star service," insisted Sandy as she cut open a roll. "Want anything else on that sandwich?"

"Fried onions and ketchup, please."

"It'll just be a few minutes," Sandy placed the steak on the sizzling grill.

"Thanks Sandy," Mr. Kendall stood at the deli counter listening to the end of *How Great Thou Art.*

"Time for the WDIA radio eight o'clock news. Governor Collins was disappointed twice today when he tried to gain the release of Karl Bontrager, a janitor at the Old Statehouse and an advocate for Delaware's playing a greater role in developing new technologies and practices. Mr. Bontrager was jailed at the Dover Police Station on charges of inciting a riot in his neighborhood this morning.

Among others; the governor was joined at the Dover Police Station by Kimberly Bontrager, Karl Bontrager's granddaughter, and a number of her fellow students from the University of Delaware. Prior to the governor's arrival, Mr. Bontrager had been transferred along with his neighbor, Kate Webster, to a psychiatric institution in upstate Delaware.

Miss Bontrager and three of her friends accompanied the governor who then flew to the institution to gain the release of Mr. Bontrager and Mrs. Webster. Upon their arrival at the institution, it was discovered that Mr. Bontrager and Miss Webster had apparently escaped with, what is believed to be, the help of a hospital orderly by the name of Brock Mattingly, a Viet Nam Veteran and a recipient of the Congressional Medal of Honor.

In a released statement, the governor assured the press that none of the three were dangerous, but were merely caught up in a big misunderstanding with Dover authorities; which snowballed into their unjustified transfer to the institution. The governor also appealed, on behalf of Miss Bontrager, for Mr. Bontrager to contact his granddaughter immediately should he be listening to the governor's statement."

"In other news, the White House has expressed concerns over nuclear centrifuges that had been covertly shipped to the Island Nation of Badasi."

Sandy turned the radio down as she placed Mr. Kendall's cheese steak in a paper bag.

"Who's this Karl Bontrager fellow?" Mr. Kendall turned to Sandy.

"Oh my, you really have been camped out at that hospital."

Mr. Kendall nodded, "I guess I've been isolated from the world for a couple of days."

"He's the talk of Delaware; I even heard that there was a story about him on the national news."

"Well what did he do, rob a bank?"

"No, on the contrary, he's given Delaware a vision of what it could and should be."

"And long overdue respect for Delaware," Joined in Carol who overheard the conversation from her place behind the cash register. "He's a hero as far as I'm concerned."

Interested, Mr. Kendall listened to the two women as they filled him in on the phenomena of Karl Bontrager and the events of the past couple of days. Hmmm, he finally thought, *Karl Kendall…that sounds pretty good.*

Pleasant Pheasant Country Club
Rehoboth Beach, Delaware 19971

"I can't see much difference between these graphite clubs and my old clubs," declared Speaker of the House Barnibus Futz. Having just completed eighteen holes, the Speaker, Congressman Oliver, Gil Hickman and House Majority Whip Schroeder headed for the clubhouse.

"Well, they'll take some getting used to, Mr. Speaker," Gil Hickman said patronizingly.

"This way to the clubhouse dining room, gentlemen," Gil Hickman held the door open for the House members.

"I've got to hand it to you, Congressman, you and your associates have certainly built an impressive golf club," Speaker Futz nodded to Congressman Oliver.

The maitre d' escorted the group to a table overlooking the course.

"With all due respect Mr. Speaker, graphite, or no graphite, there's the matter of a bet to be resolved," Oliver held up his score card. "It's right here in black and white."

"Oh yes, about my making good on our bet." The Speaker perused the menu as he talked, "What kind of legislation did you have in mind?"

Congressman Oliver placed his shrimp fork on the table as Gil Hickman and Majority Whip Schroeder listened intently, "It's in response to the problems that we've been having in the governor's race."

"Oh yes," Speaker Futz added, "I understand that you've lost considerable ground in the polls. Apparently, that janitor has caused quite a stir."

"He has, Mr. Speaker," Hickman cut in, "before the debate, Congressman Oliver was ahead in the polls, but since the debate we've been lagging the governor substantially."

"But my people have told me that both you and Collins were verbally attacked by Bontrager. How can the governor continue to maintain such a margin?"

Hickman sipped his wine before answering, "Immediately after the debate, Governor Collins was running around the state trying to win Bontrager's release. The public has been hood winked. They think that the governor is an honorable man by fighting for the rights of his foe and that Bontrager is a hero because he's fighting for the public's rights."

"That's right, I had heard that he was mistakenly jailed," said the Speaker.

"But my advisor had told me that Bontrager's whereabouts are unknown. That he escaped or something, before Governor Collins could locate him. How much of a threat can this man be? He's nothing more than a janitor, right?"

"Bontrager has caught Delaware's attention," said Hickman.

"And he's already catching the nation's attention," Majority Whip Schroeder insisted. "I've seen a couple of stories on the national news. They paint him as some kind of down-to-earth character with a common sense approach to problems. Someone who is legitimately concerned with the needs of the average person rather than special interest groups."

"A janitor with a following, Mr. Speaker," reminded Congressman Oliver.

"Students, farmers, businessmen, laborers and housewives are organizing in support of Bontrager's vision despite his disappearance and each additional day that he is gone, his popularity increases. He's become a phenomenon."

"The Congressman's Washington office has been getting barraged by phone calls, telegrams and mail in favor of a bill that will embrace Bontrager's ideas," Hickman held out his hands helplessly.

"Mr. Speaker." Congressman Oliver turned to Futz, "I need to have your help if I'm to have any chance of winning Delaware's State House for the party."

"So what's this bill got to do with your race?" asked the Speaker. "It sounds dangerous. How are we supposed to generate the funds that we need to run for public office without contributions from corporations and special interest groups?"

"And Bontrager has these hair-brained ideas about developing solutions with Delaware know-how," Hickman scoffed. "He wants to use Delaware as a clearing house for solving problems. A place where the development of solutions can be performed on a small scale with small budgets, ensuring their success prior to implementation on a larger scale with big budgets."

"Do you realize the uproar that this would cause in Congress?" Majority Whip Schroeder spoke leaning across the table. "The efficient use of funds is not a high priority when you have 535 members in the House and Senate crying for money to appease the constituencies in their home states."

"I see what you mean," Speaker Futz agreed. "He could overturn a few apple carts if he's not stopped, but how do you propose to both stop him and gain the edge in your state's governor's race?"

Gil Hickman motioned to Alan Bean who had been sitting patiently at the next table and brought a briefcase to Congressman Oliver's press aide.

"Thank you Alan," Hickman took the briefcase from the man. "This is a rough draft of a bill that Congressman Oliver is going to submit for committee review. In short it asks for the program that Bontrager proposed during the debate."

"What?" the Speaker exploded, "I just thought that we agreed that Bontrager's ideas were dangerous!"

"They are," Hickman grinned, "but his ideas will never materialize."

"How so," Majority Whip Schroeder leaned forward.

"Well, you give Bontrager and his followers a carrot. A very short carrot that will give him a chance to test his theory."

"But what if he succeeds?" asked the speaker. "Then we'll be obligated to continue funding his program."

"We're talking about a janitor not a nuclear scientist," Hickman explained.

"Oh, I see," observed Speaker Futz.

"The key is that you give him a test that he won't possibly be able to succeed at," Congressman Oliver jumped in, "a problem that no one has been able to solve and least of all an untrained janitor without political experience."

"Right, then after he fails," Hickman winked, "you can cut off the funds and go back to business as usual. As an outcome, Congressman Oliver will receive a ground swell of support for being such a dedicated supporter of Bontrager's and that support will carry him into the governor's office."

"So what pitch do we throw him?" asked the speaker.

"Well, we have a lot to choose from," the Majority Whip pondered, "Crime, pollution, hunger, health care, war…you name it."

"That's quite a smorgasbord. I vote for world hunger," said the speaker.

"Not visible enough." Hickman disagreed.

"What do you mean, not visible enough?" objected the speaker.

"Well, what do you do when you see those commercials on television? The ones to feed starving children in far-off lands. Do you run to your phone and make a contribution?" Hickman paused momentarily for any takers. "That's what I thought; you turn the channel and watch something else.

It's a topic that Americans for the most part are uncomfortable with and one that won't cast a death blow to the program. We need a problem that will emphasize the shortcomings of Bontrager's ideas and their inability to solve a major problem, like drugs."

"Man you're out for blood," the majority whip snickered, "the federal government can't even stop drugs, the public will see right through your scheme if you use that as Bontrager's test subject."

Hickman sighed, "Don't worry about it. We still have some time to figure out what problem we can throw at Bontrager. In the end, we'll look good and you'll look good.

"All we need is your help Mr. Speaker," appealed Oliver, "and yours Schroeder, to get the bill promptly out of the subcommittee and onto the House floor for a vote before the election."

"What do you think?" Speaker Futz turned to the majority whip, "Can it be done on such short notice?"

"It will take some hard work, but I have a lot of favors that I can call in from the aftermath of that check-bouncing thing," Schroeder added thoughtfully. "I'll have my staff start with the phone calls on Monday."

"Good, how about if I schedule a vote for mid-October? That will give us a good month to get all of our ducks in a row, and it will give you a few weeks post-passage to get some mileage out of it on the campaign trail," the Speaker pointed to Congressman Oliver.

"Sounds good, Mr. Speaker," the congressman agreed with a big grin.

"When can you have that final bill ready for my review?" the majority leader turned to Gil Hickman.

"You can have this copy of the rough draft for the time being," Gil handed Congressman Schroeder a large envelope. "I don't envision it changing much in its final version, Congressman, mostly t's to cross and i's to dot."

"Gentlemen, this will finally put to rest this Bontrager phenomena and score us some deeply needed points with our constituencies in the process," assured of success, Congressman Oliver raised his wine glass.

"Very well then," House Speaker Futz rose from his seat, "I'll be seeing you all back in Washington on Monday. I have a prayer breakfast to preside over tomorrow morning in Nashville."

CHAPTER 8

Roughing It

The Nemours Estate
Wilmington, Delaware 19899

"Well, here it is, the servant's entrance," Brock stood triumphantly at a gate located at the back of the mansion.

"How do you know that no one is here?" asked Kate.

"Nemours is closed from the fall until spring."

"Okay, but how do you know that this place isn't alarmed?" asked Karl.

"Oh, but it is, that's why I have this," The orderly pulled a second key from his pocket. "After being called out on numerous false alarms such as rabbits and migrating birds roaming the grounds, the local police insisted on a means to disable the system without having to wait for Nemours staffers. So back in the '50's they came up with this two-key method to disarm the security system. The sensors in the lawn, the cameras on the grounds, and around the perimeter of the mansion, you name it. But it's useless unless you know where the lock is, as well as the proper sequence to operate it."

Starting with the wall to the left of the gate, Brock ran his hand along the middle row of stones, "Here we are." He removed a false front to the block exposing a key lock with a red and illuminated light-emitting-diode (LED). Then he felt along the middle row of stones along the right side of the gate. Once again removing a false front and exposing another key lock with a corresponding illuminated red LED.

"It'll take two of us in unison," said Brock shaking his head. "The guy who designed this system must have worked at an ICBM installation at sometime.

It's too great a distance for one man to turn both keys simultaneously. Take this key and insert it in the right lock but do not turn it."

He handed the key to Karl who promptly inserted the key and awaited further instructions.

Brock inserted his key, "Listen, after I count three, then we both turn our keys together. I'll count, one, two, three and turn. Understand?"

"I've got it," answered Karl, "you'll count one, two, three and turn."

"Okay, here goes, man your keys," cautioned Brock watching Karl, "one, two, three and turn." The two men turned their keys simultaneously and the red LEDs disappeared to be replaced with glowing green LEDs.

"Great," said Brock who promptly removed each key and replaced the false fronts to the stone wall, "now for the gate," He took one of the keys and unlocked the gate pushing it in for his fellow fugitives.

Christiana Towers Dormitory
University of Delaware in Newark 19716

"We've done all that we can for your grandfather, Kimberly," concluded Dan firmly as the foursome entered the dormitory, "and the governor said that he would let you know as soon as he hears anything."

"That's true; at least your grandfather is free," added Anne. "That's the most important thing. Now we just have to wait for a phone call or for him to come walking through your door."

"Hey now, you can't blame her for being worried," Eric sympathized. "What if he was your grandfather? I'm sure that you would be wondering where he was."

"That's the problem," Kimberly sighed, "I have no idea where he is. He could be out in the cold, freezing, for all I know and who knows when he last ate."

"Hey, you once said that he was on a flight crew in the air force, right?" asked Eric. "He must have gone through some sort of survival training then. All of those aviation types have to. I know for a fact; my cousin is a P-3 Charlie pilot for the Navy—one of those planes that searches for submarines off the coast. He told me that the Navy sent him to school out West for survival training and that he learned how to live off of the land. He said that he became so hungry that he even ate a snake. I'm sure that your grandfather had similar training."

"Sure he did," Dan agreed, "and I recall this movie where these people crashed into the side of the Andes Mountains and they resorted to cannibalism to survive."

"That's just what I needed to hear," said a rattled Kimberly. "My grandfather may not only be freezing to death; but he may be eating poisonous snakes and God forbid fellow human beings."

"What do they know, Kimberly?" Anne looked at Dan and Eric with a look of condemnation. "I know your grandfather and he's no cannibal and believe it, or not, you two," Anne shot the two men another scornful look, "I've never seen Mr. Bontrager eat a snake or any reptile for that matter."

"Hey, hey, this is getting out of hand. No one's accusing Kimberly's grandfather of being a cannibal," Dan chided.

"That's right," Eric added, "we're just trying to reassure Kimberly that her grandfather will be okay."

"Right," said Dan, "and what about that guy who apparently sprung your grandfather from the hospital?"

"Brock?" asked Eric.

"Yeah, that's him," Dan remembered, "He was in Vietnam and everyone knows that Vietnam wasn't any picnic."

"And one of the orderlies at the hospital told the governor that Brock had received the Congressional Medal of Honor while in Vietnam." Eric jumped into the conversation, "they don't hand those out in boxes of Cracker Jacks. If someone can get your grandfather through this ordeal, it sounds like this Brock guy can."

"I know what you need to do," Anne said as she led Kimberly to a chair, "and we can help. We all need to start working on some of the solutions to problems that your grandfather had talked about during the debate."

"Now that's a great idea!" Eric jumped on the suggestion thinking that it might help Kimberly out of her depressed state. "Good thinking Anne." Eric took Kimberly's hand, "The best way to stop worrying about your grandfather is for you to start laying the ground work that will fulfill his dreams. We can mobilize the student body to come up with real solutions to the problems that face the world."

A bit of a glow began to return to Kimberly's face, "Real solutions though," she said. "None of this hocus pocus stuff that you hear these transcendental gurus talking about. You know my grandfather is a strong believer in common sense and doesn't take kindly to these fanatical types who would just as soon kill a person to save a tree."

"I agree," Eric nodded, "we need engineers, scientists and proven problem solvers who can identify the problems and develop a consensus as to how to handle them."

"We also need compromise from all parties involved, whether it is industry, the government, or the civil sector," said Anne. "Without these groups talking face to face, nothing will be accomplished."

The Nemours Estate
Wilmington, Delaware 19899

"Welcome to *Life Styles of the Fugitive and Famous*," Brock struck a lighter as he led Kate and Karl into the dark mansion.

"This place gives me the creeps," said Kate.

They stood beneath a massive chandelier in the grand foyer of the mansion. Brock held the lighter higher so Kate and Karl could check out the accommodations for the evening. They could see a vaulted ceiling and a well appointed interior. In addition, a long stairway curved up to the second floor.

"This will do for the night," Karl said.

"Well it's all that I could reserve on the spur of the moment," Brock quipped sarcastically.

"Nonsense, it's incredible," said Kate, missing Brock's sarcasm.

"Yeah Brock, I bet Robin Leach himself couldn't have done any better on such a short notice," kidded Karl.

"Who's this?" Kate pointed to a painting of a distinguished looking gentleman in a dark suit. Brock stepped forward to get a better look.

"It's Alfred, Alfred I. du Pont," Brock exclaimed. "This mansion and the surrounding 300 hundred acres were his."

"Where's the light switch?" asked Kate.

"No light switches," protested Brock who lit a candle that sat on an antique table. "Even though we've disarmed the security system we don't want to chance a passing police car seeing our lights from the road."

Holding the candle; Brock searched the large room, "There," he pointed, "the fireplace. Karl, see if you can get the fire started while I search the pantry for some food and be sure to open the damper."

Kate watched Karl as he lit a candle for her and one for himself. After opening the damper; he organized a couple of logs and after several attempts finally got a steady burn.

They were admiring the flames jumping to life when Brock returned, "They must have cleaned the pantry when the staff closed up for the winter months," he complained.

"I'm feeling pretty hungry," said Kate, "we did a lot of walking today."

"Same here," said Karl, "I've been operating on two cups of coffee and a stale sandwich that they gave me at the police station this morning. I was hungry even before we escaped from the hospital."

"No problem," said Brock. "There's a phone in the office," Brock started down the hall.

Thirty-five minutes later a buzzer was heard at the rear of the house and after close scrutiny Brock and Karl walked to the service gate.

"Two of Amilio's Grosso Pizza Italiano, that'll be eighteen dollars," a teenage boy wearing an Amilio's green, white, and red jacket; and baseball cap handed over the boxes. "I didn't think that anyone lived in this house."

"They don't, we're just here for the annual séance," Brock said solemnly as he paid the boy.

"Annual séance?" inquired the awestruck young man.

"Sure," Brock exclaimed coolly, "each year we contact some of the former inhabitants of the mansion."

"Wow!" sputtered the excited boy wide-eyed, "I thought that sort of thing was a hoax."

"Oh, no," Brock scoffed, "that's why we ordered pizza."

"Say what?" said the boy.

"Yeah, they didn't like the Mexican food that we got them last year, heartburn," Karl patted his chest with his fist.

"Man that's incredible! Wait until I tell the guys at school."

"Look Kyle," Brock read the boys name tag, "for the next several nights we'll be contacting a lot of former inhabitants of the mansion and we can't afford to have any disturbances, you know kids staring through windows that sort of thing.

It would disrupt the séances and everything and I'd have to file a report to the American Seance Association. You know, telling them that intrusions by you and your friends disrupted the séance. So how about holding off telling your friends for say, another week and as long as our séances go off without any disturbances, we'll use you as a caterer to the beyond; by the way they tend to be pretty big tippers." Brock handed the boy a twenty in addition to the eighteen dollars that he had already given for the pizza. The delivery boy's eyes grew large as he looked at the bill.

"You don't have to worry about me," the delivery boy made a zipping motion across his lips. "Hey do you think that they might be interested in a menu? Amilio makes great lasagna and no heartburn."

"Well, I feel sure that they would," said Brock.

"I feel the same," said Karl. "I seem to remember Mrs. Peacock asking for some lasagna."

"Great!" The delivery boy reached into his coat pocket and pulled out several of Amilio's menus. "Here and good luck with the séance. In fact, you might check with them to see if anyone's interested in a franchise. I heard Amilio talking about expanding his operation and as far as I know the sky's the limit."

Karl took the two pizzas and the menus from Kyle, the pizza boy.

"Sure," Brock nodded, "we'll ask them."

Karl and Brock watched the elated delivery boy get into his Yugo and drive away.

"No wonder our school system gets such a bad rap. Look what they've got to work with," complained Karl, shaking his head.

"Mexican food, heartburn and the kicker Mrs. Peacock, I think you've been playing too much of that board game, *CLUE*, Karl," Brock laughed.

"Oh yeah! Well it's not as bad as you with your *Amazing Kreskin* routine. Séances! Hungry deceased former inhabitants!" Karl rolled his eyes.

"Hey the bottom line is that it worked and we finally have something to eat."

"You don't have to tell me twice," Karl was already aiming the pizzas at the servant's entrance door.

Kate was waiting when they reentered the house, "What took so long? My stomach is making noises," she moaned, holding the door open wide for Karl who carried two large boxes.

"Had to tip the delivery boy," said Brock.

"Man, this place gives me the creeps," Kate closed the door behind the two men; then led them to the living room with her candle.

"I see the fire is coming along nicely," Brock smiled as Kate cleared the antique table of museum pieces for the pizzas.

"I don't suppose that you thought to order something to drink?" asked Kate of Brock.

"No, I can't say that I did," answered Brock with a note of self-reproach. He thought for a second, "Give me a minute." Brock took one of the candles and proceeded down the hall, disappearing into a room where doors could be heard opening and closing. He returned minutes later carrying a dusty wine magnum in one hand and a cork screw in the other, "It's not *Diet Coke* but I've been assured that it's top of the line stuff."

"Now you're what I call a tour guide," Kate cheered her host as she removed three crystal goblets from a hutch and passed them around. Brock opened the bottle with the cork screw. He took a moment to check the bouquet of the wine by holding the cork under his nostrils as he inhaled. "I hope 1903 was a good year," he said pouring the first glass.

"The same year that the Wright Brothers made their first flight," Karl reminded him.

"Well then, it couldn't have been that bad of a year then, now could it?" said Kate holding a filled wine goblet.

Karl waited for Brock to finish filling the final goblet before proposing a toast, "To our liberator Brock Mattingly."

"Here, Here," Kate raised her goblet.

"Now I'd like to propose a toast," said Brock topping off the three goblets, "to the people who liberated me from Doctor Hoffman and to their successful escape."

Their goblets once again met in ceremony.

"I too have a toast," said Kate as she waited for her goblet to be topped off for the second time. "To something very dear to my heart," she hesitated; "to pizza!" she screamed then darted to the large orange and white Amilio pizza boxes.

For several minutes the three trespassers sat in leather back chairs that were positioned around the crackling fire, and gorged on pepperoni pizza, washing it down with red wine.

Karl finished his second slice when he looked up from his plate which was engraved with a colorful depiction of George Washington crossing the Delaware, "Hey Brock!"

Brock withheld the slice of pizza which was about to enter his mouth, "what is it Karl?"

"When you're finished stuffing your face would you mind passing the *Grey Poupon*?" Karl asked with a grin.

Brock patted his shirt pockets as if looking for the elusive condiment, "Why, I seem to have misplaced the *Grey Poupon* Karl, but how about one of these?"

Brock reached into his shirt pocket and pulled out some cigars.

Karl, being a pipe smoker, wasted no time in accepting the after-dinner treat. "Why thank you Brock."

"Kate?" Brock offered her a cigar.

"I'll pass, you two enjoy yourselves while I clear the table," Kate began taking the dirty plates into an adjacent room. Karl lit Brock's cigar with a candle then lit his own. He took one puff then held the cigar while admiring its aromatic flavor.

"They're Cuban," said Brock, "Mr. du Pont had extremely good taste."

"I should say so," agreed Karl, taking another puff, "my granddaughter would give me an earful if she saw me with this right now. She's been after me to stop smoking a pipe for years."

"That's good she's thinking about you, she cares about your well-being."

"She's quite a young woman," said Karl proudly. "I'm all that she's got now." He continued, "My son and daughter-in-law died in a flash flood while doing missionary work in Bangladesh."

"I'm sorry to hear that," Brock consoled Karl.

"There's nothing to be sorry about," said Karl, "they're with the Lord now, the Lord and my wife." Karl looked toward the flickering ceiling, "Apparently God had a greater mission in mind for them. Someday he may have a greater mission for me."

"Maybe that someday is today? I don't know if you realize it, but you've made quite an impact during the debate. Sure there were some doubters, but you got people in this state talking again, talking possibilities instead of limitations, talking solutions instead of fears."

In fact, I'm the best example that you could have. I was disgruntled with the system, with my workplace and the people in authority who didn't exercise their power to make needed changes. Political and business leaders who are more concerned about their tee-off times than their responsibilities. I'm telling you Karl, your vision has the possibilities of making a real difference. It's a message of self-help and helping others instead of relying on government help.

That's what attracted me to it; I've seen the worst that man has to offer both in war and in peace. In some ways there's not much difference between the two. In war there is more visible damage like blood and broken bodies while in peace, spirits are sometimes broken; I've seen plenty at the hospital.

People who couldn't put the pieces of their lives back together after a traumatic incident. They may be suffering from the loss of a loved one, experimentation with drugs, financial collapse or who knows what; but they're aching just as much as those people with the physical wounds; maybe more so. The doctors can sometimes help and things get better every once in a while for the patient, but sometimes their efforts fail for one reason or another and after seeing results that often fall short, I was burned out and due for a change. Your idea gave me the inspiration for the change that I needed."

"How about one of you throwing another log on the fire," Waving her hands to dissipate the cigar smoke, Kate had returned for the empty pizza boxes, "it's dying down."

"Sure thing Kate," answered Karl taking a puff from his stogie.

"By the way," Kate paused before exiting the room with the boxes, "where do we sleep tonight?"

Brock thought for a second before responding. "Karl and I can just sleep here in a couple of living room chairs. As for you, you can sleep in the office down the hall. It's where the tour guides used to take their breaks, there's even a fold-out couch."

"I'll have to check it out," said Kate as she exited the room.

C-5B Galaxy Cargo Plane
in
Vrodkutskan Airspace

"If you think that was bad, you should have seen some of the arguments that my parents had," Sergeant Ariel Najar leaned back in his flight engineers seat to address the pilot and co-pilot seated at the controls of the massive C-5B Galaxy cargo plane.

"My father is Syrian and my mother is Jewish. Oh, the discussions that they used to have about my barmitzvah. It was like the Seven-Day War all over again."

Aircraft Commander Colonel Henry McIntyre and his co-pilot Captain Lucas Stoneking had been laughing at the flight engineers routine for several minutes.

It helped to break up some of the monotony of the arduosly long trip which took them from Dover Air Force Base in Delaware across the Atlantic, then over Western Europe.

Although the C-5 carries enough fuel for the average American car to make 31 trips around the world it was necessary for a refueling stop at Rein Mein Air Force Base, in the newly reunited Germany. Their flight then continued into what was considered, just a few months before, hostile air space over the former Warsaw Pact countries of Eastern Europe and the former Soviet Republics themselves.

Despite the length of their mission of mercy, the five man crew was afforded a relatively comfortable ride from the C-5B's four General Electric turbofans that were capable of winging the aircraft along at a speed of 571 miles per hour and at a ceiling of 35,750 feet.

The largest aircraft in the Western Hemisphere, the aircraft's cargo carrying capacity was renowned. Incredibly, it was capable of lifting six transcontinental buses, 48 Cadillacs, 106 mustangs, or 25,844,746 ping pong balls. More suitable to its mission, the cargo plane could carry 2 M1A1 Abrams battle tanks, 7 complete UH-1 Huey Helicopters, 8 complete F-5 fighter planes, or 270 troops. Furthermore, its 222 foot long wingspan was capable of supporting a take off weight of 837,000 pounds and its cargo hold was longer than the Wright Brothers first flight. On this mission though, the palletized freight contained relatively light food stuffs and clothing that were bound for the people of Vrodkutsk.

"You should take that routine on the road when you leave the Air Force Sergeant Najar," said Captain Stoneking.

"You think that it's that good, sir," asked the flight engineer as he checked his fuel gauges.

"It's better than some of the skits that I've heard on television; or for that matter, the reservation," said the Native American co-pilot. "Speaking of reservation; did I ever tell you how I got the name Lucas?" asked Captain Stoneking.

"You're going to regret this Sergeant Najar! You've got him started now," said Colonel McIntyre.

"Well you see, Sergeant, my parents despised all white men for the longest time." Captain Stoneking's eyes searched the air space ahead for other aircraft as he started to tell his story. "That is until they got their first television set. Do you know what it's like trying to get a cable hookup on the reservation?"

The copilot didn't bother to turn around to check for a response from the flight engineer.

"I'm telling you it's not easy. That pale-faced cable guy must have searched the inside of that tee pee for a good hour looking for a place to bring in the signal," Captain Stoneking waited for the laughter of his fellow crewmen to die down before proceeding with his story.

"Well, to make a long story short; my parents were watching a rerun of the *Rifle Man*, when they saw Lucas McCane shoot General Custer's horse out from under him before the battle of Little Bighorn. He became an instant hero on the reservation and when they heard that Chuck Connors was part Cherokee, well that sealed it-Lucas Stoneking."

"I'm happy that you didn't write the history books Captain," said a relieved Colonel Macintyre. "Otherwise you may be sitting in the left seat now instead of me."

"Yes sir, and you'd be on the white man's reservation," laughed the Captain.

"What do you think of that, Sergeant Najar?" a grinning McIntyre looked back for a second to see the response of his flight engineer.

"I'm the wrong person to ask, sir. Half of me wants to give up the Gaza strip and the other half of me wants to keep it," quipped Najar, who was logging fuel levels in a note book.

"That's quite a dilemma, Sergeant," laughed McIntyre while turning some switches on his radio transmitter. "It's time to check in with Vrodkutsk tower."

"Vrodkutsk Tower, this is MAC 454 inbound from Dover, over." The commander waited momentarily for a response."

"Roger, MAC 454 this is Vrodkutsk tower. Be advised…snow with cross winds of 20+ knots…poor visibility below."

The colonel keyed his microphone, "Roger Vrodkutsk Tower. This is MAC Flight 454…present altitude three two thousand."

"Roger MAC 454…have you locked at 100 miles. Whiskey one is yours."

"Roger whiskey one Vrodkutsk Tower…MAC 454 out." Colonel McIntyre switched off his transmitter.

"Vrodkutsk Tower just reported snow on the ground and 20 plus knot cross winds," said Colonel McIntyre. "We're designated to land on whiskey one, Captain Stoneking."

"Roger, Commander," Captain Stoneking broke out the pre-landing check list.

CHAPTER 9

Special Delivery

Emilio's Pizza
Wilmington, Delaware 19899

"That's him!" shouted the excited delivery boy pointing at the large screen television in the corner of the restaurant.

"That's who?" asked Amilio who continued slicing a combination mushroom and pepperoni.

"That's the guy that I told you about last night. Remember, the séance delivery at the du Pont estate? You know the Nemours Mansion," shouted the excited boy recognizing Karl Bontrager's face as it was flashed on the screen during a news report.

"Oh no," said Amilio rolling his eyes sarcastically, "the pizza franchise for dead people. We really need to get this drug problem under control in this country. If you kids would stay off drugs you wouldn't have these crazy ideas."

"I'm telling you Amilio, it's the truth," insisted the boy as he walked around the counter toward the television.

"Right and I'm Leonardo Da Vinci," unimpressed, Amilio closed the pizza box. With a twist of the volume control, the boy could hear reporter Ron Mathew's voice grow louder over the speaker. Karl's still picture was suddenly replaced by film of an interview that the reporter had conducted with Kimberly Bontrager at the Christiana Towers dormitory. Kimberly wore a button that simply said KARL and she was flanked by Eric, Anne, Dan and other college classmates.

"Apparently, Mr. Bontrager and his companions still believe that they are being pursued by Delaware authorities. Is that the way you see it Miss Bontrager?"

"Yes Ron; I've heard nothing from my grandfather and I would appreciate it if anyone with information to his whereabouts would contact me," a concerned Kimberly pleaded.

"I'm sure that if our listeners have any information on your grandfather's whereabouts, that they will contact you Miss Bontrager," Mathews assured Kimberly. "As our listeners should know; the governor has assured me that Karl Bontrager, Kate Webster and Brock Mattingly are not wanted by Delaware authorities and that the three are welcomed to return freely to their homes without any repercussions," the reporter added.

"Thank you for bringing up that point Ron. My grandfather has done nothing to deserve this treatment," said Kimberly forcefully and to the delight of her fellow students. "I'm just waiting for him to come home."

"I can't imagine what it must feel like not to know where your grandfather is. How are you dealing with it?" asked Mathews holding the microphone outstretched for Kimberly's comments.

"It's strenuous;" said Kimberly, "but I and these students, faculty and concerned citizens you see here do not plan to sit around waiting and worrying.

As a group, we've decided that when opportunities present themselves, we are going to do our best effort to use my grandfather's principles.

"It sounds very interesting, but don't you think that it's a bit naive of you to lead people into thinking that you and fellow Delawareans can solve their problems? I mean you're not the first person who's attempted to tackle these problems. There have been many good intentioned and unsuccessful attempts prior to yours."

"It's naive to ignore our problems," shot back Kimberly. "I don't claim to have the answers to any or all of these problems but to do nothing is to be a fool who's destined for defeat.

I might add that our group is just one example of what's happening throughout the state of Delaware. After hearing my grandfather's inspiring message during the gubernatorial debate, Miss Zoey Nielson, a school teacher from Sussex County quickly organized a food and clothing drive among Delaware schools, churches, businesses and military installations. Aware that Dover Air Force Base had been flying relief missions to the former Soviet Republic of Vrodkutsk, Miss Nielson got an agreement from the base to airlift these goods. This is a demonstration of our support to their new independence."

"The airlift sounds like a good idea, but I'm sorry, some aspects of your organization still sound like something that was left over from the hippy movement," Mathews grimaced. "Like those groups in the desert that take sledge hammers to missile silos. It sounds far fetched and if you'll excuse me, kooky."

Kimberly bristled at the reporters comments, "Look, do you see any love beads around my neck or daisies in my hair?"

The reporter shook his head from side to side. "Okay then, give it a rest," Kimberly barked.

Regaining her composure, Kimberly attempted to reason with the reporter, "Look Rob, we've tried to think this thing through without being too unrealistic. For the most part, we as students realize that we will have to work and live in this world upon graduation; therefore, we have a stake in whatever actions we undertake while in school.

In the aftermath of my grandfather's speech, I would never have guessed that I would have been contacted by so many people who are interested in helping to make his vision a reality.

I'd venture to say that we have students ready to pitch in from nearly every major, here at the University, as well as students from Delaware State College, Delaware Tech and other institutions. This coupled with the experience of interested farmers, fisherman, housewives, educators, businessmen, professionals and other areas that have contacted us.

I tell you now, you will not find us standing in protest atop a missile silo swinging a sledge hammer. You will not find us endangering the lives of loggers by driving two inch spikes into trees. You will not see us condoning drug use or violence.

What you will see is our turning our attention from the studies of Shakespeare, to more timely and practical undertakings, such as; finding solutions that are derived from hard work and common sense, solutions which have been purged of weaknesses and which are born from practicality, and above all; solutions which have proven their effectiveness."

"It sounds like a tool that could be used by a political group or special interest group," Mathews probed for flaws in the plan.

"We've taken great steps to assure that this doesn't happen and anyone who attempts to do so will be met with great resistance. We are not a political or special interest group and as far as we are concerned the law of the land will be the boundaries within which we will work.

We are concerned citizens that want to carefully think through the engineering, social or economic problems that the world faces. Then we will test possible solutions on a small scale and after gaining a consensus as to what works and what doesn't work, we will implement the best solution for a given problem. What political bodies do with our conclusions is secondary.

Our goal is to start the search for answers, but we're not that naive to think that we will come up with the best possible solutions every time."

"I have to admit you sound very determined Miss Bontrager. I wish you and those involved good luck on your efforts," With that segue; Ron Mathews signed off before being replaced by another news story.

Kyle turned down the volume on the television, "So that's what they were up to. They're actually members of this Delaware group. I thought that séance stuff sounded a bit unusual," Kyle said scratching his head as he walked behind the counter. He lifted the receiver from the wall phone.

"What do you think that you are doing?" challenged Amilio who was preparing some deliveries.

"You heard what the reporter said, that Bontrager guy's granddaughter wants to know his whereabouts." The delivery boy pressed the buttons.

"You have a delivery to make," scolded the businessman.

"It'll only take a minute," said the boy as he waited for someone to answer the phone, "Hello…yes maam, I have some information about that Bontrager guy."

Vrodkutsk International Airport
Vrodkutsk, Commonwealth of Independent States

Maxwell Alexander had opted for the comfort of the back seat of his limousine rather than brave the bitter snowstorm that had engulfed the Vrodkutskan airfield in near zero visibility. He had seen many changes during his assignment as both a low level operative with the State Department at the U.S. Embassy in Moscow, and as the newly appointed Charge'd'Affaires to Vrodkutsk.

Only 27, he had anticipated years of waiting and hard work before getting such an assignment; but the '91 revolution had changed all of that. It was a text book case of him being in the right place at the right time.

Overnight, the superpower which had been the Soviet Union for the greater part of the twentieth century had disintegrated into a commonwealth of numerous and weakened countries eager to regain their independence.

Countries such as Byelorussia, the Ukraine, Azerbaydzhan and Vrodkutsk had been sovereign states prior to their seizure by Russia during World War II. They were just four of the fifteen countries who had fallen prey to the claws of *the Russian Bear* during this chaotic period of world history.

With the recent breakups of the Soviet Union came the State Department appointments to the hastily reestablished governments. Subsequently, Alexander's timely laughs at poorly told dinner party jokes; his animated discussions regarding the latest Tom Clancy novel with top State Department officials; and his adeptness at diplomatic receptions paid off.

Despite the fact that it didn't have the appeal of his first choice for an assignment—Bern, Switzerland—he had accepted the appointment.

For that matter Vrodkutsk didn't have many paved roads or indoor facilities. Nevertheless; Maxwell Alexander was the Charge'd'Affaires of Vrodkutsk, a region better known within the State Department as Russia's answer to Camden, New Jersey.

Alexander was startled from his reading of *Patriot Games* by a tap at the limo window. A soldier standing outside the limousine had given the Foreign Service officer a thumbs up and had motioned toward the skyline above the end of the runway.

The Charge' quickly marked his place in the excellent read, buttoned his long black overcoat and put on his Muscovite fur hat. The driver opened the car door and Max stepped onto the snow covered taxiway that ran adjacent to the runway. It was a cutting cold wind that immediately reddened Alexander's face.

As he raised his head into the blizzard, the familiar high pitched scream of four powerful General Electric engines was heard in the distance, but the heavy snowfall made it impossible to see the aircraft. Max was rubbing his eyes when the soldier shouted a second time; once again pointing above the end of the air strip.

The ghostly outline of an immense camouflaged C-5B Galaxy had suddenly become visible over the end of the airfield and the whining of its jet engines grew more intense as each second passed. Gradually, the twenty eight wheels, resembling the poised talons of an eagle about to snatch its unsuspecting prey from a meadow, could be seen hanging from the undercarriage of the mammoth cargo carrier.

Max watched, as ailerons corrected the Galaxy's roll while it descended through the intense crosswinds. Several feet off of the ground it began its flair, and vortices of snow flakes began to appear spinning off of its outstretched wing tips and towering T-tail.

Of the many flights that the new charge' had seen arriving from Dover this was by far the most exciting that he had witnessed. The skill, the professionalism, the precision and the raw guts that it took to bring this warehouse with wings into Vrodkutsk field were apparent, and he had seen it demonstrated countless times before, although not quite as dramatically.

As the wheels made contact with the runway, the snow violently thrust out from the bottom of the fuselage. It forced the charge' to look away as a tsunami of air and flurries passed through his position beside the limousine. By the time he was able to raise his head again, the pitch of the engines had shifted. The aircraft commander had pulled the throttles back and the thrust reversers had been engaged in an attempt to slow the aircraft's ground speed to a stop.

To bring such inertia under control before the end of the airstrip was like trying to ride a Brahma bull with your spurs imbedded in its hind quarters.

Surprisingly though, the plane quickly dumped its speed, coming to a stand still at the end of the runway. Its engines now idled at a low pitched whine for a couple of minutes, while it waited for a *follow-me* truck to lead it to a parking space.

The U.S. Air Force had requisitioned a Vrodkutskan army truck for the purpose of directing the plane to a berth beside the freight terminal and fortunately; the exhausted crew did not have to wait long for it to arrive. The truck's flashing yellow lights moved past the fuselage of the big bird and immediately took up its position at the nose of the plane. As the truck slowly moved forward over the snow covered strip, the whining pitch of the engines picked up and the C-5 started its creep forward in a procession of follow-the-leader.

Within minutes the aerial behemoth had been brought to a stop beside the freight terminal and the crew had shut down its four engines which continued to spin freely from the brisk air currents that flowed between its nearly six-foot long fan blades.

The freezing charge' could see the pilot and co-pilot through the cockpit window. They sat some 30 feet above the ground in relative comfort going through their post-flight checklist while Max waited patiently on the tarmac.

Russian soldiers surrounded the aircraft and a line of green army trucks moved into position behind the plane in preparation for offloading.

In time the forward door had opened and a ladder had been extended from the fuselage. Meanwhile, a sergeant assisted some passengers down the ladder of the aircraft.

The charge' briskly stepped forward to greet an attractive woman wearing a green fur lined coat that the air force must have given her.

"You must be Miss Nielson," asked the charge'.

"That's me," answered the young woman, "Zoey Nielson."

"I'm the acting Charge' for Vrodkutsk, Miss Nielson, welcome to sunny Vrodkutsk." Max extended his gloved hand to the woman.

"Alexander, Maxwell Alexander," proclaimed the charge' in his best James Bond. "I'll be your liaison during your stay," he stated with authority.

"Very good," she smiled.

"We greatly appreciate your leading Delaware's efforts to bring these badly needed goods to the Commonwealth of Independent States, Miss Nielson. It's a deeply needed show of support for these courageous people."

"Thank you Mr. Alexander, I hope that it can get to the people who most need it," She spoke while shielding her face from the driving snow.

"We'll do our best to see that it does," assured Max.

"That's all that I ask," she smiled and quickly introduced her group to the charge'.

"I have some other business to attend to here but I'll be joining you later at a reception that's being held for you at the Embassy. For the present, I'll turn you over to Mr. Jefferson. The charge' steered her to an escort who took her to a waiting bus.

The next group to trickle down the ramp was the crew. Colonel Macintyre and Captain Stoneking were the last to deplane and Maxwell Alexander was waiting for them.

"Couldn't stay away I see," bantered Alexander.

"We couldn't pass up the balmy weather," countered the colonel; holding his cap to his head.

"You guys can socialize; I'm getting into the terminal before I freeze my butt off," shouted Stoneking.

"Oh come on now Lucas, you're destroying my image of the Native American. I've always had this image of a brave warrior sitting on horseback in the driving snow with his head held high and you've got to go ruin it for me," quipped the colonel.

"That wasn't my tribe," objected the captain, "my tribe was the one where the young strong brave sat in a warm teepee drinking a hot cup of coffee while his shapely squaw gave him a back rub."

Captain Stoneking made for the door of the freight terminal and disappeared inside. A moment later Colonel Macintyre and the charge' caught up to him. The rest of the crew was enjoying some badly needed coffee and exchanging war stories with some Russian soldiers who had sought shelter from the storm. During the interim, Russia still kept troops in some of its former states.

As usual, at the conclusion of these flights a frenzy of trading broke out between the former adversaries. Russian vodka, hats, patches, hammer & sickle pins, and photographs were exchanged for American patches, hats, jackets and cigarettes. These moments were truly historic and both groups of men wanted their pictures taken shaking each other's hands or wearing each other's hats to prove that they had been a part of it.

"How do you like your coffee, Colonel?" the charge' asked as he poured a cup for the Galaxy's commander.

"Blonde and Sweet," the colonel requested as he brushed the snow from his uniform.

The charge' added some cream and sugar then passed the paper cup to the colonel.

"We've got a special delivery for you to make, Colonel."

"It must be important for you to come here personally to tell me about it," said Macintyre.

"The Secretary of State himself approved it after conferring with the president. You know how adamant the U.S. has been pertaining to nuclear proliferation."

Colonel Macintyre nodded.

"Well, you'll be tasked with the medivac of a Russian nuclear engineer who has a serious heart ailment."

"What's that have to do with stopping nuclear proliferation?"

"This Nuclear Engineer is the Direktor of the Vrodkutsk Nuclear Research Center just outside of town and apparently, he's the main reason that a mass exodus of Soviet nuclear scientist and technicians hasn't occurred. So far he's been the conscience that has kept most of them in place by invoking ethics, patriotism and scriptures from the bible, how about that one for a switch?" Max shook his head. "I tell you, Colonel, there are real fears that if he doesn't resume his post soon, his fellow scientists and technicians will flee the country in search of better opportunities."

"Why can't he get treatment here?"

"They don't have the facilities, equipment, or medicine to treat his heart condition. Tell me, Colonel; when do you think you can be ready for your return to Dover?"

A tired Macintyre drew out his answer, "Mr. Alexander, we can be turned around within 24 hours."

"Good then," Max raised his cup of coffee in a toast to the aircraft commander and smiled, "Good indeed Colonel."

CHAPTER 10

Pizza Special Surprise

The Nemours Estate
Wilmington, Delaware 19899

"What time is it?" a disheveled Karl Bontrager entered the kitchen.

Brock checked his wristwatch, "Zero-eight-thirty,"

"That cross-country excursion you took us on yesterday must have worn me out," Karl took a seat at the kitchen table, "I don't remember the last time that I've slept this late." Then Karl's eyes quickly lit up when he detected a familiar aroma, "Is that coffee?" Karl asked.

"Sure is?" Brock reached for the pot.

Karl looked puzzled, "Pizza is one thing, but don't tell me that they have coffee delivery in this upscale neighborhood too."

"It's surprising what the staff leaves around here when they close up for the winter," Brock pointed to an open box on the counter, "have a *Pop-Tart.*"

Karl removed a packet from the box, "Where's Kate?"

"She's freshening up," answered Brock smiling as he filled a cup.

"Do I detect some interest?" Karl asked.

Brock turned from the kitchen counter, "That girl is definitely a sparkplug and she's easy on the eyes too."

"Well you can add feisty to cute," Karl bragged, "that girl has some fight in her. Why you should have seen her when the media was staked out on my front lawn," Karl looked as if he were talking proudly of his own child."

"I could see that when we were making our way from the institution, she's got determination," Brock passed a cup to Karl.

As Karl accepted the coffee from Brock's outstretched hand he noticed a ring that he was wearing.

"That's quite a ring you're wearing Brock," Karl's memory was at work. "There's something familiar about that design," said Karl, "it must have cost you a fortune."

"More than you'll ever know," said Brock.

"Mind if I take a closer look?" Karl read the inscription that encircled a large gold star that contained two figures, one of which held a shield. An inscription read, *Fair winds and following seas.*

"My goodness, I had no idea, "Karl looked at Brock as if he were in the company of General George Patton, himself. "That design is from *the Congressional Medal of Honor*," Karl drew back in reverence.

"That sounds familiar, what's *the Congressional Medal of Honor*?" asked Kate walking into the room while brushing her freshly washed hair.

"It's only the highest honor that can be bestowed upon a member of the U.S. military," answered Karl, "and it's only awarded to those who have displayed extraordinary acts of heroism in action."

"Now that is something," Kate moved in close to look at the ring, "how did you receive it?"

"Vietnam, but there were a lot of guys who deserved it more than I did and they never got one."

"Yep, he's a *Congressional Medal of Honor* recipient," said Karl. "I've only had the honor of meeting a couple during my thirty years in the Air Force, but they had this modest attitude about receiving it."

"Well, tell us more Brock about what you did to receive it?" Kate was both impressed and curious when it came to Brock. Early on she had thought that there was more beneath the surface of this resourceful machine-like human who at no time seemed to need a break during their cross country escape from the hospital.

"Ever here of the Navy SEALs?"

"You mean like the animal?" Kate replied.

"You had said you were in the Navy, but a SEAL too?" Karl interrupted, "they're only the premier special forces group in the military. SEAL is an acronym Kate; it stands for Sea, Air, and Land; they're trained to operate in all three environments. The bottom line is…they don't take any cow manure off of anyone."

"Gee you make us sound bigger than life Karl," Brock protested, "and you're about to make me blush."

"So what happened?" Kate insisted.

"Well, I was in a unit that was conducting maneuvers north of the DMZ." Brock continued, "Our orders were to penetrate a North Vietnamese fortress under the cover of darkness and to grab its Commanding Officer for questioning back at Da Nang. It was supposed to go off without a hitch, *in-and-out*, with no gunfire if all went according to plan; but they were waiting for us. Someone had tipped them off. They allowed us to get inside the compound and then they let us have it. A fire fight broke out.

Two of our men were hit immediately and all but one of us managed to fight our way out. Once on the outside, we heard screams coming from inside the NVA compound. It was our wounded team member that we'd left behind. We knew that the NVA would give him a slow and painful death if we left him, so there was no real decision to be made. While three of my buddies suppressed enemy fire, I went back in and greased a group of V.C. who were approaching our wounded team member. I then carried him outside of the compound where we managed to elude the NVA and eventually made it to safety by swimming to our rendezvous…a waiting submarine in the Gulf of Tonkin. Years later, a buddy of mine, who worked for the National Security Agency, said that the NVA had more than likely been tipped off by using crypto information that John Walker had supplied them."

"Walker," Karl remembered the name, "the submarine radioman who was convicted of spying for the Soviet Union."

"That's right," Brock acknowledged in disgust. "It turned out that the man that I had the privilege of saving was himself a recipient of the Congressional Medal of Honor from a previous tour of duty in Vietnam. He's the one that had this ring specially made for me," Brock flexed his hand, "I've worn it ever since."

"Sounds like Rambo," Kate said without thinking.

"You can forget that crap that you see in the movies," objected Brock, "that day I was scared numb."

"That has got to be the most heroic act that I've ever heard of," Karl was obviously moved. "When I was a young airman I sometimes saw the bodies of dead soldiers and wondered what I'd do in a situation like that; a situation where I'd be placed at risk."

"Well, it's not something to be sought after believe me," Brock insisted, "You opened yourself up to risk when you spoke out during the debate. Look at what happened, you've lost your job, you've been jailed and now you're on the run from the authorities. It takes no small act of courage to speak out for what you believe and you did just that Karl."

"You might say that Karl deserves Delaware's Medal of Honor," interjected Kate.

"Please Kate, there's no comparison between me speaking my mind during the debate and Brock's saving a soldier's life while under enemy fire," Karl felt patronized. "What I'd like to know is how did a Medal of Honor winner end up as an orderly in a psychiatric hospital? You must have had some opportunities after receiving the Medal."

"I did," confirmed Brock with a sigh, "I was offered an appointment to the Naval Academy, but I turned it down. After hearing about some friends being spat upon when they returned stateside in their uniforms and then watching Congress micromanage the war, I decided that I didn't want to remain one of their chess pieces any longer. I wanted to get away from it as much as I could."

"So you went to the institution?" asked Kate.

"Not at first, I took a hiatus from the world for a few years, working odd jobs such as the tour guide. Eventually, I was contacted by a friend who knew that I was looking to try something else. He suggested the institution and they hired me.

I felt good about it at first and worked with a few good doctors who seemed to care about their patients, but I gradually grew discouraged over the blatant greed and disinterest displayed by the likes of Doctor Hoffman. Under Hoffman many patients were considered ill until their medical insurance ran out; then suddenly, a miracle cure would be found. You and Kate were an opportunity for me to get out of there and to get my adrenalin pumping again and I'm glad that I took it."

"Well, you came to the right people," Kate assured Brock.

Then, Karl stood up from the table to stretch his legs when he glimpsed something through the window, "Police car!" he shouted.

Brock and Kate leapt up from the table to see the police car parked by the servant's entrance.

"A news van," said Kate nervously, "behind that wall. I can see its satellite dish."

Brock rushed to a front window of the mansion, "They've got ladders and they're coming over the wall, there must be a dozen of 'em carrying microphones and cameras."

"They've got us outnumbered, Brock," Karl joined Brock at the front of the mansion. "Do some of your Medal of Honor stuff and quick!"

"Do you believe this, for you to survive Vietnam only to be done in by a pizza delivery boy?" said Kate who had followed the two men into the room.

"Not quite," disagreed Brock, "hurry! Follow me." He led the pair down a hallway, then down a stairway that ducked into a sub ground level room.

They could hear the swarm of reporters shouting as the mob crossed the perfectly landscaped grounds of the Nemour's mansion, getting ever closer. The servant's entrance gate had since been opened at the rear of the house and a swarm of reporters flooded into the compound. This, in conjunction with their co-patriots who were rushing the front of the house resulted in a pincer maneuver, an attempt to cut off their prey from any escape.

"What is this room?" Kate asked.

"I heard it was a small research laboratory of some sort," explained Brock as he searched a wall with his hands. "As a safety precaution, an emergency exit was installed. That's what I'm looking for, the exit!" He continued scouring the wall for the door that blended in perfectly with the papered wall.

"Uh huh!" Karl cleared his throat, "Tell me Brock, does this exit fold into the wall and does it have a backing of four inches of steel," Karl asked mockingly as he stood leaning against the entrance to the newly discovered portal.

"That's it," said a relieved Brock. "Quick!" he coaxed Kate and Karl through the opening to their escape route. The sound of reporters simultaneously rushing in through both the front and rear doors could be heard as Brock stepped into the dark tunnel pulling the door shut behind him to conceal their means of escape.

Vrodkutsk International Airport
Vrodkutsk, Commonwealth of Independent States

"That's it," shouted Loadmaster Serello to his men from the rear cargo access. "Let's get this booster secured," he ordered stepping onto the C-5's rear loading ramp.

"How's the load going, Sergeant Serello?" asked Colonel Macintyre. He had just stepped from around the fuselage of the aircraft to the foot of the ramp. Charge'd'Affaires Maxwell Alexander and Nuclear Engineer Viktor Belenko were with him.

"So far no problems sir," answered the sergeant.

"Good job. We'll be taking off shortly sergeant," said the Colonel.

"Yes sir, all that's left is to finish securing the booster in place, sir. I'll give the Russians credit, they make some big rocket motors," said the loadmaster. "It was a tight fit."

"Za energia rocket boosters are za largest in za world," Belenko spoke proudly in broken English. "No other rocket motor can produce zuch thrust."

"No doubt and the U.S. is lucky to get this remarkable piece of technology," Charge' Alexander admitted.

"And at bargain basement prices," added an American soldier who was standing on the back of the truck. Charge' Alexander shot the American youth a censuring look. True; the United States was in the midst of cashing in on the former Soviet Union's Red Sale of high-tech goods; but Charge' Alexander was well aware that the pride of its people was still alive and well and he was extremely sensitive to comments that might offend their dignity.

"Do you think that I could see Direktor Gaslov before you leave Colonel?" asked Engineer Belenko.

"Certainly, Mr. Belenko, now if you'll follow me gentlemen," Colonel Macintyre led Engineer Belenko and Charge' Alexander onto the after ramp of the cargo plane and then to the ladder that led to the after troop compartment of the C-5 Galaxy.

Once to the top of the ladder the three men approached the stretcher upon which Direktor Gaslov lay. An American doctor and nurse, on loan from the U.S. Embassy in Vrodkutsk, tended to the patient's needs.

"How's Direktor Gaslov doing Doctor?" asked Charge' Alexander.

"We presently have him on beta blockers," answered the embassy physician, "they should help break up the arterial blockage."

Engineer Belenko stepped to Direktor Gaslov's side, "Can you hear me Direktor Gaslov?" whispered Belenko.

Direktor Gaslov's eyes opened, "Viktor."

"Yes, Direktor Gaslov," answered Belenko moving closer to better hear his boss.

"They're taking me to America, Viktor," Gaslov managed a smile.

"Yes, I know sir, they have the equipment and medicine that you need and the doctors will treat you very well there."

"I wish that you were coming along."

"I would like that very much, going to America, but comrade I'm afraid that my responsibilities are at the plant. I have to try to continue your excellent tradition as head of research...that will be an enormous task during your absence."

"The officials have made a good choice my friend," Engineer Belenko's tired looking mentor tried to encourage him. "You will do fine Viktor, they're good men, they just need some guidance at times. Tell them that I look forward to seeing them again."

"And we will look forward to your return, Direktor," responded Belenko.

"I'm sorry gentlemen but Direktor Gaslov has a long flight ahead of him and we must prepare for our departure," interrupted the embassy doctor.

"It sounds as if I must be on my way," the direktor smiled wanly.

"Yes sir." Engineer Belenko stood at attention as he gave the direktor a thumbs-up. Colonel Macintyre led Engineer Belenko and Charge' Alexander to the ladder that was located at the rear of the compartment. It dropped down to the after cargo area of the Galaxy aircraft.

Charge' Alexander climbed down the ladder first, waiting for Belenko and Macintyre.

"Well then, it looks as if Direktor Gaslov is in good hands," Alexander assured the Engineer.

"Da," agreed Belenko, "I am sure Direktor Gaslov vill receive very good care in America."

"And, Colonel, I wish you the best on your flight," the Charge' extended his hand to the Air Force officer. "I trust that Direktor Gaslov will have a smooth flight," the Charge' added confidently.

"Yes, good flying to you Colonel Macintyre," Belenko shook the Colonel's hand, "and please keep us up to date on Direktor Gaslov's progress."

"I'll pass that on to his doctors," Colonel Macintyre assured Engineer Belenko.

"Thank you Colonel," Belenko followed Charge' Alexander down the ramp at the rear of the aircraft. Colonel Macintyre watched the men exit the C-5 then walked forward to join Captain Stoneking who was making preflight preparations in the cockpit.

The Russian and the diplomat walked to Charge' Alexander's waiting limousine. They watched the crew and ground support personnel prepare the large cargo carrier for flight. One of the ground crew, who wore a pair of mouse ears, stood well in front of the nose of the Galaxy.

He gave hand signals as each of the massive engines came to life. The sound was deafening and it caused the men to shout while communicating.

"I'm amazed every time I see one that's about to take off," shouted the charge'.

"It's a fantastic sight," agreed Belenko. "I am pleased that they have good weather today."

"I'm sure the colonel agrees with you," the charge' cupped his hands about his mouth so that the engineer could better hear him.

They watched for several minutes, as the Galaxy moved from its parking place and followed a truck to end of the airstrip where the Galaxy came to a stop. Its engines remained at idle while Colonel Macintyre waited for the truck to move off of the runway. Moments later, the throttles were opened and the C-5 began its takeoff roll; rapidly accelerating down the runway. After several hundred feet, its nose rotated upward and the aircraft's camouflaged fuselage made a quick ascent toward the clouds.

"Direktor Belenko, need a lift?" asked Alexander of the new interim direktor of the Yakustk Research Center.

It took Belenko a moment to respond. For the first time someone had called him by his new title and the responsibilities that went with that title were felt by him for the first time. It would be a heavy burden filling the shoes of the man who was presently en route to the United States.

"Well, Direktor?" Alexander asked a second time.

"Da," replied Belenko, snapping out of his daydream, "I would appreciate that very much, Mr. Alexander."

The charge' opened the car door for the Russian Engineer and Belenko took a final look at the far horizon before getting into the limousine. The C-5 Galaxy could be seen fading into the distance, racing the Direktor toward the United States where a former foe would soon try to save the old man's life.

CHAPTER 11

The Tunnel

The Nemours Estate
Wilmington, Delaware 19899

"This reminds me of one of those after-life experiences," said Kate groping in the faint light given off by Karl's lighter. "You walk through a dark tunnel and when you come out the other end you see your deceased relatives and pets."

"Quiet," warned Brock, "we don't want to tip them off. They could be standing on just the other side of this door."

"Well let's get moving then," whispered Karl holding the light high to illuminate the tunnel.

"This way," Brock beckoned, leading his two fellow escapees into the darkness. They walked for several yards feeling their way along the walls.

"Eeeeek!" Kate suddenly screamed grabbing her chest which was pounding violently. "Watch out!" she squealed.

"What is it?" asked a startled Karl.

"Someone's in here, I just saw him," she moved behind Karl for protection.

Brock and Karl peered intently into the darkness when Karl's lighter caught the reflection of two eyes peering back. Karl stopped, "Maybe it's the police."

For a moment they waited for the person to react, but it did not. It stood motionless, the outline of its face flickering in the jumping light as its eyes locked onto the three intruders.

"Who are you?" asked Karl of the stoic person.

There was no response. Karl moved his lighter from side to side but the stranger's eyes remained fixed. It made no sound, and it made no attempt to challenge them. It just seemed to be waiting for their next move.

"Dummy," said Brock softly.

"I wouldn't try to provoke him Brock, he may get mad," Kate cautioned.

"No Kate," Brock shook his head from side to side, "It's a dummy, a mannequin. At times they used them for props. Apparently, they've decided to store them in here during the off-season. It's a good dry place. Let me see your lighter, Karl." With the lighter held high, Brock walked toward the figure, "Yep, we've got ourselves a mannequin. A well dressed one and from the looks of it he's got company," Brock referred to some other mannequins that lined the side of the tunnel. They wore clothing from the early 20th century.

"Now follow me," said Brock, stepping around the human likeness, "and be careful, who knows what they may have stored in here."

"Hey!" said Kate as she observed one of the figures close up, "I've got an idea."

Kate quickly pulled a brunette wig over her blonde hair, "Hurry, put these on." She handed Karl a pair of wire rim glasses that she took off of one of the mannequins, "Hopefully, that will change your appearance enough that people won't recognize you,"

She then removed Brock's lab coat and replaced it with a brown jacket that she had removed from yet another mannequin, "The sleeves are a bit short, but it'll do."

"This jacket is tight," complained Brock.

"Would you rather be taken back to the hospital?" responded Kate, "I'm sure a straightjacket would be even tighter."

Suddenly, the sound of footsteps and voices could be heard coming through the walls and floors of the house.

"They're in the house, come on," Brock said in a whisper. He turned quickly and moved into the darkness with a lighter as his only illumination.

"Where's this tunnel come out at?" asked Karl as he cautiously followed Kate, who followed Brock.

"I'm not sure, but someone once told me that it had an exit," a couple of minutes had passed when Brock came to a stop, "There's a ladder ahead, wait here," he ordered. "I'm going up to take a look topside," handing Kate his lighter, Brock quickly climbed the ladder that followed the tunnel shaft upward. Several seconds passed before he came halfway down again, pausing on one of the rungs. "We're in luck; we're just outside of the chauffeur's quarters."

Brock started back up the ladder with Kate and Karl close behind. He cracked open a lid to make another quick check of the area before pushing it open fully.

"All right, there's no one in sight...let's be quick," Brock said exiting the tunnel. He waited above helping Kate and Karl from the tunnel and then closed the exit to cover their trail, "Hurry, into the garage."

The building was situated a hundred yards from the main chateau but only fifteen yards or so from the tunnel exit. The three fugitives ran the short distance to the door that led to the chauffeurs living quarters and darted inside through a side door.

It was a two-story structure in the style of the French architecture used for the main house, but much more modest. The second floor was once used as the living quarters for the chauffeur's family and it had a couple of balconies that overlooked the pastoral settings of the Nemours estate.

The first floor contained a machine shop that was separate from a large garage area which contained several limousines once used by Alfred I. du Pont and his family during outings.

"Get into this one," motioned Brock, pointing to the '51 Roll's Royce Silver Shadow. Kate and Karl wasted no time following his instructions as Brock removed a chain barrier that was used to keep tour groups out of reach of the vehicles; he then pressed a button next to the large oak garage door. It slowly rose while Brock jumped into the chauffeur's seat of the classic automobile, and Kate and Karl, in wig and glasses, opted for the backseat.

Brock opened the glove compartment where a set of conveniently placed keys sat as if pre-positioned for their escape. The automobile started on his first try and he stopped it momentarily outside of the garage; returning to close the oak door.

"We've got to cover our tracks," he cautioned, getting back into the luxury automobile."

Brock put the Rolls in gear for the short trip to the main gate and freedom.

Once at the gate, he stopped the car, pulling down the sun visor to expose a key card that he promptly inserted into the gate's electronic scanner. The gate slowly opened and Brock drove the car through the opening and over the grounds of the A.I. du Pont Institute, a non-profit hospital for seriously ill children. The institute sat on grounds adjacent to the du Pont estate. Seconds later, Brock pulled the Silver Shadow onto Rockland road. Successfully departing the

Nemours grounds undetected, the three were on the lamb, but this time, in style.

C-5B Galaxy Cargo Plane
over the Atlantic

"There she is…right on schedule," announced a relieved Captain Stoneking.

"Where?" Colonel Macintyre searched the heavens, "I still don't see it."

"At eleven o'clock," answered the co-pilot.

Colonel Macintyre strained his eyes through his Polaroid sunglasses, "You must have eyes like a hawk Lucas; I don't see anything but an empty sky."

"At eleven o'clock, Colonel, its flying straight and level," insisted Captain Stoneking.

There was silence for several seconds. To help sensitize his eyes, Colonel Macintyre turned his head away from the sunlight that was streaming in through the cockpit windscreen. After a moments rest, he resumed his search for the elusive KC-10. Then, the tanker's thin vapor trail became visible to the Aircraft Commander's strained eyes. To facilitate getting airborne with the heavy Energia rocket motor, the Galaxy had taken off light on fuel from Vrodkutsk, and the tanker had flown from its base in Reykjavik, Iceland for the sole purpose of topping off the cargo planes fuel tanks.

"You win again, what is it this time?" asked Macintyre, "another steak with all the trimmings at the O-club?"

"Sounds good," responded Captain Stoneking with a sly grin, "that'll be medium-well, sir." Stoneking was not immune from gloating.

"From now on I think we should call you *Captain Eagle Eye*," Macintyre nodded as he banked the Galaxy toward the KC-10, "I've only heard of one other person that could see as well as you do, Lucas."

"Who's that, Colonel?" asked Stoneking.

"Chuck Yeager, I read his biography. He contributed much of his success as a fighter pilot during WWII to his eyesight.

"No kidding."

"Sure, in fact he could spot the enemy well before any of the other pilots in his squadron and he used this advantage to get the jump on his apparently nearsighted opponents in the German Luftwaffe."

"What kind of plane did he fly?" asked Stoneking.

"He became an ace flying the supercharged P-51 Mustang. He even shot down a German jet once, an amazing accomplishment when you consider that his P-51 was a propeller driven aircraft. It's no wonder that he was selected to break the sound barrier."

"Maybe I shouldn't have passed up becoming a fighter jock…might have a couple of Iraqi Migs to my credit by now," Stoneking motioned with his index finger as if chalking up two kills.

"MAC 454, this is Texaco 21." The UHF communications receiver interrupted Colonel Macintyre's war story as he promptly reached for the UHF microphone. It was located amongst numerous communications and navigation equipment boxes that were housed together in a large console on the floor between the Aircraft Commander's and Co-pilot's seats. "Roger, Texaco 21, this is MAC 454, have you visually at ARIP." Colonel Macintyre was referring to the Air Refueling Initial Point, an area located upstream from the designated refueling area where the receiving aircraft initiates a rendezvous with the tanker. "Altitude two one thousand…Heading two seven zero…Speed mach seven five…over," Colonel Macintyre un-keyed his microphone.

"Roger, MAC 454, have you at ARIP and commencing air refueling track."

In preparation for the air refueling rendezvous, The KC-10 broke off from its orbit over the Atlantic and now flew due west, several miles ahead of the thirsty C-5B Galaxy cargo plane. In accordance with air refueling procedures, the tanker maintained an altitude of 22,000 feet, one thousand feet above that of the trailing Galaxy.

Colonel Macintyre increased the throttles to Mach 0.77 to close the distance on the tanker. At six nautical miles from the air refueling control point, Captain Stoneking started to run down the pre-contact checklist for the refueling.

He scanned the multitude of switches, buttons and levers that surrounded his seat, verifying and, if necessary, positioning them accordingly; *IFF…set…anti-collision/strobe lights…on…*He stopped for a moment pointing above the colonel, "The air refueling door, Colonel?"

Macintyre flipped a switch located above his head, "Refueling door cleared to open," he assured Stoneking, who continued down the checklist. *No smoking light…on…Rudder limit switch…Min Q.*

Simultaneously at the Flight Engineer's desk, Sergeant Najar was running down his pre-contact checklist; *Aux and Extd Range Boost Pump Switches…off…Left and Right Separation Valves…open…Fill valve switches…open…Aux and Extd Range Refuel Switches…set…Electrical Power Switch…REF…Boom Latch Switch…Norm…Air Refueling Isolation Valve Switches…REF…Air Refueling Door Switch…Open, Lights On…*

At one half of a nautical mile from the Air Refueling Control Point, Colonel Macintyre reduced the throttles to .65 mach (270 knots) and pulled back on the control yoke. The Galaxy's nose pointed upward, beginning a gradual thirty degree climb toward the tanker's tail end.

The KC-10's underbelly grew larger in the C-5's windscreen as separation steadily decreased. Colonel Macintyre could now see the boom operator looking down from his observation window at the tail of the tanker. The airborne service station seemed close enough for the boom operator to take a squeegee to the C-5's windscreen. He extended the refueling probe to supply the Galaxy with the JP5 that it needed to complete its flight to the states. Through the use of a joystick, the boom operator operated ruddervators which extended from either side of the refueling probe, in the process correcting for the probe's position.

Captain Stoneking watched intently as the probe slowly moved above the Galaxy's cockpit, disappearing as it passed behind the Galaxy's windshield toward the receptacle located on the centerline of the cargo jet's fuselage.

Watching a series of Pilot Direktor Lights, located on the underbelly of the tanker, Colonel Macintyre gradually nudged the massive airframe closer and higher. He thought about the principles that he conveyed to his students in Aerodynamics 201; a class that he taught as a part-time instructor to Delaware Tech's aviation students.

The Galaxy's huge black nose generated a bow wave, of sorts, that was similar to that of a boat. The cushion of air that preceded the cargo plane actually pushed the tanker forward at a greater rate than the KC-10's thrust was allowing.

When talking to civilians or his student aviators; Colonel Macintyre often compared it to the drafting techniques that he had seen NASCAR drivers employ at Dover Downs *Monster Mile*. On countless occasions he sat in its grand stand watching the likes of Richard Petty and Dale Earnhardt who extended the fuel consumption of their cars by drafting off of one another. The rear car's nose tucked so closely to the rear bumper of the lead car that it actually pushed the lead car from behind through a cushion of air. A feat not for the faint hearted at 160 miles an hour!

A feat made even more difficult when the mass and inertia of two aircraft, with a combined length of over one and a half football fields, is flying at Mach 0.6 and an altitude of 21,000 feet.

Up, down, forward and aft; Colonel Macintyre made minute adjustments to the C-5's throttles, elevators and rudder to correct for the turbulence that the

KC-10's number three engine was generating around the Galaxy's towering vertical stabilizer.

Simultaneously, Captain Stoneking double checked the separation between the aircraft, while Sergeant Najar sat at his Flight Engineer's desk awaiting the 170,000 pounds of fuel from the tanker.

After a few minutes, Colonel Macintyre finally found the sweet spot as it was called by the Galaxy crews—a pocket of relatively low air turbulence that the aircraft could hover in during the fuel transfer. At that point the Pilot Director Lights transitioned from red to green and the flight crew could hear the probe's nozzle sliding across the fuselage above their heads, then; into the refueling slipway, located 12 feet behind the C-5's windshield. With a thump it finally made contact with the Galaxy's receiver.

"We're taking fuel, sir," announced Flight Engineer Najar. The cargo plane was receiving 9,000 pounds of fuel per minute and it was Colonel Macintyre's job to keep the Galaxy in position for the nineteen minutes needed for the transfer.

C-5B Galaxy troop compartment.

Back in the troop compartment, Direktor Gaslov was unaware of the mid air refueling that was presently taking place. The Galaxy's large airframe provided him with a comfortable ride as he rested under the supervision of the embassy's medical team, or more specifically, Nurse Baxter.

Just an hour before the nurse had relieved Doctor Bryant of his two hour shift. He was taking a nap in one of the seventy five seats of the troop compartment, all of which with the exception of his were empty.

An IV stuck out from Direktor Gaslov's arm and several electrodes were pasted over his chest. Nurse Baxter monitored his vital signs on portable electrocardiograph and blood pressure monitors. An opened defibrillator unit sat within easy reach.

It seemed like an extremely long hour to the nurse, who watched the phosphorus glow of the cardio rhythm on the cathode ray tube. It had a tranquilizing effect as it pulsed up and down at a consistent rate, scanning across the screen, from left to right. The strain that it placed on her green eyes prompted the nurse to rub them back into focus.

"Coffee?" a voice asked from the rear of the troop compartment. Sergeant Scarelli was standing at the coffee mess at the aft rear corner of the troop compartment. He saw the nurse's fatigue as a way of making some conversation with the pretty red head.

She pulled her hands from her eyes to see the loadmaster with an out-stretched steaming cup.

"Coffee," Scarelli repeated.

"Yes, I could use some," she patted her skirt down as she stood up, and then walked to the rear of the compartment to accept the hot cup from the sergeant. Out of the corner of her ear, she continued to listen for the rhythmic beep that accompanied each of the pulses that appeared on the electrocardiograph's screen.

Beep…beep…beep…"Thank you," she said to the blushing young man. "Watch it ma'am." Beep…beep…beep…Its awfully hot," he said handing the young woman the coffee cup, "Cream or sugar?"

Beep…beep…beep…"Sugar, please," She held the cup as the sergeant added the sugar.

"So how long have you been a nurse?" Scarelli asked.

Beep…beep…beep…"Seven years," she answered after taking a sip of the refreshing brew. "Four in the states, two in Moscow before the breakup and the last year in beautiful Vrodkutsk," she laughed.

Beep…beep…beep…"How long have you been flying?" she asked.

"Flying?" Scarelli repeated, as if surprised. He walked over to the small window in the side of the Galaxy's fuselage and looked through it. "My god, we are flying," he said with a frightened look. "Some Russian guy told me that this was a freight elevator…at least I think that's what he told me. I'm afraid that my Russian's not very good." Nurse Baxter started laughing so hard that some of her drink spilled over the edge of her cup. Her laughter was short lived!

Beep…beep…beep…beep…beep…beep…beep…beep…beep…beep… beep…beep…beep…

"V-tach!" shouted the nurse, quickly setting her coffee down. Doctor Bryant abruptly awoke from his nap. Direktor Gaslov had just entered Ventricular Tachycardia; the ventricle of his heart had become blocked—due to a great part to the high cholesterol diets of his homeland.

"What happened?" he asked urgently.

"He's in V-tach, Doctor," the nurse shouted a second time while placing an oxygen mask over Gaslov's nose and mouth. She checked his blood pressure on the monitor, "BP 100 over 50." Direktor Gaslov's breathing was shallow and labored.

"Lidocaine 5cc's stat," ordered the doctor in an attempt to relieve Gaslov's pain. The nurse removed a lidocaine syringe from a black case and handed it to Doctor Bryant, who promptly inserted it into Direktor Gaslov's IV.

"Calan, 5cc's," was the physician's next demand—a move to reduce Gaslov's heart rate. Nurse Baxter pulled a second syringe from the black case and Doctor Bryant injected it just as he had the lidocaine-via Gaslov's IV.

"Prepare to cardiovert, 50 joules!" Doctor Bryant commanded while absorbing the information from the monitors.

Thinking ahead, the nurse had already begun applying conductive paste to the defibrillator paddles and set the power controls for 50 joules as Doctor Bryant had ordered. She handed the paddles to the waiting Doctor who shouted,

"Clear!" then placing the two paddles, one on Gaslov's upper sternum and the other on Gaslov's left side at the fifth intercostal, Doctor Bryant discharged the unit and Gaslov's body jerked in response. After a moment's hesitation, the rhythmic beep…beep…beep…of a beating heart had returned. A relieved Doctor Bryant and Nurse Baxter attended the director to ensure he didn't have a relapse, while Scarelli got on the phone to the cockpit.

C-5B Galaxy Cargo Plane
Cockpit

Captain Stoneking returned the phone to its receiver, "We've got a medical emergency in the troop compartment; Gaslov's had a heart attack!"

Macintyre didn't even acknowledge Stoneking, but remained focused on the tail end of the KC-10. His adrenalin was already at an elevated pitch before the Captain had informed him of the emergency in the Troop Compartment and for thirteen minutes he had been fighting and finessing the Galaxy to maintain a safe, yet constant, separation from the tanker. The fatigue was tremendous and an error on his part could mean a catastrophic midair collision over the Atlantic Ocean. Such an accident would, more than likely, result in their disappearing with little if any trace, followed by solemn visits by Air Force officers to families of the crew of the two aircraft.

Colonel Macintyre was not going to let that happen though! He was responsible for a state-of-the-art Energia rocket booster, his crew and the safety of the crew of the tanker, a C-5B Galaxy cargo plane, the largest aircraft in the U.S. Government's inventory, and a highly important Russian research scientist who was in danger of losing his life.

"What's the status of the fuel level?" Macintyre asked his flight engineer.

Sergeant Najar turned from the gauges at his flight engineers station. "We've taken 120,000 pounds with 50,000 pounds to go, sir. It'll be six more minutes at best."

At that moment atmospheric forces conspired against the two aircraft and the Galaxy hit a violent air pocket. It surged the cargo plane dangerously close to the rear of the KC-10 forcing the tanker's refueling probe from the C-5's receptacle. The Galaxy's crew had seen this scenario during many hours spent in the refueling simulator at Dover. But this time they weren't refueling with a model KC-10. That was a full size tanker outside of the cockpit window with a real crew and the possibility of a disaster occurring was a given.

Their training was well spent, they responded automatically and quickly. "Texaco two-one! Breakaway! Breakaway! Breakaway!" called out Captain Stoneking into the microphone of the UHF transmitter. Colonel Macintyre pressed the *Air/Refuel Disconnect*; then retarded the throttles to idle. The nose of the Galaxy quickly dropped and Macintyre checked the cargo planes rate of descent with the control yoke, ensuring the C-5's large T-tail didn't pivot up into the underbelly of the tanker as the Galaxy went into its evasive dive beneath the flying gas station.

Observing Breakaway procedures, the tanker accelerated away from the Galaxy while maintaining altitude. Captain Stoneking could see that the red rotating beacon, located on the bottom of the tanker, had been turned on.

A shaken Colonel Macintyre leveled the Galaxy off at 20,000 feet; then turned to his flight engineer, "With the 120,000 pounds from the tanker; we should have enough fuel to make it into Dover. Do you agree, Sergeant?"

"Yes sir, we have 240,000 pounds total. It gives us a fair margin for safety- that is if we don't wander off of the track too far," answered Sergeant Najar who was still breathing heavily from the sudden dive.

The Colonel picked up the microphone to the UHF set.

"Texaco two-one...this is MAC 454...at altitude two-zero thousand. Have taken one-two-zero pounds and are proceeding to Dover with a medical emergency."

"Roger MAC 454...good luck and out."

Delaware Souvenirs
Lewes, Delaware 19958

"Thank you," Mike handed the clipboard to the UPS driver and took custody of a large cardboard box.

"Here it is," exclaimed the elated store owner. His wife Wendy and son Sean had no idea what he was talking about.

"Here's what?" Sean questioned.

"Just the one thing that'll give us some cash flow during the off season," answered Mike, who placed the box on the counter top and began opening it.

Wendy and Sean looked on in interest as Mike reached into the box and pulled out a blue and gold tee-shirt, "I plan on selling a truckload of these." Mike held the shirt up proudly," So whatta ya think?"

Wendy and Sean read the inscription on the front of the T-Shirt.

Bontrager
4
Governor

The words were printed over the silhouette of the state of Delaware.

"I don't get it," a puzzled Sean said.

"What do you mean that you don't get it?" asked Mike of the 22 year old. "Haven't you heard of Karl Bontrager?" Mike continued.

Sean stood silently with a dead-pan look.

"Don't you kids read newspapers?" asked a baffled Mike."

"Well, I think it's a good idea," interjected Wendy trying to divert her husbands questioning, "It's about that janitor who's missing, right?"

"What janitor?" Sean's face was a blank.

"The one who interrupted the debate between the governor and Congressman Oliver the other night," exclaimed Mike.

"Debate for what?" nothing registered with Sean who was seemingly unphased by the whole thing.

"Didn't you tell me that you voted in the last election?" Mike was beside himself.

"Yes, I voted," Sean answered.

Mike scratched his head, "Well how did you learn about the issues and determine who you were going to vote for without picking up a newspaper, or watching the news?"

"MTV," Sean responded.

CHAPTER 12

On a Wing and a Prayer

Summit Aviation, Middletown
Delaware 19709

"Turn in here," Karl gave Brock directions from the back seat of the Rolls Royce. With the exception of some strange looks by passing motorists, their twenty-five minute trip from Nemours was uneventful. Thus far they had eluded state authorities and most importantly the press.

"What, this airfield?" Brock looked dubiously at the well kept but seemingly deserted structures of the little airfield.

"Yes," Karl insisted. "Just park her in there, that's a good hiding place." Karl pointed to an empty space inside one of the hangars and Brock drove the automobile through the open hangar door.

"Yes, this is good Brock; we can leave the car here," Karl instructed. "Be sure to give the old girl a good rubdown, will you?"

Brock didn't appear amused.

"Sorry," Karl apologized, "couldn't resist the opportunity. You know, it doesn't take long for power to corrupt a person from the back seat of a chauffeur driven Rolls Royce," Karl patted the leather arm rest.

"Apparently not," huffed Brock into the rear view mirror.

"Well, what are we doing here?" asked Kate anxiously looking at the array of vintage World War II aircraft that sat around the field.

"This is our ticket out of here," Karl declared. "There she is," Karl Bontrager's eyes suddenly lit up at the sight of a Douglas DC-3 that was parked at the edge of the small airfield. The plane was painted olive green and its fuselage and wings were set off by a black insignia that had a star centered inside of a chevron. It was the familiar marking that was used to distinguish U.S. combat aircraft from those of the axis powers during World War II.

"Just as I remember her," Karl sighed in retrospect as he stepped out of the Rolls, and then held the door open for Kate.

"What, that?" objected Brock who had abandoned the driver's seat. He stood next to the automobile and looked through the rear opening of the hangar. "You're not serious! Who says it will even get off the ground, it's an antique," observed Brock.

"Nonsense, she's in prime condition. I helped refurbish it myself and it's even registered with the Confederate Air Force."

"Well, what about the pilot? I don't happen to have Pappy Boyington with me," Brock was apprehensive.

"You're looking at the pilot," answered Karl proudly.

"You?" Brock said in a surprised voice.

Karl opened his wallet and showed Brock a card. It was a discolored and dog-eared pilot's license with Karl's name on it.

"It's expired!"

"Nonsense, flying is like riding a bicycle. Once you've done it you never forget," countered Karl.

"What if the owner happens along?"

"Belongs to a friend of mine," Karl explained. "He was a Tuskegee Airman, you know, the famous black fighter squadron called the Red Tails? He flew in the big one, WWII. The Red Tails had an impeccable record during the war and when I was a young man he used to take me up all the time. He even got me checked out in her."

"Are you sure Karl, can you fly this plane? I mean without killing us all," asked a nervous Kate.

"Look, I wouldn't risk your lives anymore than I would my own children. Now any minute the police, the press, or who knows who could come in here and apprehend us all; we could end up back at the institution. As for me I choose freedom," Karl pointed emphatically toward the beautifully restored cargo aircraft, "and folks, that is our ticket out of here."

Brock saw the same look in Karl's eyes and heard the same assurance in his voice that he had exhibited during the gubernatorial debate; the look and sound of confidence.

"Okay Karl I'm in, you've convinced me. Where do we fly to though?" asked Brock.

"To a friend of mine, the owner of this plane. We can lay low there until the heat subsides," he answered.

U.S. Congress (Committee Room)
Washington, D.C. 20515

"This is unadulterated pork barreling," pontificated the congressman from Alaska, "It's yet another case of throwing money at problems."

"Problems that need to be solved," shouted Majority Whip Schroeder.

"That's right," agreed Congressman Oliver, "They're problems that we all face and something needs to be done, so why not little Delaware?"

"Don't give me that *holier-than-thou* routine, Oliver," argued the Alaskan. "The last thing that you're interested in is solving problems. You're only concern is for your chances of capturing Delaware's State House."

"That's enough," shouted Schroeder, "I won't tolerate this kind of behavior in the committee room. Now let's see a show of hands, those for sending the Oliver/Bontrager Bill to the House floor."

Six hands went into the air while two did not.

"That's it then," announced Schroeder the bill goes to the House floor for a vote."

Summit Aviation
Middletown, Delaware 19709

"You flown much Brock?" Karl asked as he strapped himself into the left seat of the DC-3.

"As a passenger," Brock answered reluctantly. "I used to have to jump out of perfectly good airplanes, but don't ask me how they work. Remember, I was a SEAL, not a *Jet Jockey*."

"I've flown before," interrupted Kate. "My uncle had a crop dusting operation and took me up a few times. He even let me operate the controls while we were airborne," she added nervously.

"Great! You can be my co-pilot," Karl checked the DC-3's fuel situation, then pointed to the right seat, "and Brock you can sit in the jump seat." Karl pointed to a seat that was located behind his.

"Just listen to me Kate and do as I say," Karl explained as Kate strapped herself into the right seat.

"Roger Captain," she said with a timid smile.

"That's the spirit Kate" Karl looked up after having set the wing flap and landing gear latch levers in the neutral position.

"Hand me that check list," Kate handed Karl some laminated sheets that sat atop the control console.

"Let me see," Karl murmured to himself, "*battery master switch on.*" He flipped a toggle switch along the bottom of the control panel. "*Fuel tank selector-set. Booster pump on.* Okay Kate open your side window and check that no one is standing around the #2 engine."

"Its all clear," she said looking at the *Pratt & Whitney* on the right wing.

"Good, now holler out *clear* just to be safe."

Kate let out the code word that was used to alert anyone that an engine was about to be started. There was no response, "All clear, Captain."

"All clear, aye," confirmed Karl reaching for the starter switch on the forward centerline of the ceiling. The inertia starter in the #2 engine made a whirring sound for a few seconds before the engine slowly sputtered to life.

After priming the engine, Karl set the throttles to 1200 rpm while waiting for the oil pressure and temperature to meet specs. Once the engine was running smoothly he shut off the booster pump and made a pressure check of the right engine hydraulic pump by cycling the flaps. Within several seconds Karl was satisfied with the operation of the #2 engine and he had repeated the procedure after he started the #1 engine. Black exhaust fumes, now trailed behind the left and right wings, forcing the grass to wave frantically in the torrent of air.

Karl next checked the flight instruments: *Airspeed indicator, Vertical velocity indicator, Turn-and-slip indicator, Directional indicators* and *Attitude indicators.*

He ran the engines up to 1700 rpm and cycled the props. The even growl was a welcome sound.

"All right, this is it." with a gleam in his eye and a broad grin, Karl gave a thumbs-up and released the brakes. The aircraft slowly bounced forward onto the asphalt runway. Looking to each wing, Karl moved the control yoke to check for free movement of the control surfaces. "Wing flaps up. Cowl flaps in trail," Karl advanced the throttle to maximum power. At 45 knots (52 miles per hour), Karl could sense the tail rising to a level flight attitude and at 70 knots (80 miles per hour) he pulled back on the control yoke and the DC-3 was airborne.

New Castle County Airport
Wilmington, Delaware 19720

"Newcastle Control, this is MAC 454 Medivac. Request clearance for emergency landing," Colonel Macintyre didn't have to wait long for the air traffic controller to respond.

"MAC 454 Medivac...have cleared immediate airspace, you're cleared to land runway 1."

The air traffic controllers at Delaware's largest civilian airport had been aware of the medical emergency for three hours. Someone in the chain of command, either the U.S. State Department or the Air Force had decided to have Direktor Gaslov flown upstate where the larger Wilmington area hospitals could better treat his heart ailment. Whoever made the decision opted not to waste valuable time having the Galaxy land at Dover Air Force Base, only to have the research scientist subjected to a lengthy transfer to an air ambulance. Gaslov would have had to have been flown the 46 miles upstate anyway and time was not a commodity that Gaslov had plenty of.

The only catch was that no one had ever attempted a landing of the largest aircraft in the Western Hemisphere on the relatively short, 7,000 foot long, airstrips of the New Castle County Airport. To make matters worse, this particular Galaxy was carrying a massive Energia rocket booster. A lot of weight and inertia to add to the cargo planes 374,000 pound operating weight.

Colonel Macintyre had driven by the airport, via route 13, on many occasions. Once he was even summoned there by the vice president, who was campaigning and took advantage of the opportunity to recognize Macintyre for his record setting number of flights during the Persian Gulf War.

But Colonel Macintyre had flown into the airport only once, with a friend of his that flew the C-130 Hercules for Delaware's Air National Guard. He recalled that the guard's facilities were at the northwest corner of the airfield; on the opposite side of the main runway as those for the civilian airlines.

"New Castle tower, commencing turn for final approach," announced Macintyre over the VHF radio. He had started the most critical and dangerous maneuver of flight, the landing.

"Roger MAC 454 Medivac," answered the air traffic controller.

Four miles from the field, Macintyre turned the control wheel. The ailerons shifted in response, banking the Galaxy north for the final approach. He next lowered the complement of 28 wheels that comprised the landing gear.

Colonel Macintyre looked seriously at his co-pilot, "As soon as the nose gear touches down, I want you to hit the reversers. I'll be plenty busy with the brakes."

"Yes sir," assured Captain Stoneking. A second later he was distracted. "What in the world is that?" he asked.

Macintyre looked in the direction of Captain Stoneking's index finger.

"Well I'll be," exclaimed a surprised Macintyre. A few miles distant, an aircraft was skirting the Western edge of the airfield. It did not seem to be posing a problem for the Galaxy's flight path, but the aircraft commander did not appreciate the misleading assurances, of the airspace being clear, that the tower had just given him moments before.

The Colonel snatched the VHF microphone from its rest, "New Castle control...this is MAC 454 Medivac, I thought you had cleared the immediate airspace!"

"MAC 454 Medivac, sorry about that, am attempting to contact unidentified aircraft at this time," responded New Castle Control.

"Roger, New Castle Control," Colonel Macintyre placed the microphone back on its receiver.

"You don't see too many of those anymore," said Macintyre briefly admiring the aircraft. "An old Douglas DC-3...in war paint no less." Macintyre watched as the plane cruised southward and finally out of his field of vision.

"Full flaps," the colonel ordered. Captain Stoneking immediately shifted a lever on the central control console. A whirring sound followed and finally a thump as the flaps extended fully to their landing position, in effect, giving the Galaxy's wings a greater curvature and greater lift for the slower landing speeds. To do otherwise would result in a stall and most likely a fiery crash short of the runway.

Macintyre adjusted the throttles for a landing speed of 120 knots and quickly stabilized the Galaxy's descent rate; 6 feet-per-second according to the vertical speed indicator. The aircraft's nose now looked over the tier of landing lights that stretched across busily traveled route 13, and ended a couple of hundred yards beyond, at the foot of the runway. The lights sat atop several bright orange steel girders and grew successively shorter in height as they got closer to the foot of the runway.

Macintyre made minor adjustments to the control yoke and rudder pedals as Captain Stoneking called out the altitude.

"One-hundred...seventy...fifty...thirty...twenty...main down, nose down!" While Captain Stoneking activated the thrust reversers, Colonel Macintyre cut back on the throttles, activated the spoiler, and then engaged the brakes.

As the cargo plane rolled quickly down the paved runway its four engines, hanging from wings which extended considerably beyond the confines of the pavement, kicked up a column of dust and torrents of spinning debris.

Colonel Macintyre used the entire 7,000 foot long runway to finally bring the *City of Dover* to a stop. Taxiing the big bird was another consideration. It was difficult maneuvering the cargo plane within the confines of the relatively small airfield. Colonel Macintyre and Captain Stoneking watched intently as the Galaxy's massive wing moved dangerously close to the civil aircraft and buildings along the apron next to the terminal.

An ambulance and two state police cars sat in front of the building's glass facade, awaiting Direktor Gaslov's arrival, their red and blue lights flashing out of unison.

Within minutes Scarelli had Direktor Gaslov downloaded from the troop compartment above the cargo bay and onto a gurney. Macintyre and Stoneking were still doing their post flight checks in the cockpit, when they saw Gaslov's ambulance and police escort leave the apron for the fifteen minute trip to Christiana Medical Center.

Colonel Macintyre turned to his co-pilot, "Well, we've got a rocket booster to deliver Luke, next stop, Cape Kennedy."

Vrodkutsk, Commonwealth of Independent States

"All right then, if you'll just sign on the bottom line Comrade Kuryakin, the deal will be finalized," Maynard Price pushed the document across the table while an interpreter translated. The nuclear technician looked over the document which had just been thrust under his nose. The contract was in both English and Russian, the Russian translation appearing in (parens) after its English counterpart.

Kuryakin, who was without counsel, carefully examined each page of the document as if it were as important as the U235 that he had become responsible for at the Vrodkutsk Nuclear Research Center. Inside, he struggled with the need to feed and house his family and his loyalty to the people of Vrodkutsk. He knew that his friend Direktor Gaslov would be most displeased to hear of his decision and it caused him to hesitate with pen in hand.

"You're making a wise decision Comrade," Maynard Price held up a fist full of rubles that were to become Kuryakin's signing bonus.

Kuryakin didn't need a translation for Maynard's words of encouragement, nor the incentive to ratify the contract. His mind had been made up when his wife, Riasa, had their fifth child. Their cramped three room apartment had become entirely too small and the food was becoming increasingly scarce.

Yes, Kuryakin knew all too well that Maynard Price's world was one of greed. The world of the high-tech headhunter, Price was a man with little if any conscience or national loyalty. His god was the almighty dollar and for the right price he could get an up and coming third world power the technical expertise that it needed to become a dangerous up and coming third world power. That is if *the Price was right* and that had been the case with Amin in Uganda, Pol Pot in Cambodia, Qaddafi in Libya, Noriega in Panama, Hussein in Iraq and now with Jonathan Doe in Badasi.

Kuryakin's hesitation was brief. His hand navigated the pen over the contract with the precision of an argon laser. It was finished. For the next five years, with the option to extend of course, Kuryakin was to be the property of the people of Badasi.

As a sign of gratitude, a beaming Maynard Price rolled a tiny nugget across the table. Kuryakin picked the stone up and after a second of close examination exclaimed in Russian, "Platinum?"

"That's right," leered Price who quickly snatched up the contract and shoveled it into his open briefcase, "and there's more where that came from." Price insinuated with a devilish laugh. "By the way," Price reached inside of his billfold, "Here's my card." He quickly scribbled a phone number on the back of the card and handed it to Kuryakin who needed the translator's assistance to read its gold embossed script.

Head Hunters, Inc.
Maynard $. Price
Kingston, Jamaica

"Be sure to tell your nuke buddies that I'm staying at the Vrodkutsk Hilton downtown, I'll be expecting them."

CHAPTER 13

The Pork Barrel

Douglas DC-3
New Castle, Delaware Airspace

"A C-5, that's odd; I don't recall a Galaxy ever flying into New Castle. Must be for an air show or something," Karl spotted the cargo jet through the cockpit window. It was a couple miles east of the DC-3's position and making its final approach at New Castle County Airport.

"DE17384 this is New Castle tower, we have a medivac flight inbound, what are your intentions?" the tower was calling the DC-3 on its VHF radio. The message was repeated a second time before Karl noted that a small metal plaque mounted over the radio was inscribed with the same call sign, DE17384.

"New Castle tower, this is DE17384…presently leaving your airspace."

"Roger that DE17384…tower out," the radio went silent.

"Well, I guess no one's missed the plane," said Karl placing the microphone back on its hook.

"Yet!" Brock quickly added from the jump seat.

"What next?" asked Kate.

"We'll continue south until we get to Milton, Delaware, that's where the owner of this plane lives. We can use it as a safe haven from the police and news media." Following Route 13, Karl put the DC-3 on a southward track.

Woodburn, the Governor's Mansion
Dover, Delaware 19903

Governor Collins and his aid Sarah Watkins were watching the results of the Oliver-Bontrager vote on C-Span.

"The final vote is 238 yeas and 197 neas. The yeas have it…the *Oliver-Bontrager bill* passes.

"Mr. Speaker," Douglas Oliver stood at one of the microphones in the House Chamber.

"The floor recognizes the distinguished congressman from the state of Delaware," announced the speaker.

"I'd like to say a couple of things in the aftermath of the vote. First I'd like to thank those of my colleagues who helped me to pass the bill and second I'd like to say that it's a good day for Delaware, a good day for Delawareans, a good day for our country and a good day for the world. That's all that I have to say, Mr. Speaker.

"Very well, Mr. Oliver, the floor motions for a recess until two o'clock," the speaker banged his gavel and the room started to clear rapidly.

"Turn off the TV, Sarah," ordered the governor. Sarah hit the remote and the screen went blank.

"How do you feel, Governor?"

"Mixed feelings," he answered. "I'd be happy that the bill passed if I thought that it would do any good, but I'm not sure. I've found that more direct action by people always showed greater results. You know how it is when government gets involved with issues of this nature, the bureaucracy takes over and nothing much ever really happens. There's no real impetus for the government to do much unless it benefits some politician and it's usually just a waste of money." Governor Collins scratched his bald head. "Unless people are interested in solving the problems, the incentive for change isn't really there and progress then gets bogged down until it comes to a complete stop. On top of that, the fact that Oliver is involved doesn't help matters any, it only worsens them."

Christiana Hospital,
Newark, Delaware 19718

Doctor Bryant and Nurse Baxter escorted Direktor Gaslov's gurney inside of the Medical Center. The hospital staff had been waiting for Gaslov's arrival and took him immediately into surgery. Six hours later his bypass was complete.

After an hour of observation in the recovery room; he was taken to a room in the intensive care unit where he was able to get some much needed rest.

Island of Badasi
Southwestern Africa

Nuclear Technician Kuryakin was greeted at the Badasi International Airport by Georgi Fyodor, another transplanted Russian technician. Georgi helped Kuryakin load his bags into the Land Rover for the trip to Badasi's research center. The journey was one of contrasts; affluent dwellings graced the surrounding hillsides while peasant villages dotted the lowlands. In some ways it reminded Kuryakin of his homeland; where he had seen magnificent buildings erected by the communist party, while at the same time people stood in long lines for the basic food stuffs needed to maintain life.

"So where do you come from," asked Georgi.

"Vrodkutsk," answered Kuryakin, "the research center."

"How about you?"

"The Soviet Navy…submarines," Georgi turned off the main road and onto a heavily traveled artery.

"Ahh," Kuryakin smiled, "tired of sea duty were you?"

"It was an opportunity that I couldn't pass up," Georgi turned to Kuryakin, "The money you know, it's very appealing. I can feed and clothe my family properly now."

"My reason also, a wife and five kids," Kuryakin refrained from showing Georgi pictures of his family. "What kind of work do you do here?"

"I'm assigned to the rod control mechanism for the reactor," answered Georgi proudly. "We are in the process of installing it."

"Sounds like a big undertaking."

"Oh it is, a considerable one," assured Georgi. "The logistics are tremendous, getting all of the equipment in place; then testing the controls and safe guards."

"I'm eager to see it. I work primarily with fueling."

"Then we should see a lot of each other," Georgi smiled.

The Land Rover stopped at a gate at the foot of a hill. Georgi showed one of the guards a pass and was promptly waved through. The road was nestled between two hills and when the Land Rover reached the crest Kuryakin could see the dome like containment building of the nuclear reactor in the valley below.

Milton, Delaware 19968

Jeb Wheeler was sitting in his living room watching Green Bay beat Philadelphia 14-3 late in the second quarter when he clapped his hands together in celebration, "that kid has got a cannon arm," he shouted aloud.

"Are you talking to the television again?" his wife Deanna asked as she entered the living room. Deanna set a tray on the coffee table, "Now what's all of this shouting about?"

"The Packers have some new quarterback named Brett Favre," Jeb said excitedly. "Man can he really throw that football. With him at the controls I think the Packers will win their 12th NFL championship," Jeb was obviously elated at the young quarterbacks play.

"Well, I brought you a snack," Deanna had made him a tuna fish sandwich and a glass of ice tea and it didn't go unnoticed by his Chesapeake Bay retriever, Red Tail.

"I'll be back in a minute," Deanna said," exiting for the kitchen.

Meanwhile, the dog sat attentively next to the La-Z-Boy hoping for a piece of the sandwich and Jeb's faithful companion didn't have to wait long, his master tore off a generous piece which Red Tail quickly swallowed.

Then, Deanna returned from the kitchen with a plate of freshly made chocolate chip cookies.

"How was the sandwich," she asked.

"It was fine honey, how about another?" Jeb watched John Madden go over the half time statistics.

"I wasn't asking you, I was asking Red Tail," his wife said sarcastically as she observed the dog licking his chops clean.

Knowing that Deanna didn't like Jeb feeding the dog snacks, Jeb nearly turned red in the face and would have if it wasn't for his dark complexion. So he tried to change the subject to avoid his wife's wrath, "chocolate chip, my favorite sweetie," he said with a grin. Deanna lowered the plate in front of Jeb's nose so that he could smell the wonderful aroma, then she teasingly picked the biggest cookie on the plate and gave it to Red Tail whose tail was wagging full throttle.

"Hey," Jeb objected, "Those are my cookies." Deanna placed the plate on top of the television set.

"How much longer is this game on," she asked impatiently, "I'd like to watch something else.

"Deanna, how often do I get to watch the Packers play?" he waited for a response that never came. "Well not too often in Delaware," he argued, "unless they're playing the Eagles, or the Redskins, I don't get to see them."

Her arms were folded now, "How long Jeb?"

"There's only thirty minutes of playing time left Deanna," his voice contorted as he strained his ear to hear the commentator over Deanna.

"Oh no," I know what that means. With all of the time outs…that means that there's two hours yet." She knew his routine well. There was no winning against a football fan, even less a lifelong Packer fan.

"Okay then, you can watch your football but after the game, you're taking me out to dinner." During their forty five years of marriage, Deanna had learned to become an excellent halftime plea bargainer. From new shoes to her choice of summer vacation spots, Deanna had acquired the skills of a seasoned prosecuting attorney and all during the halftime shows of professional football games.

"You've gotta date Sugar," he said happily, "now please let me watch the game."

Although she did not wrestle control of the television from her husband, Deanna returned to the kitchen having won her concession and Jeb took a drink of his tea.

Three minutes into the third quarter Jeb was comfortably settled back in his chair when Red Tail started barking and ran to the rear door. The retriever was excited about something but Jeb was in no mood to break his concentration from the game; the Packers had the ball!

The retriever knew how to get his master's attention though; he ran from the door and stood in front of Jeb barking like he had seen Lassie do in several black and white reruns on the Nickelodeon channel.

"Red, you're blocking the TV boy, move it," Before Jeb could get out of his chair to remove the persistent beast, the familiar sound of two growling *Pratt & Whitney* engines was heard over the house. Jeb jumped from his chair and followed the canine to the back screen door, pushing it open. Coming around for a second pass was Jeb's restored Douglas DC-3 and as it made its second approach, he could see the plane's wings rotating up and down in a waving motion. The aircraft was now flying tree top level and as it passed over Jeb's and Red Tail's position, Jeb identified the pilot at the controls, "Why that old fart," he said to himself.

"What's all the commotion?" Deanna shot out through the back door; she had been interrupted while trying a dress on for her and Jeb's dinner date.

"It's Karl!" Jeb pointed to the DC-3 which was circling for the third time.

"There goes my dinner date," groaned Deanna disappointedly.

Karl caught sight of Jeb, standing in back of his house, through the cockpit window, "There he is," said Karl making minor adjustments to the DC-3's control yoke. "Stand by for landing," he called out to Kate and Brock as he banked the plane toward a soy bean field that was adjacent to Jeb's property.

Red Tail barked as the plane approached then bounced across the field. Once the aircraft taxied to a stop it was only a matter of seconds before the side door opened and Brock and Kate Webster appeared. They climbed down the ladder while Karl went through his post flight in the cockpit. Karl followed his friends shortly thereafter and promptly received a warm greeting from his old flight instructor and buddy.

"What in the world, Karl!" Jeb Wheeler asked.

"Hope you don't mind me borrowing your plane," Karl grinned sheepishly.

"You must have a good reason," sighed Jeb. "What's going on?"

"It's a long story," Karl leaned over to pet Red Tail, "one that I'll be more than happy to tell you over some of Deanna's homemade cookin'." Karl gestured to his friends, "This is Kate Webster and Brock."

"I recognize you from TV," said Jeb.

"TV," asked Kate.

"Sure, you're the talk of the state...and the country for that matter," said Jeb. "You're all heroes."

"Heroes?" Karl looked shocked.

"Sure," said Jeb, "you've acquired a real following since that little scene that you made during the debate. Got the whole state supporting you and your ideas now. They've even passed a bill in Congress with your name on it."

"Then why have they been chasing us from one end of the state to the other," asked Kate.

"Oh! You must mean the riot. The governor has since pardoned you, haven't you read any papers or listened to the radio? He said it was a mistake or something like that," Jeb explained.

"Well someone forgot to tell the news media, Dover police, a Judge, and a mad doctor," bristled Karl. "We've been attacked, jailed, insulted and sent to a psychiatric institution. Some people aren't getting the word."

"Well, all that I can say is that you've all been pardoned. It's all a big mistake," insisted Jeb.

"Like Karl said, someone's been chasing us," declared an angry Brock, "we've been running, like fugitives, from one end of the state to the other. Just the other morning we were found out at the Nemours mansion."

"That's right," agreed Kate. "We've been imprisoned, hunted and disgraced. There's been no sense in the way that we've been treated. It's been as if someone's been out to get us."

"How many for dinner?" their heated conversation was interrupted by Deanna, who had come out to the field from the house.

"Deanna!" Karl waved and shouted hello to Jeb's wife.

"Karl Bontrager, where have you been? Everyone's been looking for you," she shouted back.

"I know! I can't go to my house, town, or the bathroom without someone waiting behind a bush for me?"

"I've been following your story on television, it's better than my soap opera, *The Young and the Wealthy*."

"Oh you watch *The Young and the Wealthy*," squealed Kate who suddenly perked up. "I've missed a week of stories. How's Chad Slade doing? Did he run off with his boss' wife?"

Karl gave Kate a look of disbelief, "There's a time and a place for everything Kate, you can catch up with *The Young & The Senseless* later on…you know after we've solved some problems in the real world. Now about these clowns who've been chasing us," Karl continued.

"You know the news media. They smell a story and they're on the trail like blood hounds," Jeb complained.

"Yeah, I know the news media, you can trust them about as far as you can throw them," quipped Karl.

"By the way, have you called Kim yet," asked Deanna, "she's been calling all over trying to find you."

"No, I haven't," I've been too busy trying to save our skins.

"My goodness, do you think I could use your phone, I need to call my daughter," a worried Kate asked of Deanna.

"Certainly, let's move this conversation indoors and I'll put the coffee on," Deanna led Kate to the house.

University of Delaware
Newark, Delaware 19716

A knock on the door interrupted Kimberly as she was getting ready for class.

"What is it?" she shouted.

"Call on the lobby phone," came the reply from the other side of the door.

"Thanks," Kimberly picked up the books for her first class and rushed out of her room; she found the lobby phone hanging by its cord.

"Hello," Kimberly bubbled excitedly, "Granddad, where have you been? I've been worried sick!" There were a few seconds of silence. "Well I don't care," Kimberly scolded, "you should have called earlier."

Students that had been watching *The Price is Right* on the lobby television overheard Kim's conversation and began gathering around the overjoyed junior. Her jubilation was contagious and the students quickly asked for a meeting with Karl Bontrager the Delawarean, speaker, leader, folk hero, former fugitive, and janitor, even more, the man who had caught the imagination of *the First State*.

CHAPTER 14

Decisions, Decisions

Seaford, Delaware 19973

"Good news Doug," Gil Hickman flashed the headline in front of Congressman Oliver's eyes. *Oliver leads Collins in race for Statehouse.* "That Oliver/Bontrager bill was a brilliant idea…you're ahead in the latest poll, Congressman."

"It's about time," Oliver straightened up in the chair behind his desk. "I thought that stunt that we pulled with the shrink was going to do us in," he grumbled as he grabbed the paper from his press aide's hands.

"I told you not to worry about that. As it turned out, it was to our benefit. The fact that we had Bontrager institutionalized just made him more popular and now you're looked upon as his ally. Now when Bontrager's popularity goes up, so does yours and no ones the wiser," Hickman winked.

"Sounds good in theory," Oliver looked up from the newspaper, "I just hope it works."

"With just two weeks until the election you can count on it," Hickman assured him.

"If your theory proves right, then we'll just have to ensure that Bontrager's popularity remains high," Oliver's eyebrows arched.

"Well that's taken care of," Hickman placed his hands on Oliver's desk as he addressed the congressman, "ever since he escaped from that institution, he's been looked upon as a martyr, a folk hero, you name it; and the best part about it is that no one knows his whereabouts. As long as he is out of sight he becomes an asset for us."

Christiana Hospital,
Newark, Delaware 19718

"How are you feeling Direktor Gaslov?" asked a familiar voice. When Direktor Gaslov opened his eyes he recognized Doctor Bryant and Nurse Baxter standing over his hospital bed.

"Good morning, do you remember who we are?" asked the doctor.

"Yes," answered a drowsy Gaslov in a hoarse voice, "you are from the cargo plane."

"That's right," nodded Doctor Bryant.

Nurse Baxter gave Gaslov a drink of water.

"Thank you," said Gaslov more clearly.

"You've had a heart bypass operation Mr. Gaslov, are you experiencing any pain?" asked the Doctor.

"Chest...sore."

"Nurse Baxter has something for that," The Doctor nodded to the pretty red head.

"It's time for your medication," she propped Gaslov up and gave him some pills that were followed by more water.

"Very good," the doctor commented, turning to the bank of monitors that were located above Gaslov's bed. "I see your EKG...your heart rate has improved."

"Where am I?" asked Gaslov.

"Delaware, in the United States of America."

"How long will I be here?"

"If you do well here, you will be moved to another room in a couple of days. Then, you'll be there for a couple of weeks until you heal from the surgery and then it's back to Vrodkutsk, I suppose."

"Gaslov smiled," Yes, I must return to the research center in Vrodkutsk."

"Don't you worry about that...I don't want you to do anything but rest and maybe watch some television. By the way you have a visitor."

Nurse Baxter opened the door and waved for someone to come in.

"Dimitri!" shouted a woman running to Gaslov's bedside. It was Gaslov's wife who was followed in by a State Department official. She kissed her husband on the forehead and he smiled taking her hand, "Tatya," he murmured.

"Well everything seems to be all right here," observed the State Department official, "I think I'll give them some privacy."

"Sounds like a good idea," the doctor agreed, "but only five minutes. He needs his rest."

Doctor Bryant and the State Department official followed Nurse Baxter out of the room.

Milton, Delaware 19968

"As always, that was a fantastic meal Deanna," Karl leaned back in his chair and patted his stomach.

"I second that," commented Brock as he worked on his second piece of apple pie.

"Yes thank you very much for your hospitality Mrs. Wheeler," said Kate.

"Deanna, call me Deanna," The smiling woman insisted.

"Can I help you with the dishes, Deanna?" asked Kate standing from her chair.

"Nonsense, you must be dead tired," Deanna motioned her to sit down.

"Not at all, now that I know that my little girl is fine I'm wide awake."

"Well, all right then," Deanna picked up a plate and headed for the kitchen and Kate followed.

While the women cleared the table; Jeb led Karl and Brock out to the back porch where Karl and he lit up their pipes.

"Nice looking barn you have back there Jeb, new isn't it?" asked Karl.

"Yep, Elias Yoder and his sons put it up for me."

"No one can build a barn like the Amish," said Karl admiring the structure. "Ever see a barn raising?" Karl turned to Brock, tapping his pipe against a porch post and Brock shook his head no in response.

"Well I witnessed one being raised out near Hazlettville. The frame, walls and roof were complete in one day. While the men built the barn, the women made lunch which was a smorgasbord of different meats, vegetables, breads and pies. Every man knew his job and went about his work intuitively without waiting for instructions. You know, not a harsh word was spoken during the day. You've got to take your hat off to people who can work together like that."

"Well Karl, what are you going to do now," asked Jeb, changing the subject.

"I haven't thought about it too much," Karl tapped his pipe on the railing. "I suppose I'll go back to Dover and look for another job."

"That shouldn't be too hard for the greatest Delawarean since Caesar Rodney," Jeb took a puff from his pipe.

"Caesar Rodney?" straining his comprehension, Karl shook his head.

"Yep, that's who they're comparing you to, Caesar Rodney," exclaimed Jeb.

Karl turned red from the comparison, "That's nonsense," he sputtered; all I did was speak my mind."

"Well, whatever you said, people liked it and whether you like it or not you're the modern day Caesar Rodney," Jeb laughed because he knew that Karl didn't accept flattery too well. It made him uncomfortable.

"Don't fight it, Karl," Brock insisted, "great men do great things."

The conversation was interrupted by the sound of tires upon the gravel lane, "Expecting company, Jeb?" Karl pointed to a Jeep that was coming up the driveway. It stopped at the foot of the porch.

"Granddad!" a young woman shouted from the passenger seat. Kimberly opened the door and ran to her grandfather giving him a big hug. "You dare-devil you, you had me worried sick."

"Hi, Mr. Bontrager," Eric exited the driver's side of the van while Dan and Anne had come along for the ride and the three joined every one on the porch.

After introductions Kim asked her grandfather for a favor, "Granddad, Anne would like to do an interview with you for the university paper, the Blue Hen."

"An interview," Karl exploded, "nothing against you Anne, but I've had my fill of the media!"

"Mr. Bontrager, this would be a great opportunity to clear the air," said Anne enthusiastically. "Eventually, people are going to find out that you've returned and the media is going to want interviews. You're a public figure now."

"That's right," agreed Kim, "wouldn't it be better for Anne to interview you initially and to get the facts straight than to wait for some stranger to distort the facts."

Karl scratched his head, "What do you think Jeb?"

"It's not my decision to make," said Jeb sidestepping, "that's your problem, but the girls seem to have a point. You know how the media can distort things. It may be a good idea to head them off at the pass by having someone that you can trust break the story before it starts to get out of hand."

"What do you think, Brock?" asked Karl.

"It's no problem with me; but I think that we should ask Kate."

Karl took a puff from his pipe, "I'll have to give this some thought myself."

"And we've got a lot to fill you in on," pointed out Kim proudly. "Several students have begun work on making your dream for Delaware a reality."

Seaford, Delaware 19973

"Bad news Doug," Gil Hickman burst into Congressman Oliver's office and flashed a headline in front of Congressman Oliver's eyes, *Bontrager in Milton*.

Gil Hickman repeated the headline, "Bontrager in Milton."

"Milton?" Oliver jumped up from behind his desk.

"He flew in there yesterday afternoon."

"Flew there, how?" Oliver looked aghast.

"He took a DC-3 from an air field up north," Hickman wiped some sweat from his brow, "flew it himself. Apparently, belongs to a friend of his."

"A DC-3, I thought he was a janitor!" Oliver banged on his desk. "What's a janitor doing flying an airplane?"

"Well the last time I checked, there's no law excluding janitors from flying," Hickman said sarcastically. "What can I say, he's like *The Flying Janitor*, you know like *The Flying Nun*."

"This is no time to be making jokes, we've underestimated Bontrager," Oliver snapped back. "What's this going to mean for us? I mean, is he necessarily a threat to my campaign?"

"Maybe not," answered Hickman thoughtfully, "he may treat the Bontrager bill favorably. I mean why not, it's named after him and on the surface it utilizes his ideas."

"True," Oliver thought it over, "you never know he could conceivably endorse me."

"We'll have to wait and see."

"Yes we'll have to wait and see, "agreed Oliver sighing deeply.

CHAPTER 15

Homecoming

The Green
Dover, Delaware 19903

"It's great to be back in Dover and I'd like to thank the people who supported me during my absence," Karl waved from the steps of the Old Statehouse to the crowd that had gathered to welcome him back home. "I'd like to introduce two friends of mine," he motioned to Kate, who was holding her daughter Amanda in her arms, and Brock, who stood proudly next to Kate. "Kate Webster and Brock Mattingly, as you can imagine we've been through quite a bit over the past several days."

Kate and Brock stepped forward; smiling as they waved to the crowd.

"I didn't realize that I had created such a stir until I came out of hiding, and had a chance to speak to some friends of mine," continued Karl. "I meant what I said during the debates and with the help of people throughout Delaware we will try to put this state on the map and make it into an example that the nation can be proud of." With that, Karl, Kate and Brock gave a wave and began to walk down the steps of the Old Statehouse to meet with reporters who had been waiting anxiously.

"Mr. Bontrager, Mr. Bontrager," the reporters shouted as they jockeyed into position to ask questions.

"Please call me Karl," it was obvious that the janitor was uncomfortable with the attention.

"Do you have any political ambitions, Karl?" Ron Mathews shouted.

"That's ridiculous," laughed Karl removing the pipe from his mouth. "No I have no desire to be a politician," he answered firmly.

"Well what about your plans now that you're a state hero?" persisted the reporter.

"Hero, that's nonsense; I just said what was on my mind. I'm definitely not a hero." Karl turned to Brock, "Now he's a hero." Karl grabbed Brock by the arm, "A Congressional Medal of Honor recipient during the Vietnam War. Why don't you talk to this man, he's the hero." One of the reporters jumped on Karl's suggestion and began talking to Brock and another began to interview Kate about her part in helping Karl elude the authorities.

Meanwhile, Ron Mathews continued to hound Karl. "You must realize that you're a public hero Karl and that people are interested in your plans for the future."

"Why yes, I have plans to live as peaceful a life as possible. After I find another job, I plan to live in the same house, in the same neighborhood and with my spare time I plan to give my granddaughter and her student friends a hand with organizing interested people throughout Delaware who want to pursue some of my ideas."

"And how do you plan to do that?"

"Granted, it's easier said, than done. We're sorta breaking new ground with this idea, but we're optimistic. Now I've got a football game to go to and I don't want to be late." Karl brushed off the remaining questions and made his way through the crowd.

Delaware Stadium, University of Delaware
Newark, Delaware 19716

"In the lead car is Karl Bontrager, who is seated between Kate Webster and Brock Mattingly," exclaimed Ron Mathews into his microphone as he watched the University's Homecoming ceremony from the press box. "It's a fitting tribute for the man who put Delaware in the national spotlight for the past week. Mr. Bontrager and his friends are exiting the car to take their seats in the stands."

Christiana Hospital,
Newark, Delaware 19718

"Good morning Direktor Gaslov," Doctor Bryant startled the direktor who was watching television.

"It's an interesting sport," the direktor pointed to the screen, "but I don't fully understand it."

"Football?" Doctor Bryant watched for a moment, "It's the University of Delaware…they're a good team."

"It reminds me of ice hockey, very physical."

"And violent," the doctor added while removing a clipboard from the foot of Gaslov's bed. "I've got some very good news for you. You've improved enough that we're moving you to another room."

"One with a television I hope," asked the direktor with a laugh.

"Yes indeed," Bryant was studying the sheets attached to the clipboard.

"We need this room for more serious patients and we're going to start you on some exercises."

"Exercises?" Gaslov looked disappointed.

"Yes, you need to strengthen that heart if you plan on living a long and healthy life and the physical therapists here are very good," Doctor Bryant returned the clipboard to the foot of the bed.

"How long before I can return to my work in Vrodkutsk?"

"A few weeks if you listen to me and the physical therapists," the doctor waved his finger at the direktor as if scolding him. "But you shouldn't worry about returning to work yet; you should look at this as a vacation and start enjoying yourself."

Their conversation was interrupted by the direktor's wife who stormed into the room with several shopping bags. The State Department official was with her as always.

"We went shopping at the most beautiful store. It was huge and there were no lines. It is called the Christiana Mall and the food there was fantastic. Look what I got?" Tatya opened one of the bags and pulled out a pair of slippers with a rabbit face and ears, "these are for you."

Gaslov rolled his eyes, "What am I supposed to do with these?"

"Put them on your feet," she lifted each of Gaslov's feet from the bed and placed the slippers on them.

"I'll look like a clown," protested Gaslov with a stern look, "I'm a nuclear scientist not a clown in the Moscow circus."

"Better to look like a clown than to catch pneumonia," Tatya insisted firmly.

"Look," shouted Gaslov suddenly pointing to the television screen. "That man is hurt," the foursome watched as a stretcher was brought out on the field to a downed player who was obviously in a lot of pain.

Delaware Stadium, University of Delaware
Newark, Delaware 19716

Amidst the crowd of enthusiastic fans Karl and his entourage watched *the fightin' Blue Hens* battle the Midshipmen of Annapolis to a third quarter tie. The roar of the crowd fluctuated during each play.

Between plays, Kate looked up from the program that she had been reading, "Who's this player Rich Gannon, he sounds pretty good?"

"He is good," answered Brock, "but you won't see him playing here today."

"Why not?" asked Kate.

"Because he graduated from Delaware in '87," replied Brock, "he plays quarterback for the Minnesota Vikings now."

"You know, my father used to tell me about a Delaware halfback who played during the forties," Karl said with a smile. "I think dad said this player rushed for 220 yards on six carries in one game."

"That's incredible," Kimberly, an avid football fan, had turned in her seat to face Karl who was in deep thought.

"I believe his name was Doherty, Gerald Doherty, if I remember correctly."

"You're right Karl," agreed Brock, "his nickname was *Doc*. I read about him in the newspaper. Apparently he was something else, during WWII he left *U of D* to join the Marine Corps and even took part in the assault at Iwo Jima. Then, after the war, I read that he returned to Delaware where he played sports and was even drafted by the Baltimore Colts."

"Incredible, I guess "Doc" Doherty was literally a *fightin' Blue Hen*," reasoned Karl.

"Well, he may not have played football or landed at Iwo Jima but this is my hero," Kim grabbed her grandfathers arm, "It was great for you to come to the game, Granddad."

"How could I beat this," Karl looked across the field, "my granddaughter, my friends and I watching Delaware play the Naval Academy on a Saturday afternoon."

Delaware was lined up in Coach Raymond's *Wing-T* offense on the Navy thirty-five yard line, when the quarterback kept the ball on a misdirection play. Following the right offensive guard the quarterback had picked up the three yards for the first down, but a Navy player had forced the offensive guard to land in an awkward position, causing him to grasp at his knee.

"That's Korf!" shouted Eric, "and it must be pretty serious to bring a stretcher onto the field."

"I hope that he'll be all right," said Kim cautiously, then; everyone watched with concern as Korf was carried off of the field.

Seaford, Delaware 19973

"Once again the United States has warned Africa's island nation of Badasi to terminate its nuclear program." Ron Mathews paused, "In other news, Karl Bontrager, made a triumphant return to his hometown of Dover, Delaware yesterday after having disappeared shortly after the gubernatorial debates just over a week ago. He was joined by two fellow patriots, his neighbor Kate Webster and friend Brock Mattingly. The three had traveled together believing that authorities were searching for Mr. Bontrager and would imprison him if caught. As we said on last night's report those grounds for Mr. Bontrager's incarceration were groundless and the governor has since stopped all legal action against Mr. Bontrager, calling it, *an abuse of the legal system*. The governor also assured the public that he would get to the bottom of it and would push for an investigation."

"Great, that's just what we needed, an investigation," shouted Congressman Oliver as he switched the television off. "I told you Gil, I told you that you were going too far."

"Listen, have you forgotten that you approved my plan?" Hickman pounded on Oliver's desk.

"And what a stupid thing it was that I did," Oliver stood from his chair and began pacing. "We're up to our necks now you fool and we'll be lucky if we don't get caught and sent off to prison."

"Prison," countered Hickman in shock.

"Yes prison," screamed Oliver.

"You're blowing this whole thing out of proportion," Hickman's arms went up in the air.

"When is the last time that you've ever seen a U.S Congressman go to prison?"

Hickman paused for an answer, but there was no response.

"Never, that's when. The worst thing that could happen to you is that you could be censured by the House of Representatives and that rarely happens. Look at how many crooks are on Capitol Hill right now and note how many times that they've returned to office despite getting black eyes. House bank scandals, Check kiting, payoffs, you name it and they still get re-elected."

"Well how do you propose that we cover our tracks?" Oliver paced the floor nervously.

Before Hickman could answer, there was a knock at the door and an advisor entered the room.

"What is it Alan?" Oliver tried to compose himself.

"Your wife is on the phone, Congressman."

"I'll be right there, Alan," the advisor nodded his head and left the room closing the door behind him.

"A few phone calls are all that it will take," assured Hickman, "you know, to get everybody's story straight."

"Well you better get on it right away," the congressman growled.

"I'll call Judge Stortz, Doctor Hoffman and Lou Swetman first thing this morning," Hickman's tone was apologetic.

"Good, get started while I talk to my wife," Oliver's look was threatening as he stomped out of the room.

Woodcrest Drive
Dover, Delaware 19904

Karl's '60's era two-story colonial was somewhat like a time capsule. While his home entertainment system still included a reel-to-reel tape player and phonograph turntable; his kitchen cabinets contained both a Popeil Vegomatic and a long neglected fondue pot.

Following one of Karl's passions, his living room was conducive to reading. A hardcover copy of Anton Myer's *The Last Convertible* lay upon an end table next to a brown leather chair. The chair faced a stone fireplace and along one entire wall there was a knotty pine bookcase that contained hundreds of National Geographics, a set of World Book Encyclopedias and a multitude of dog-eared novels.

Keeping with his interests in aviation and history, a framed *Life Magazine* covering the first Apollo moon landing hung in his den.

The one common theme throughout his house was pictures. Much as his late wife had left them, family photographs taken at theme parks, barbeques and other functions spotted the walls, mantle, and tables. A few of the photographs had even captured Karl with dark hair, and a mustache that may have been discarded around the same time as his 8-track tape player.

Seemingly, the only thing missing was an olive green '67 Dodge Monaco station wagon in the driveway and a lava lamp on an end table.

It was in this atmosphere of nostalgia that students, faculty and interested Delawareans had gathered in Karl's finished basement. They were interested in participating in Karl's vision and they were discussing the provisions of *The Bontrager Bill* that was passed by the U.S. House of Representatives.

Political Science Professor Ross sat at a table with Karl, Kimberly, Kate, Brock and Eric while several other people stood around the table listening. "I've reviewed *The Bontrager Bill* and it gives us the option of tackling a test case in one of several problem areas such as education, hunger, pollution, energy, etcetera. There is quite a list to choose from.

Monies from the federal government will be set aside to fund the research and implement the undertaking which we choose. A condition is that we must choose among one of those areas in which we have the expertise and the means to accomplish the task.

In addition, means of transporting materials or services will be available through existing sources of government transportation."

Discussions throughout the room centered on the selection of problem areas.

"How long do we have to accomplish this task professor?" asked Karl.

"We have one year from the first of the year, subject to extensions that are dependent upon our progress." Professor Ross pointed to the provision in the bill. "If we accomplish our goal adequately the funds may be continued; otherwise they will be cut off."

"And who decides whether we've achieved our goal?" asked Kimberly.

"The problem area agreed upon and the plan to attack it must be submitted for approval to the Congressional Committee by December first, that only gives us a few weeks to come up with a plan," Professor Ross looked concerned.

"Do you think that will be enough time Professor?" Karl asked while lighting his pipe.

"It will have to be," Eric interjected.

"Yes, Eric is quite right. We have to come up with a comprehensive plan with specific goals and present it no later than December first. The provision is direct and without making that deadline there will be no funding of any program."

Professor Ross drummed his fingers on the table.

"Then we better get started," said Kate anxiously, "any ideas?"

"What about education?" one man suggested.

"I think that we should concentrate on our environment," a woman insisted.

"How about crime?" suggested someone else.

"I can see that we've got our work cut out for us," Karl laughed.

Christiana Hospital,
Newark, Delaware 19718

"This is your new room Direktor Gaslov," Doctor Bryant held the wheel chair as a nurse assisted the direktor into his bed. "This will give us a chance to observe you for a couple of weeks until you're released."

"I will enjoy that day very much, Doctor, I have work to do in Vrodkutsk." Direktor Gaslov seemed very determined to make that happen.

"And this is your roommate," the doctor pointed to the large young man lying in the next bed, "it's a bit unusual, but since Direktor Gaslov has come such a long way and you both have science in common, I made special arrangements to put you together in the same room."

"The name's Korf," the young man gave a friendly wave to Gaslov.

"Korf plays offensive lineman for the University of Delaware football team and he injured his knee," the doctor explained, "he's in here for surgery."

"Yes," nodded Gaslov, "I've seen your American football; it's very violent like our hockey in Vrodkutsk."

"Direktor Gaslov is a nuclear research scientist in the former Soviet Socialist Republics," Doctor Bryant exclaimed.

"Is that right?" Korf looked over at his new roommate. "That's very interesting. I've got some questions that I'd like to ask you later on."

"I thought you two might find much to talk about. Korf is a fourth year chemical engineering student at the university," the doctor turned to Gaslov, "he's in one of the best chemical engineering programs in the country at U of D."

Direktor Gaslov's eyes lit up. "Yes indeed, I will be very interested in talking to this young man," he smiled.

"Korf!" it was Kimberly, Eric, Anne and Dan. They stood in the doorway of the room. "Surprise, we came to visit you buddy," said Dan.

"How's the leg?" asked Eric.

"I go in for surgery tomorrow morning. Hey let me introduce you to a couple of friends. This is Doctor Bryant and my roommate is Direktor Gaslov...a nuclear research scientist from a former Soviet Republic." Everyone exchanged handshakes.

"It's a pleasure to meet you comrade Gaslov," Eric extended his hand to the scientist.

"So how's everything going with you?" asked Korf.

"We had a meeting on the Bontrager Bill last night," Anne replied excitedly.

"Bontrager Bill?" Korf's face had an inquisitive stare.

"A congressional bill has been passed to help test my grandfather's ideas," said Kim proudly. "It's really something else and everyone met to discuss ideas and options."

"So how did it go?"

"Let's just say that I know what they mean by gridlock on Capitol Hill, everyone seems to have a different idea about what we should do and whatever that is we need to decide soon. The congressional committee isn't going to wait forever, we need to get on the same page as far as an idea, and then submit it."

"I wish that I could've been there," Korf turned on his side to face the group, "for the past year, I've had an idea kicking around in my head."

"Really, what is it?" asked Kim.

"It may sound far fetched, but my idea is an alternative fuel car. While it hasn't been earmarked for automotive use, we've been working on both a hydrogen fuel cell and a *state-of-the-art* superconductive electric motor at the university lab. What happens is that hydrogen gas is used as fuel for the fuel cell which converts the gas to electricity. In turn, the electricity is used to operate the highly efficient superconductive electric motor. A great benefit of the system is that it doesn't emit harmful exhaust gases like an internal combustion engine; instead it only emits a harmless water vapor.

There's a catch though, as it stands right now, if we made the fuel cell small enough to fit in a car it wouldn't produce sufficient power to drive the superconductive motor. It would take considerable time and research to develop a suitable fuel cell for an automotive application and then it may not even be feasible in the short term."

"I know what you're talking about," said Eric looking at Korf, "the electrical engineering department has been working on it. There are some real challenges to making both a compact and practical hydrogen power source, but don't write that idea off just yet. You never know, if we could get the university behind us we may be able to do something with this."

The idea of a pollution free car excited Kim, "So if we had the support, do you think that we could actually build a hydrogen car?"

"I don't know, it would take a lot of time, effort and money and even then there is no guarantee that the fuel cell would work well enough. Think about it, the major automakers have research projects in a multitude of areas ranging from gas-electric, battery, and solar powered vehicles. Meanwhile, I'm still driving a Jeep with an internal combustion engine. One thing in our favor is that the automakers have been concentrating their research money in other areas and don't have an efficient superconductive electric motor like we do. On the other hand, we won't know if we can get a small hydrogen power plant to work effectively enough until we build one."

"Well it isn't called the Bontrager Bill for nothing," emphasized Kim. "If we could convince my grandfather of the idea then it should be an open and shut case."

Intrigued, Direktor Gaslov listened intently while refraining from any interruption of the conversation.

CHAPTER 16

SuperPower Brainstorming

Seaford, Delaware 19973

"I've contacted all three," Gil Hickman was elated, "the Judge, Doctor Hoffman and Swetman and they've all got their stories straight. They won't be able to connect us with anything."

"I hope you're right," Congressman Oliver sat up in his leather chair, "I don't fancy my neck being stuck out so close to the election."

"The election is in the bag," Hickman declared, "some of this Bontrager thing is rubbing off on you. You're looking good in the polls and with only two weeks before the election you'll be sitting in the Governor's office with this thing far behind you."

Christiana Hospital,
Newark, Delaware 19718

"Superconductivity at near ambient temperatures," an astounded Gaslov shook his head. "In the late '70's we conducted some superconductive research, but always had to use liquid helium to achieve a superconductive state."

Korf had been describing the university's superconductive electric motor and Gaslov couldn't believe what he was hearing.

A phenomenon first discovered in 1911, superconductivity is the ability of some materials to conduct electricity with zero resistance. The catch is that those materials had to be super cooled to minus 420 degrees Fahrenheit by using liquid helium, an extremely impractical requirement.

The benefit of conducting electricity without any resistance loss (superconductivity) would be similar to a water pump, supplying water to the faucet of an upstairs sink without having to overcome the weight of the water in the pipe leading to the sink. As a result, you could have a much smaller pump which would require much less power.

Picturing electric current flow as being similar to the water going through the pipe, and resistance as being similar to the weight of the water; the same thing applies to an electric motor. The wires carrying the electricity to the motor and comprising the motor windings have resistance and are inefficient compared to a superconductive electric motor, which has zero resistance to electric current flow.

A superconductive wire with zero resistance would result in lower operating temperatures, less power required, and longer life. These attributes could permeate every area of electricity and electronics. From incredibly efficient power generation, to super-miniaturized supercomputers, to electric cars and levitated trains, the painstakingly slow developments in superconductivity had the potential for huge payoffs.

It wasn't until 1987 that a material had been fabricated to allow superconductivity at the higher temperature of minus 300 degrees Fahrenheit. A 120 degree improvement in superconductivity over 75 years didn't seem like much, but it allowed more readily available liquid nitrogen to be used in place of the liquid helium.

Then in 1989 professor Felty, along with a group of his university colleagues, gradually developed a material that achieved superconductivity at near ambient temperatures. As an outcome the superconductive motor became their initial effort to achieve a practical use for NAS...*Near-Ambient-Superconductivity.*

By utitilizing thermodynamic principles in the design of the motor's housing and more readily available coolants, the near ambient superconductive electric motor had become a reality. Now the challenge was to find a high profile use for the motor, a use that would greatly increase public interest and demand for the new technology.

As a chemical engineering major, Korf was well aware of the upcoming decision that Felty's team was faced with. A bit of a gear-head, Korf had sometimes wondered about the practicality of putting it in an automobile. He knew that Felty's superconductive motor would be more efficient than the 340 cubic inch engine in his '72 Plymouth Duster. In fact, the automotive industry hadn't had many major breakthroughs in the area of fuel efficiency during Korf's lifetime.

Since the gas lines of the '70's, Detroit automakers had their ideas for making cars more fuel efficient. They started integrating lighter materials, such as plastics, into their product line and they also started offering smaller cars.

By the late '80's some automakers had something on the drawing board called the gas-electric engine. It was an internal combustion engine that was supplemented by an electric motor. While Korf thought of the gas-electric system as innovative, to him it appeared to be a band-aid for the world's reliance on oil when compared to the possibilities of the university's superconductive electric motor powered by a hydrogen fuel cell.

Unlike Detroit's automakers, Professor Felty and his colleagues were not restricted by Detroit's profit margins and board members. Even so, in regards to Korf's idea of putting the superconductive motor in an automobile; Felty's team was restricted by the available space. The fuel cell that produced the electricity for the electric motor would have to be downsized to make it practical for an automobile.

"So you feel that your electron pump would be sufficient to power the car's superconductive electric motor?" for hours, Korf and Direktor Gaslov had been talking about the possibility of building an efficient and pollution free automobile by using both American and former Soviet technologies.

"Yes, that's highly probable by the description that you have given me of your electron pump," Direktor Gaslov was sitting up in his bed as he explained the concept to Korf. "Our electron pump is also a fuel cell. It uses hydrogen and oxygen to produce electricity and we've used it quite successfully aboard Soviet spacecraft. The difference is that we have developed it further by being able to amplify the output from the fuel cell with the addition of the electron pump. This gives our fuel cell greater efficiency and output power for its size which is what you are looking for. I feel that with some engineering it would meet the needs of your automobile. The only thing would be the transport of the device and its technology through diplomatic channels, and the research necessary to miniaturize and interface the two technologies."

"Direktor, what if we could get such an agreement between our two governments, would you be willing to participate in the project?"

"Yes," agreed Gaslov," most indeed. Since the breakup of the Union of Soviet Socialist Republics, my government has been looking for new uses for our technologies, in addition to new ways to market them. Such a program would be just the thing to help get our economy back on its feet and I would enjoy seeing that very much."

"Then it would be a joint venture for Vrodkutsk, the Delaware venture," Korf concluded.

Courthouse
Dover, Delaware 19904

The District Attorney for the state of Delaware had questioned the three men for over two hours. His decision was whether there was enough evidence to bring them to trial for their actions against Karl Bontrager and Kate Webster.

"There just isn't enough substantiated evidence, Sam, despite how fishy this thing smells." District Attorney Raymond Lewis spoke with his aide, Sam Darrel, as they walked to the courthouse cafeteria, "Lou Swetman says that he fired Bontrager for being a poor custodian and that it had nothing to do with the debate. It's one man's word against another. Meanwhile, the Judge says that he was merely trying to protect the public, a matter of judgment, and Doc Hoffman says that in his opinion, Karl and Kate displayed aggressive tendencies, a matter of diagnosis."

"But it's obvious what happened," said Sam. "Someone got on the horn and forced Bontrager's dismissal. Then the poor guy got railroaded out of town by the judge and the doctor."

"I know, I don't like this thing anymore than you do," countered Raymond, but with the evidence that we have there's no way to have a finding of wrongdoing; then having it stick in court. Sorry Sam, but sometimes the bad guys get away."

Seaford, Delaware 19973

With a brief knock on the door the congressman's aide ran into the office bubbling with good news.

"Oh, it's you, Alan."

"Thought you'd like to see the morning paper," the aide handed Oliver the newspaper."

"Very good, thank you Alan," Alan walked out of the office and Oliver quickly looked at the front page where in a big headline it read: State Hearing finds no basis for Bontrager case.

"Beautiful," an elated Oliver said aloud to himself. He then reached for the phone to consult with Gil Hickman.

Vrodkutsk Nuclear Research Center
Commonwealth of Independent States

"Direktor Gaslov would be ashamed of you," shouted acting Direktor Belenko to the assembly of engineers and technicians. "We have a job to do here in Vrodkutsk. Are you going to sell out our homeland for dirty money?"

"Money to feed and clothe our families," grumbled one angry technician.

"Even with money, the store shelves are empty here," added an engineer, "in other countries we have opportunities to work for good wages and to feed and clothe our children."

"I know that the situation is bad," Viktor pleaded," but we must be patient for the new system to take hold in our economy, not to cut and run as you propose.

To leave your homeland and become a puppet of a tyrant is not the answer. Now that the government is giving us the freedom to do so, we must stay and rebuild our economy and homeland."

"We can't eat government promises," argued another defiant plant worker, "we've waited long enough."

"I ask you for only one thing," reasoned Viktor sincerely, "to wait for Direktor Gaslov's return."

Evans Hall University of Delaware
Newark, Delaware 19716

"What do you think, Professor Felty?" Dan asked hopefully. "Is it possible?"

"I don't know," answered the professor, "it sounds a bit like the claims of *cold fusion* from a few years back. It didn't make sense and it turned out that it didn't work. Are you sure about what Korf told you?"

"He was adamant professor," Dan looked concerned. "He said that Direktor Gaslov believes that their fuel cell along with it's electron pump would increase the cell's power output substantially enough to drive our superconductive motor."

"I don't know Dan; a lot of research has been conducted in the West on power plants and for the Soviets to have come up with something that we haven't," the professor scratched his head. "Well, I'd have to talk to Direktor Gaslov himself, but if he's correct..." the professor didn't finish his sentence out of fear that he would sound overly reactionary.

"But what professor?"

The professor hesitated, "It would be revolutionary, there I've said it; but I'm witholding any further comments until I see their fuel cell, the electron pump, and Direktor Gaslov."

"I can arrange a meeting," Dan assured with a broad smile, "it'll be my pleasure."

Old Statehouse
Dover, Delaware 19903

"And when I'm elected governor there will be more freedom for patriots like Karl Bontrager to influence our government for the betterment of all of our citizens," Congressman Oliver stood behind a podium on the steps of the Old Statehouse as he addressed a crowd of his cheering supporters. A group of dignitaries sat in chairs behind him.

"I am sure that all Delawareans will support me in helping to make Mr. Bontrager's dreams come true with the Bontrager Bill...which I authored...and am proud to say sought support for...and finally won passage of in the U.S. House of Representatives. The Bontrager Bill is a first step, a pilot project to provide for a more efficient means of developing and testing solutions to problems that Delawareans, Americans, and people around the world face." Oliver paused for applause. "Today, I am proud to introduce you to the man who was and is the inspiration for the Bontrager Bill. Ladies and gentlemen I give you Karl Bontrager."

A hesitant Karl Bontrager stood and waved to the cheering crowd. Congressman Oliver took the opportunity to shake Karl's hand for the cameras, and then adjusted the podium microphone for the tall Delawarean.

"Thank you...thank you very much," Karl's amplified voice was nearly drowned out by the crowd which insisted on showing gratitude to the man who put Delaware on the map.

"Thank you so very much for coming out today. I am not a professional speaker, but your kindness makes me feel like one. A few weeks ago, I was a janitor in this building," Karl turned to point at the red brick structure that was behind him, "at that time, with the exception of a few friends and my granddaughter, I was unknown. Now I stand before you and I tell you, I've got a lot of friends." A cheer rose through the crowd. "People who feel the same as I do and if presented with the same opportunity that I had, I believe would have done the same thing. Those people are you."

Karl pointed to the crowd, "the good people of *the first state* who are now poised to meet a challenge, the challenge of making an impact for the good of Delaware and beyond.

Benjamin Franklin called Delaware, *the Diamond State,* not because of its diamond mines, it has none, but because he considered Delaware a jewel among states. I think everyone of us here has seen the bumper sticker which reads, *Delaware Small Wonder.* I agree, Delaware is a small wonder and its people make it so. Are you with me," shouted Karl who got an immediate affirmation from the crowd. "Well that's great because with the help of Professor Felty, of the University of Delaware, I am prepared to make an announcement, Professor," Karl motioned for the Professor to join him at the podium.

"Thank you Karl. Karl has asked me to make an announcement about the intentions of the first test case for the Bontrager Bill. As you may know, the Bontrager Bill allows us to submit a plan to attack a major problem that affects Delaware, the nation, and the world.

During several meetings, many possibilities were proposed for a first test case by many concerned citizens, but we could only choose one. In making our decision we considered the feasibility of the project, its potential impact, and its cost.

A couple of areas that affect the world are alternative energy and pollution; our first test case will set out to tackle them both. As a result, we intend to develop a practical hydrogen powered automobile with a superconductive engine. After consulting with Direktor Gaslov of the Vrodkutsk Nuclear Research Center, we have concluded that such a revolutionary and pollution free power plant for an automobile is feasible.

This power plant will consist of technologies from both the former Soviet Socialist Republic of Vrodkutsk and those under development at the University of Delaware. If successful, and I wouldn't be standing here today if I didn't feel confident about this endeavor, this power plant will become the mainstay of automotive technology throughout the world. It will not be an internal combustion power plant, rather it will be an electrical power plant and as I said pollution free.

In the months ahead, our work will be cut out for us. We must mate the two technologies and build a prototype automobile that will operate efficiently; yet perform comparably to the standards of performance that we have become accustomed to with the internal combustion engine.

In addition, technical personnel and engineers from the Republic of Vrodkutsk will be used for research in the project. These individuals, whose skills are easily marketed to unfriendly countries, will be given the opportunity to stay in their homeland and work on less threatening technology to the world; in effect, helping to slow the exodus of nuclear trained personnel and their knowledge to countries with less than peaceful intentions. We will soon set in place the cornerstone that will mark the beginning of our new relationship."

The crowd was ecstatic as the Professor returned to his seat.

U.S. State Department
Washington, D.C. 20515

"What is this Phil?" questioned Rob Henderson thumbing through a folder at his desk.

"Top priority, someone high up wants it taken care of…A…S…A…P…It's a joint agreement to exchange technologies with the Commonwealth of Independent States and it's as hot as a tick on a match in the Mojave Desert."

"Are you sure? It looks like they're glossing over some of the technicalities."

"The president himself signed a directive to push this thing through. It's an election year you know," replied Phil, "has something to do with that Bontrager Bill…you know, that group in Delaware."

"No bull," said Rob excitedly.

"No bull, now let's get hot…like that tick."

Island of Badasi
Southwestern Africa

"Georgi!" Nuclear Technician Kuryakin called out as he entered the control room. Georgi Fyodor was standing at the Reactor Plant Control Panel with an engineer.

"How are you doing Comrade Kuryakin?" Georgi kept looking at the panel as he addressed the technician. "Rod control test, we're testing the electromagnets for failsafe release."

"Ah yes," said Kuryakin, "in preparation for the fueling."

"Reactor scram! Reactor scram!" announced the engineer over the power plant's intercom. The engineer had just tripped the main coolant pump breakers and, just as designed, the electromagnets de-energized, releasing the control rods into the reactor's core. In the event that the core had already been fueled with U235-which it hadn't, the graphite control rods would absorb the neutrons given off by the uranium isotope, thus preventing an uncontrolled nuclear chain reaction and steam explosion.

There were smiles all around; the test had been a success.

"So how long Georgi before these tests are finished?" asked Kuryakin. "I've got a core to fuel, you know."

"Patience comrade Kuryakin," Georgi looked down at a clipboard that he clutched in his left hand, "a week, maybe two. To rush these safeguards would be foolish...remember Chernobyl." Georgi admonished with a long face. He had lost two friends in the Soviet Union's premier nuclear power plant disaster and wisely, he didn't take the reactor safeguard examination lightly.

Christiana Hospital,
Newark, Delaware 19718

"On behalf of the peoples of the Commonwealth of Independent States, you may sign here Direktor Gaslov." The diplomat, from the former Soviet embassy in Washington D.C. pointed to a line at the bottom of the document. Gaslov had been well on his way to recovery, but hospital restrictions did not permit him to leave his wheel chair as of yet. He signed the document with a smile and a flair for theatrics as cameras clicked around the room and his wife gave him a kiss.

"And Mr. Bontrager on behalf of the United States and the state of Delaware, you may sign here," The U.S. State Department official pointed at yet another line at the bottom of the document and Karl added his signature, concluding it by accepting a kiss from his granddaughter.

Then at the front of the make shift press room at the hospital, Karl Bontrager exchanged pens with Direktor Gaslov and they shook each other's hand. Once again the clicking sound of cameras filled the room.

"Direktor Gaslov, are you sure that this new power plant is possible?" a reporter asked.

"Are you so sure that it is not possible," the direktor asked rhetorically. A collective laugh accompanied the direktor's response.

"With an answer like that, I think that Direktor Gaslov would do well as an American politician," chuckled Governor Collins over the podium microphone.

"Seriously, will it work Professor Felty?" asked another reporter. Professor Felty moved to the microphone, "I believe this historic moment was accomplished due to the fact that after Direktor Gaslov's discussions with us, that is, Mr. Bontrager, the engineering faculty of the University of Delaware, and those involved in the Bontrager brain trust, that both parties developed great confidence in each other's technology and expertise.

This will truly be the greatest scientific endeavor between the peoples of the Commonwealth of Independent States and an American based organization since the Apollo/Soyuz link up in the early '70's and I hope that it's not the last. Direktor Gaslov would you care to comment, sir?" Professor Felty adjusted the microphone for the direktor.

"I do not sign such documents without first weighing there feasibility and this is no exception. Since Premier Gorbachev's reforms and the breakup of the Soviet Union, the political climate has become fertile for a project such as this.

For me, my hopes are with the men and women of Vrodkutsk. Those people who are going without the basic necessities of life while their country is rebuilding its infrastructure. Those people, whom I left a few weeks ago, and who only want for their families; what I've seen in such abundance here in Delaware. This agreement," the Direktor raised the document in his hand, "can only be a catalyst for these things to become a reality in my homeland and for that I am very much appreciative of this opportunity."

"Direktor Gaslov, Direktor Gaslov," shouted another reporter.

"I'm sorry but there will be no more questions," Doctor Bryant interrupted, "Direktor Gaslov is scheduled for physical therapy shortly."

"In that case I'll be happy to take more questions," laughed Gaslov not looking forward to the daily workout.

CHAPTER 17

Back in the U.S.S.R.

Vrodkutsk Nuclear Research Center
Vrodkutsk Commonwealth of Independent States

"Welcome home, Direktor Gaslov," Engineer Viktor Belenko greeted his super-visor at the front entrance to the facility. He noticed that the direktor was now equipped with a cane to help with his bad leg. "How's your health, sir?"

"I'm doing well, Viktor," replied a cheerful Gaslov. "How's everything been during my absence?"

"I'm afraid not very good, sir. We lost Kuryakin."

The direktor stopped in his tracks with a look of deep concern.

"Badasi, he left a couple of weeks ago. The same old story, he said that he had hung on as long as he could. The family you know."

"Anyone else?"

"Not yet, but the dam is about to burst wide open, I'm afraid. Frankly, I'm surprised that some stayed on as long as they have," Viktor shrugged. "There's been a headhunter by the name of Maynard Price; he's been trying to recruit men for Badasi. He's staying in town and some of the men are thinking about talking to him."

"Then we don't have any time to waste," said Gaslov. "Assemble the off shift immediately; I don't care if they're at home or wherever they may be. I've got some important news for them and I want them here now."

"Yes Direktor, may I ask what the news is?"

"You'll find out along with the rest of the men, Viktor," Gaslov was deeply worried.

Seaford, Delaware 19973

"How's the next governor of Delaware doing this morning?" Gil Hickman entered Oliver's office and tossed a newspaper on the congressman's desk.

The headline read: *Oliver Fifteen Point Favorite.*

"Fifteen points," shouted the wide eyed politician, "this Bontrager thing was the best thing that ever happened to us!"

"You could probably ride his coattails right into the White House," Hickman was jubilant.

"Yeah, it's too bad that I'm only running for governor, Gil." Oliver had been laughing more freely since the district attorney's preliminary hearing failed to finger him. "With three days left until the election, do you think that you can get me on the ballot in all fifty?"

"Hey, I'm not a miracle worker," laughed Hickman with a sly wink. "By the way, Alan's been telling me to start referring to him as the Budget Czar."

Oliver's eyebrows twitched as his smile receded somewhat, "Ah yes, the cabinet position."

Gil sensed that there was something suddenly wrong with Oliver's demeanor, "What is it?"

"Well, remember that big contributor from Hockessin, Charlotte Whittaker?"

Hickman nodded his head, "What about it?"

"Well, she's had an eye on that cabinet position for some time," Oliver frowned.

"She's got to be seventy years old," objected Hickman.

"Not for her, for her granddaughter, she works as an accountant for a reputable firm in downtown Wilmington. The last time I ran for congress she pulled out her checkbook and basically said that she may come to me for a favor someday and it turns out that day is today."

"You know how hard Alan's been working on this campaign, you can't pull the rug out from under him now," Hickman was irate.

"Well, four years ago I had no idea that she had any interest in that position until I received a phone call from her the other day," Oliver stood up. "She's got too many connections; I just can't give that position to Alan, that's all that there is to it."

Vrodkutsk Nuclear Research Center
Commonwealth of Independent States

"Comrades, thank you for assembling on such a short notice, but I have very important news for you," Direktor Gaslov stood atop a catwalk that overlooked the maintenance room.

The men seemed to be pleased at the fact that the direktor appeared to be in such good health, while at the same time disturbed that they had been recalled. They had heard so many pep talks over the past year that held out many promises of better food or housing conditions which never materialized that they were not looking forward to yet another one.

"As you know, I have spent the last several weeks in the United States of America, at a hospital in the province of Delaware. During my stay there I received excellent medical care and met many interesting people. The United States is truly a prosperous country where foods are plentiful and the standard of living is very high. The store shelves are full of high quality goods...and there are no long lines. A great deal of the population lives in single family dwellings that are comparable to a politburo member's country dacha, with indoor plumbing and the latest of modern conveniences. Everyone, it seems, has a shiny new automobile and nice clothes to wear.

I do not say these things to make you feel bad my comrades; I say these things to show you the possibilities that exist for us here in Vrodkutsk," sporadic laughter broke out amongst the men.

"Yes, you laugh," Gaslov conceded, "but I have seen these things for myself. The capitalist system works and it can work here in Vrodkutsk. Are we not men like those of the United States? Men with a will to set and accomplish goals, goals for the future of our families and our country which now has new found freedoms to pursue those goals! Freedoms to search and strive to new heights. I say yes. We can do these things that others in far away places have done before us. It is the easy road to give up, to turn your backs on our homeland. Any man can take the easy road. It is for the strong and the determined to take the hard road, the road to a better future for Vrodkutsk and its people and the Americans have made that road wider for us."

Gaslov braced himself with the cane as he held up a document in his right hand. "This can be the beginning of a new future for Vrodkutsk and its people. During my stay in America, I signed an agreement that was approved by both the United States and the Commonwealth of Independent States. This is a joint agreement to develop a revolutionary, pollution free, automotive power plant to be used in automobiles of the future. This engine will be electric in nature and will consist of components from both Delaware and the Vrodkutsk Research Center."

The men grew more interested as Direktor Gaslov continued.

"The United States government is underwriting most of the cost; ensuring you a paycheck. One of the basic principles of the agreement is to infuse a capitalist mind-set into those participating in the project. This will mean an exchange of personnel between the two countries and our learning the building blocks of starting and running a business. That means learning the meaning of terms such as profit margin and overhead; I still need to learn the meaning of those terms myself."

A smiling Gaslov had sensed that he was breaking through to his men and women from the eager looks on their faces and could see that they wanted to hear more.

"You may wonder how this will translate into an improvement in our standard of living. Well, it will mean a steady paycheck for the near term and possibly profit sharing in the long run. What is profit sharing, you ask? Someday, should the power plant become a success and then sold around the world, you employees as part owners of the company, may receive a portion of the money from the sale of the engine.

Then, you will explain how capitalism works to your relatives and friends and they will hopefully start their own businesses."

Direktor Gaslov was caught off guard by a technician with his hand raised.

"Yes, you have a question Andrei?"

"Yes sir, what is to be the name of this endeavor?"

"That is a good question Andrei. After much debate in America, we decided upon, SuperPower Automotive."

Dover, Delaware 19904

"These are for you, Elizabeth," Karl placed the flowers next to the marble headstone which read:

Elizabeth May Bontrager
1 May 1931–1 May 1986

"So much has happened to me since I was last here. I was fired from my job, placed in jail, sent to a psychiatric hospital and then gained notoriety all because I spoke my mind to the governor during a political debate.

Before I knew it, my whole life was turned on its ear and I was on the run, just like that David Jansen fella in *the Fugitive*. It was really something. It got the blood pumping in the old arteries again and gave me something to live for. In fact, I haven't felt this alive in years, Elizabeth.

Beth, it turns out that when I piped off during the debate, a lot of people heard my ideas and they think that they're pretty good. I wish you were here to be with me, but until we're together again, Kimberly has been keeping me on the straight and narrow. She's a wonderful granddaughter, reminds me a lot of you.

Well I guess I better be moving on. The grounds keeper has been watching me and is starting to think that I'm talking to myself. I love you Beth."

Seaford, Delaware 19973

"Everything's been arranged at the The Hotel Nanticoke for tomorrow night," said Hickman. "It'll be a great place to watch the returns and stuff our faces before Collins concedes. There's plenty of room for your supporters and we should have a great evening.

"Excellent Gil," smiled Oliver looking up from his desk. "I was just working on my acceptance speech. When I finish I want you to look at it."

"Yes sir, Governor Oliver!" chuckled Hickman.

"Now don't jinx me," he cautioned, "we still have one more day until the election."

"Just a technicality with your overwhelming lead in the polls," quipped Hickman. "I suppose Collins has already cleaned his desk out."

"You're a bit premature, Gil, but keep that thought."

Woodburn, the Governor's Mansion
Dover, Delaware 19904

"Sarah, sometime in the next few weeks, we'll be sending our furniture to our cottage in Bethany Beach." Governor Collins eased back in his chair, his look was shallow.

"Are you conceding already," asked the governor's aide? "This isn't the governor that I know, the one that doesn't go down without a fight."

"Hey! I'm just facing reality. The only thing that's left is for the fat lady to sing and tomorrow night she's taking her place at center stage."

"Regardless of what the outcome may be, there's no big rush to move the furniture," Sarah pointed out.

"No I've already decided that I'll be spending the balance of my time as governor by the ocean. You know, get in some fishing and relaxation," The governor motioned as if reeling in a fish.

"I'm sorry Bob," Sarah looked at her boss who was showing signs of stress. "Maybe I could have done something differently to give you a better chance during the campaign."

"Sarah, you did everything you could." Governor Collins became very serious, "Oliver took the Bontrager issue and ran with it. It's apparently working for him and tomorrow the people of Delaware will make their decision. I guess we'll just have to wait and see whether you can fool some of the people some of the time or all of the people all of the time."

Newark, Delaware 19711

"Thank you all for coming to my home this evening." Professor Felty stood in front of his living room fireplace. Chairs had been assembled in a half circle facing the professor and Korf who was still on crutches, sat in the front row with Karl, Kimberly, Eric, Dan, Anne, Kate Webster and Brock Mattingly. The rest of the participants had a wide range of occupations and had come from their homes throughout Delaware.

"The purpose of this meeting is to select an initial group to fly to the Republic of Vrodkutsk. This group will help to lay the groundwork for Super-Power Automotive and will establish the design parameters to make the electron pump and superconductive motor compatible with each other. It is very important that these initial figures be precise so as not to cause a loss of time later down the road. A mockup of the superconductive motor will be taken on this trip and Direktor Gaslov, his engineers, and technicians will be briefed as to its operation.

Direktor Gaslov had informed me prior to his departure that his workers are unfamiliar with the workings of the capitalist system and need to be enlightened to them. In addition, one of the goals of this trip will be to introduce the people in the surrounding areas of the Vrodkutsk Research Center to the capitalist system. Many of the people of these outlying areas earn their living through an inefficient agricultural system that historically hasn't had incentives or rewards for greater output; therefore, there is a need for agriculturalists and businessmen on the trip. Are there any questions?" Seemingly, every hand went up in response to Professor Felty's opening.

Vrodkutsk Nuclear Research Center
Commonwealth of Independent States

"So what do you think, Viktor?" Direktor Gaslov confided in Engineer Belenko.

"Do you think the men are behind the idea?"

"Well, you got their attention. I don't think that we'll see any defections for awhile. That is, as long as the men have hope in this plan."

"Good then, we'll have to move quickly to show them that we are serious about this. As I said, there will be exchanges of personnel between here and Delaware, the first of which will be next week when a contingent arrives here, in Vrodkutsk. We need to start preparing now and we'll need our best men to brief the Delawareans on the electron pump.

Also, we'll need schedules for the men to be briefed by the Americans on the superconductive motor. Although this is a test project, we must also introduce the men and the people in the outlying areas to the fundamentals of capitalism."

"Yes sir, I'll get on it right away." Viktor set about his newly assigned tasks optimistically. The knowledge that the center would be turning its energy from those associated with war to those of free enterprise was comforting to the scientist. Since the collapse of the Soviet Union, the research center had lumbered along searching for a purpose and a goal, it's workforce knowing that without change the center would become obsolete in this new age of improved East/West relations.

CHAPTER 18

All of the People Some of the Time

The Hotel Nanticoke
Seaford, Delaware 19973

"I just received a phone call from Governor Collins," Governor-elect Oliver waved his hands to quiet his cheering followers. "He wished me good luck and he offered me any assistance that I may need during the transition period.

Let me say that this is a victory for you," Oliver pointed to the joyful crowd.

"Working together we will guide Delaware toward the next century. This will be a time for Delaware's voice to be heard throughout the country and around the world."

Vrodkutsk Nuclear Research Center
Commonwealth of Independent States

"Welcome," Direktor Gaslov greeted the group of Delawareans. "Let me introduce you to my assistant, Engineer Viktor Belenko."

Karl Bontrager extended his hand, "It's a pleasure and this is our group from Delaware," Karl introduced the faculty, students, farmers and business-men who had made the trip from Delaware.

"A very distinguished group," said Gaslov. "I'm eager to talk to all of you, but first I'd like to take you all on a tour of our facility and have you meet some more of our people."

"Sounds good," agreed Karl. "I believe our people are just as eager to exchange ideas with your people on the project, and the sooner the better."

Direktor Gaslov and Viktor Belenko led the group throughout the facility for two hours, stopping to talk to several engineers and technicians along the way.

"This is our main research laboratory," Direktor Gaslov led the Delawareans into a large room with white walls and a red tile floor. It was spotless and seemed to have much of the equipment that one would expect in its American counterpart. There were men and women, wearing white lab coats, standing in front of work benches that were outfitted with oscilloscopes, power supplies, digital multimeters, spectrum analyzers and other measuring equipment. Despite all of the shortages that had beset Vrodkutsk, the former Soviet Union had outfitted the important *Cold War* research center with a full complement of test equipment; much of it purchased from the West.

The workers greeted their guests with broad smiles as the direktor, who was obviously proud of his facility, walked between the benches pointing out the various types of studies that were underway. "As you can see, although a great deal of our research is in the field of nuclear power, we are conducting research into many other areas such as the electron pump."

Gaslov stopped in front of a platform that supported the mechanism. The device was primarily a metal cube of approximately 2 meters and attached to one end of the cube was a smaller box which had its side cover removed. Inside the smaller box were circuit boards and wires. Professor Felty correctly assumed that the box contained the power supply and central processing unit for the electron pump, but there was some other hardware that he couldn't account for.

One of the engineers approached the group and Direktor Gaslov introduced the woman, "This is Doktor Petrova Marchenko. She is in charge of the research into the electron pump and will brief your group on its operation."

Karl noted that Petrova didn't look like the stereo typical Russian Nuclear Scientist. Her deep blue eyes were unobstructed by glasses and her dark medium length hair surrounded an angelic face. In addition, she had obviously taken care of herself and Karl guessed her age to be in the late forties while she was actually in her mid-fifties.

As a young woman in the West, Petrova could have possibly been a model, but little did Karl and his group know that her dossier included work on projects ranging from the Soyuz space station to the Soviet Union's response to the United States Strategic Defense Initiative (SDI). During the cold war, defections were a real possibility. Therefore, she was deemed too valuable by the Kremlin to allow her travel in the West as some of her colleagues had.

Nevertheless she had gained an impeccable command of the English language through schooling and numerous diplomatic receptions that she had attended in Moscow for foreign dignitaries.

Petrova moved toward the device, "This larger cube contains the fuel for the fuel cell portion of the electron pump, "started Petrova. "Hydrogen is the fuel and it is embedded in these removable sheets. Of course, the hydrogen combining with oxygen is what supplies the free electrons that power whatever electric device you desire. That's where this smaller cube comes into play. It houses a cathode, an anode, a specially developed polymer, associated circuitry and the actual electron pump."

Petrova continued through her briefing for some time, emphasizing that the problem with the system that they had was that it needed to be reduced in size to make it a practical power source for the automotive industry.

Much of Petrova's briefing was foreign to Karl, but he didn't seem to mind as long as she was conducting it.

After the briefing, Direktor Gaslov introduced the two, "This is Karl Bontrager," Karl was caught off guard and blushed slightly as he shook Petrova's hand.

"Yes, I've heard much about you, Mr. Bontrager," Petrova smiled, "your inspiration is fascinating and I look forward to working with you and your associates."

Petrova turned as she looked at Karl's friends.

"And we are looking forward to working with you, Doktor," interjected Professor Felty. "I'm looking forward to your lectures."

"We'll have plenty of time for work after lunch," Gaslov reminded them. "Would you care to join us, Doktor Marchenko?"

"Yes, very much so," Petrova graciously accepted.

Island of Badasi
Southwestern Africa

"So we meet again, Kuryakin," Georgi was filling his lunch tray. "How do you find your work here, comrade?"

Kuryakin's look was glum. "Do you have a few minutes to talk?" asked the technician as he chose the stroganoff.

"This sounds serious," Georgi placed a glass of tea on his tray.

"Yes sit with me at my table. I'll introduce you to some of the engineers that work in the control room."

"No," objected Kuryakin, "I must speak to you alone."

Georgi was surprised at his friend's insistence to talk alone. "All right Kury-akin," Georgi pointed with his tray, "there's an empty table…we can talk there."

The two men had resumed their conversation at the unoccupied table, "What is N-1?" asked Kurykin.

Georgi stopped the fork short of his mouth, "Where did you hear about N-1?" he asked in a whisper. His eyes darted around to see if anyone was watching.

"I'm in fueling, remember?" whispered Kuryakin. "People talk and I was bound to find out sooner or later. I just found out sooner."

Woodburn, the Governor's Mansion
Dover, Delaware 19903

"Well it's done," Governor Collins said in a relieved tone, "The election is finally over and I can go back to being average *Joe Citizen* again."

"You seem to be taking this pretty well Bob," Sarah Watkins said with a forced smile.

"Oh I began preparing myself a couple of weeks ago," The governor took a seat at his desk. "We knew the race was lost when Oliver got the Bontrager Bill through congress. It won the people over."

"No sour grapes?" Sarah asked.

"I'd be lying if I said no. You know I like Karl Bontrager and what he's try-ing to do, but…," Governor Collins hesitated.

"But what Bob?"

"But I'll never understand how Oliver fooled so many people; I mean to win the race and everything with his track record."

"Sometimes the good guys don't win, Governor," Sarah tried to ease the incumbent's mind. "There are people through history who didn't win every election that they entered, yet they went on to have a great political career."

"Well the only thing that I want to see is the reel end of a fishing pole for the next few weeks," insisted the governor. "My political career is on hold for the foreseeable future."

Vrodkutsk
Commonwealth of Independent States

The contingent of Delawareans was meeting with the citizens of Vrodkutsk, Delaware farmers meeting with Vrodkutskan farmers, Delaware businessmen meeting with Vrodkutsk's future entrepreneurs, and Delaware educators and scientists meeting with their Vrodkutskan counterparts.

The exchange of information between the two factions was sparked by the desire for technological breakthroughs as well as the goal for improving the standard of living of the Vrodkutskan people. Such endeavors would have been forbidden a few short years before, but in the post glasnost era such cooperation was encouraged.

Karl Bontrager, who just a few weeks before was tasked with emptying trash baskets for the Delaware Legislature had been catapulted into the world of international politics as an innovator. A man of dreams who would watch them become reality. Karl was living the dream of so many people who would never realize their own. He was the hourly factory worker who dreamt of owning his own company, the child who aspired to become an astronaut, the store clerk who desired to write the great novel, the single mother who yearned for a better job, and the bus driver with an idea for the better mousetrap.

Karl had succeeded where others had failed because he seized the moment. There were many people who were seated in the Old Statehouse on that evening which changed his life, but Karl was the only one to seize the opportunity. His fifteen minutes of fame touched the hearts and souls of the people who are often left without a voice. Karl had become their voice and in a sense those people had seized the moment when they called on Karl to have his say that evening in Delaware's Old Statehouse.

Karl could now stand on the sidelines if he desired and could watch others carry out his vision; but he was learning the meaning of living life to its fullest and he was enjoying it too much to stand idly by. He now yearned to learn from those that he had inspired, the future astronaut, the farmer, the housewife, the grocery clerk, the businessperson, the bus driver, the educator and the scientist.

Communal Farm
Vrodkutsk, Commonwealth of Independent States

"This is a communal farm," Churkin, a Vrodkutskan, addressed his remarks to Bill and Lori Lessard. The three wore rubber boots and heavy coats as they ventured through the farm, "We raise cattle, hogs and chickens," the proud Vrodkutskan boasted.

"That sounds like our farm in Delaware," exclaimed Lori Lessard.

"How big is your farm?" asked Churkin.

"Two hundred acres," replied Bill.

Churkin was surprised at the size, "You must have many workers helping you?"

"We stay pretty busy," Lori interjected.

"We also stay busy," said Churkin as he opened a gate and ushered the Lessard's through. "The government allows us to keep some of the crops as partial payment for our work. These we can sell on the open market. The problem is that much of the machinery we have is in disrepair. This is due to a shortage of parts which leaves us little choice but to do much of the planting and harvesting by hand."

"That is a big problem," consoled Bill, "but over time maybe some of our ideas can be of help to you and your fellow farmers."

Churkin led Bill and Alice into a house on the communal farm grounds. Inside sat men and women who had gathered to hear about the farming methods used in Delaware. Many of them looked as if they had worked long and hard during their lifetimes. Their hands were calloused and their faces were wrinkled. Some had survived through the hardships and privations of Stalin, a shameful period in Soviet history that rewarded hard work with tyranny, empty promises, and the Gulag.

These were truly people who had known the meaning of living on the bare necessities. The Lessard's understood that they could not cram Western ideology, technology, or practices down the throats of these people and expect it to take hold overnight. It would take time and understanding of Vrodkutsk, its people, and its special problems.

"This is Bill and Lori Lessard," Churkin acting as translator, introduced them in Russian. "They're our special guests from the United States, and they have come to tell us about their farm in Delaware." The Vrodkutskans welcomed the visitors.

"The Lessards will start with a video of their farm and will answer your questions at its conclusion," Churkin addressed the group as Bill set up the portable video equipment that he had brought with him. Within a few minutes the lights were darkened and the Vrodkutskans were getting their first uncensored look at farm life under capitalism.

The scene was being repeated in and around Vrodkutsk. Business people from Delaware showed their videos and spoke of the advantages of capitalism over communism; seemingly everyone that had heard of the Delawareans and their seminars took advantage of the opportunity.

The Vrodkutskans were shown videos of large department and grocery stores that were stocked with modern goods and foods that they had only dreamt of. Streets with beautiful homes and plenty of shiny new automobiles. "These are the promises that the Communist party always made but never fulfilled," the Delawareans would hear time after time at the seminars. "We too want to be prosperous," was another familiar phrase that was common among the Vrodkutskans.

Meanwhile, Direktor Gaslov, Karl Bontrager, Professor Felty, his colleagues and the handful of students who had accompanied them on the trip continued their indoctrination on the electron pump by Doktor Marchenko. She stood in front of the seated group at a lectern. An overhead projector sat upon a nearby table.

"The electron pump is similar to a battery in that it uses a chemical reaction to produce a flow of electrons between two terminals. It differs from a battery though in that it uses hydrogen and oxygen rather than two dissimilar metals submersed in an electrolyte."

Doktor Marchenko placed the first overhead slide on the overhead projector, "As you can see a membrane allows the protons to pass directly to the cathode, but the only path available for the electrons is through an external circuit. Of course, the electrons flowing through the external circuit will power your superconductive motor. The advantage of this system is that it is extremely efficient and produces no harmful hydrocarbons. The only resulting byproduct is water vapor.

In fact, our newest Soyuz space station uses this method of power in conjunction with solar panels and it's operated for months in space before requiring periodic replacement of the hydrogen impregnated sheets by cosmonauts."

Doktor Marchenko placed another slide on the overhead, "The membrane stays in tact and can last for an extended period of time barring any unforeseen problems.

One of the distinguishing differences between our electron pump and your fuel cell back in Delaware is the addition of the electron pump itself. The electron pump portion of our fuel cell actually boosts the output of the fuel cell, somewhat like a transistor can be used as an amplifier to boost an audio signal," during the lecture Doktor Marchenko went into great technical detail of the operation of the electron pump. She also fielded many questions from the visiting professors and dignitaries.

"In conclusion, we feel that the electron pump, in conjunction with the superconductive motor, will serve as a viable power plant for an alternative power automobile," with that Doktor Marchenko was greeted with a standing ovation and a round of applause from the visiting Delawareans. While the mathematics and science became overwhelming, at times, Karl had been to so many indoctrinations on the electron pump that he had acquired a practical knowledge of the device.

"You must return with us on our return trip, Doktor," Professor Felty extended his hand to Marchenko. "We will need your expertise to bring the project together."

"Yes, of course," she smiled modestly, "that is if Direktor Gaslov gives me his okay."

Direktor Gaslov nodded, "We must have our best working alongside our Delaware colleagues," he said with a guttural laugh.

CHAPTER 19

Back in the U.S. of A.

Dover AFB
Dover, Delaware 19902

"Granddad! Grandad!" Karl Bontrager entered the terminal to see his grand-daughter waving frantically.

"Kim!" He threw his arms around her and gave her a big hug.

"How was your flight?" she asked.

"Well it wasn't PanAm but it wasn't bad as the Air Force goes," he kidded.

"I'd like you to meet a friend of mine from Vrodkutsk," Karl turned around. "This is Doktor Petrova Marchenko of the Vrodkutsk Nuclear Research Center."

"Welcome to Delaware, Doktor Marchenko," Kim had a good feeling about Marchenko.

"Your grandfather has told me much about you, Kim. A university student I understand."

"Yes Doktor...at U of D," acknowledged Kim.

"Your grandfather is truly a visionary and I look forward to implementing his ideas with the help of Professor Felty and his colleagues."

At that moment Professor Felty and Eric Emerson carried their bags into the terminal.

"Eric!" Kim gave her boyfriend a hug followed by a kiss, "How was your trip?"

"Fantastic! You wouldn't believe the laboratory that Doktor Petrova has in Vrodkutsk and I think the project is off to a good start."

"Ditto," Professor Felty nodded as he put his suit case on the floor, "I think that we've hit the ground running. There's still a lot of work to do though, but it looks very promising."

Woodburn, the Governor's Mansion
Dover, Delaware 19903

"Well this is it," boasted Governor Oliver, "everything we've worked for during the past several months and it's finally become a reality."

Gil Hickman removed two cigars from his coat pocket. He lit one and handed it to the newly elected official. The two men stood in the governor's office puffing away for minutes while they savored the moment.

"What about Bontrager?" the thought popped into Oliver's head.

"What about him?" asked Hickman, nonchalantly.

"Well, we're going to start receiving pressure from the speaker to cut his program. That was one of the stipulations in the agreement, remember?"

"You're in the governor's mansion now, you're the boss."

"Well yes, but what do we tell them?" Oliver was concerned.

"It's too chancy," Hickman pointed out. "To start any trouble with Bontrager now would be political suicide for us and the Congress."

"Maybe you're right," Oliver reflected, snuffing out his cigar in an ashtray.

"We were lucky not to get fingered in the cover-up. We shouldn't press our luck while we're ahead," insisted Hickman.

There will be time to take care of that," Oliver shook his head. "Before we decide what to do about Bontrager, I have to break the news to Alan, send him in."

Worldwide Oil Corporation
Houston, Texas 77002

"Have you read this press release about the Bontrager Bill, Mr. Hollister?"

CEO Dennis Hollister looked up from his desk.

"You mean that bill involving Delaware?"

"Yes that's the one," said James Clark. "In the hopes of producing a revolutionary hydrogen power plant for automobiles; they're integrating Soviet and American technologies through a company called SuperPower Automotive and from the sound of it, an engine that could prove to be very bad for our business down the road."

"Someone's always trying to come up with an alternative power automobile, look at the big three. They've sunk millions into different systems; but their efforts, for the most part, have resulted in little more than a show for the EPA. They haven't been able to produce a practical power plant and I don't think that we should be too concerned about this new challenge to the combustion engine."

"Yes sir, but I thought that I should bring this to your attention since the scientific community seems to be awfully high on the idea."

"I'll tell you what," Hollister had a smug look on his face. "Keep me informed in case they come up with something, but be discreet. We've got enough bad exposure from that tanker mishap off of Nova Scotia. We don't need anymore bad press, got it?"

"Yes sir, Mr. Hollister," Clark responded like an obedient lap animal, "I'll keep you informed."

The Blue Coat Inn
-Overlooking Silver Lake-
Dover, Delaware 19901

Karl's choice of the colonial restaurant, with its exposed beams and scenic overlook of ice-covered Silver Lake, was an endearing coup with the beautiful Petrova Marchenko. The warmth of the stone fireplace and the snowfall outside just made it that more surreal.

"The crab imperial is delicious Karl," Petrova was not only pleased, but she was stunning in the glow of the fire, as well.

In the brief time that they had known each other, Petrova's intellect and warm personality had won Karl over; but this was the first time that Karl had seen her away from the lab and her lab coat. Petrova's alluring evening attire had simply made it impossible for Karl to concentrate on his stuffed pork chops. While Karl was no longer a twenty-year-old airman in the Air Force, he was still a man, a man who had become seduced by Petrova and her charms.

"Karl...Karl..." Petrova caught his ogling red-handed, but seemed amused by her dinner partner's poorly concealed glances.

"Oh...what?" a blushing Karl finally stammered back to the conversation with an awkward smile.

"Oh, this dinner is just a little Delaware hospitality," feeling much like an immature schoolboy, he sat appreciating this gem of science who would be greatly responsible for bringing his ideas to reality. "I thought that you might like to relax a bit before continuing your work at the university," her beauty, manner and presence made Karl's heart beat a bit faster.

He was unaware that he, his ideas, his sense of adventure, and Bontrager optimism, had the same effect on Petrova. "Well I appreciate it," she blushed, her face illuminated by the fire. "From what I've seen, the people here are most generous and I'm sure that my colleagues will find it so; when they arrive next week. Now Karl, I would like you to tell me about yourself."

Karl cleared his throat, "I was born and raised in Georgetown, Delaware. It's a small town about 30 miles south of here."

Petrova noted Karl's grin as he briefly revisited the path that had been his life.

"Then, at eighteen," Karl continued, "I enlisted in the air force and became a flight engineer on cargo planes. As a result, I've traveled throughout the world hitting a mixture of your major tourist attractions and international hotspots. Eventually, I was stationed back in Delaware, at Dover Air Force Base, where I finally retired."

"How about you, where are you from?" he asked tapping his pipe on an ashtray.

"Kazan, it is a city on the Volga River. My father was a tug boat captain there."

"Well, how did you become a scientist?" Karl asked.

"The Soviet government administered many tests to me and my classmates as a child. One time it was a test of physical endurance, such as running or other physical challenges. Other times it was a test of creativity, such as music, or art. Sometimes, a classmate would be removed from my school then sent to another; such as those for gymnastics, or music."

Petrova sipped her wine, "I was at the age of eight when I was given a test in mathematics. As a result, my childhood was spent attending the Izhevsk Science Academy, where the government had groomed me for a career in the defense industry. I took subjects ranging from aerodynamics to English at the academy.

Later, at my first assignment at the Antonov aircraft works in the Ukraine, I met my husband who was a test pilot. He died during a test flight of the Mig-15." Karl noticed tears forming at the corner of Petrova's blue eyes and touched her hand reassuringly.

"I'm sorry to hear that," Karl consoled, "I lost my wife in 1986 after a long illness."

Later that evening at Karl's Woodcrest home, he and Petrova discussed many of the aspects of the joint venture between their countries.

Alan Bean
Dover, Delaware 19901

If it hadn't been for Gil Hickman tipping him off, Alan Bean would have unloaded on the newly elected governor. While angered and in turmoil over losing his promised cabinet position, Alan had time to compose himself before getting the word from Governor Oliver. He had played it off as disappointing, telling Oliver that he was a team player for the new administration.

In reality, for over a year Alan Bean had worked vigorously for something that he greatly desired and he hadn't had the last word, yet. His efforts, time and desire outweighed any real loyalty that he once had to Oliver, and he was in such a state of mind that he wanted to make that point painfully clear to the new administration.

Worldwide Oil Corporation
Houston, Texas 77002

"The bottom line is that our stockholders are scared. Have you seen today's paper?" Frank Womack stabbed at the paper with his index finger, "down more than half a point for the third straight day and you can't blame them. All that they know is that Bontrager's group has something in the works, and that it could turn this company on its ear when it comes to profits."

"They're overreacting," countered Dennis Hollister from his seat at the head of the mahogany table, "so far there is nothing to substantiate that Bontrager's people have made any progress. From what I understand they've merely started work on the project and still have a long way to go."

"Whether or not they've made progress is of little consequence," interrupted Holly Johnson, "It's what the public perceives that is at the heart of the problem. What they do know is that articles in magazines such as *Popular Science* and *Mechanics Illustrated* have talked of Bontrager's group using a marriage of proven American and Soviet technologies. A marriage made in heaven so to speak. A marriage between two former foes that have come to an understanding post Cold War."

"That's right," agreed another board member, "the public loves these types of stories about the superpowers. Once at odds with each other, now forging a better tomorrow for the world."

"I think that we've all overlooked something," James Clark stood up from his leather backed chair. "What if this isn't just public perception? What if this new engine works and works well? I've obtained information that although it's only in the early stages of development, such an engine may be feasible. Then what? What will we do after the fact, when this thing becomes reality? If you think our stock has started to take a nose dive now, just wait for the ride ahead." Clark looked at each of the frowning board members, "To do nothing now is to give into defeat."

"And what do you propose that we do?" asked one of the board members sarcastically, "kill Bontrager?"

"Of course not, answered Clark with a stern look, "we merely kill his funding. Remember it was a House Bill that gave him the tools to enact his ideas. No bucks, no Buck Rogers I believe that's what they said in the film *The Right Stuff*. Well Mr. Bontrager is about to become Buck Rogers without a rocket ship."

"And how do you propose to do that?" asked Holly Johnson.

"Listen, I understand the situation," Hollister stood up from the table buttoning his suit jacket, "but James and I have a teleconference scheduled with our Qatar operation right now. We'll pick this conversation up at the next meeting."

The CEO and James Clark left the boardroom for Hollister's office down the hall.

"I want you to start having our lobbyists put a full court press on the Congress," Hollister was telling Clark the things that he had wanted to hear. "Concentrate on the ones that we've made campaign contributions to. I want you to get them back in line. You know, use the old stick and carrot routine; threaten to pull the contributions if they don't start poking holes in this Bontrager thing. On the other hand, promise them the usual perks and contributions if they terminate the funding. Be sure that you're firm, I don't care if it flys in the face of any existing agreement that they have with Bontrager, I just want those funds terminated."

Island of Badasi
Southwest Africa

"I want to know why N-1 is behind schedule." Jonathan Doe shouted at Chief Engineer Handel Koernig.

"The refueling sir," answered the German in his own defense. "It's taken us longer than expected to finish fueling the reactor and it will take months for us to process the plutonium for the device."

"That's not good enough," Jonathan Doe grew angrier. "I told you to cut corners on the testing, prior to fueling, so you could meet my deadline; but you didn't listen to my instructions."

"But to do otherwise would jeopardize the safety of the project," the chief engineer had to select his words carefully for Doe's reputation was notorious for his ruthlessness. "We needed those tests to ensure the safe operation of the reactor."

"That's it! I don't want to hear anymore, you're off the project. Pack your bags; I want you off of the island today. Schmidt will take over for you."

Woodburn, the Governor's Mansion
Dover, Delaware 19903

"We've got problems!" Gil Hickman rushed into Governor Oliver's office slamming the door behind him.

A startled Oliver turned from a window to see his aide, "What kind of problems?"

"Blackmail," groaned Hickman, "someone knows about your skimming the lottery commission, the strings that you pulled to get your cousin's construction company a contract on the road projects, and about the Bontrager fiasco."

"How?" a shocked Oliver turned pale.

"I don't know how and I don't know who. All I do know is that I received an anonymous phone call just a minute ago and the person said to have the Bontrager funds cutoff or they would disclose everything.

The White House
Washington, D.C. 20500

"Good morning, Mr. President." Security Advisor Burt Jennings entered the Oval Office just as the president was hanging up the phone, "What do you have for me this morning, Burt?"

"I'm afraid that our worst fears are becoming a reality, Mr. President. The body of Handel Koernig, a renowned German scientist, has been recovered from the wreckage of a plane crash on the continent of Africa." Jennings removed some photographs of the crash scene from his briefcase and placed them on the president's desk. "The CIA is still trying to determine if foul play was involved but they're certain that one of the crash victims was Koernig."

"Well this gives us yet another piece of the puzzle," the president leaned forward in his chair to get a better look at the photos. "Any estimates on when they could have a weapon?"

"Nothing concrete, from what we could tell from the recon satellites, the reactor has become operational in the last week. A best guess would be six months to a year to process the plutonium."

"Burt, if Jonathan Doe gets his hands on a weapon, the entire continent of Africa will be under his thumb."

The president removed his glasses, "Have Watkins cancel my flight to Anchorage. I want a meeting with the security counsel this afternoon and Burt have the speaker, minority and majority whips present. They should finally be in on this thing."

"Yes sir, Mr. President," Jennings placed the photos back into his briefcase.

College of Engineering, University of Delaware
Newark, Delaware 19716

"Welcome to the University of Delaware," Professor Felty and his colleagues exchanged handshakes with the Vrodkutskan delegation.

"And how are you doing Doktor Marchenko?" Direktor Gaslov had a big grin on his face. "Have you been behaving yourself in America?"

"She's been invaluable," interrupted Professor Felty. "With Doktor Marchenko's insight into the electron pump, we've been able to make up some preliminary drawings for the project."

"Very good!" Gaslov was pleased, "our people in Vrodkutsk are eager to get to work. They've already begun getting the materials together for the electron pump that will power your motor."

"Well, things seem to be coming along on schedule," Doktor Marchenko commented.

"What about the car, have you made any provisions for it yet?" Gaslov said excitedly.

"The university's materials lab is coming up with a graphite-composite to use for the body and frame," answered Professor Felty. "It should make it stronger and lighter than using metals."

"Excellent idea," Direktor Gaslov was impressed by the progress that had been made thus far, "it's best to eliminate any unnecessary weight to the vehicle."

"Korf wanted to put the electron pump and electric motor in his old Plymouth Duster," laughed Professor Felty, "but the engineering staff opted to build from the ground up."

Professor Felty led the group to a Computer Aided Drafting (CAD) terminal where Eric Emerson was seated, "Bring up some of the SuperCar drawings, Eric." Eric clicked the mouse and a colorful schematic appeared on the screen.

"Here you can see the electric motor in blue under the hood of the car, coupled to your electron pump in red," Eric began to explain, "from the figures that Doktor Marchenko had supplied us, we've reengineered and rearranged the electron pump into a 7" thick wafer that's housed in the car's frame under the passenger compartment. The hydrogen impregnated fuel sheets are located where a conventional gas tank would be located."

"I see," said Direktor Gaslov who was looking at the monitor, "very impressive. We need to get these drawings to Vrodkutsk so they can start fabricating the reconfigured electron pump.

"Now here's a rough drawing of the car," continued Eric, "of course, this is subject to considerable change depending on the problems that we may encounter, but as you can see, with its aerodynamic styling it is aesthetically appealing."

"It will be a most beautiful machine," agreed Gaslov, "a machine which maximizes the potential of our engineering."

"A machine that ought to retire a few gas guzzlers," quipped Eric.

The Vrodkutskan delegation was obviously pleased with Eric's CAD drawings and the comments of both Professor Felty and Direktor Gaslov.

"Well then," Professor Felty rubbed his hands together, "what do you say we have some lunch; then get to work building this thing?"

Woodburn, the Governor's Mansion
Dover, Delaware 19903

"I've got it," announced Gil Hickman. "Didn't that press release say that Super-Power Automotive was a corporation?"

"So, what's your point?" asked Governor Oliver glibly.

"Well nothing in the Bontrager Bill had set aside funds for the profit of any individuals, be they Vrodkutskan, or American." Hickman looked seriously into the governor's eyes, "We've got them. It would be a misappropriation of funds for congress to continue payments for the Bontrager Bill.

Congress can't fund an organization that bills itself as nonprofit when there are Vrodkutskan shareholders. I distinctly remember the press release saying that shareholding was an incentive for the Vrodkutskans to participate in SuperPower Automotive."

"Gil, I think you're onto something." Oliver sat up in his chair, "I not only think you've got something; I know you've got something. I want you to take care of it.

Plant the idea through the press or something, but whatever you do don't get our fingerprints on it. I don't want anything connecting us to this."

A quick knock and his aide hurried in.

"Yes Alan what is it?"

"You're scheduled for that meeting with the Board of Education, Governor."

"Oh yes," Oliver picked up some papers from his desk, "put this in the car for me, I'll be along in a minute."

"Yes, Governor," Alan took the papers and exited the room, closing the door behind him.

"Now back to our conversation," Oliver pointed to Hickman, "remember no fingerprints."

"No fingerprints," repeated Hickman assuredly.

CHAPTER 20

The Buck Stops Here

Student Center, University of Delaware
Newark, Delaware 19716

"With the evidence presented during this hearing, we have no other choice but to move to terminate any and all funding for the Bontrager Bill," Speaker of the House Futz led the proceedings. "All those in favor say Yeah!"

"Yeah!" was the overwhelming response.

"All of those opposed?" Futz asked.

"Neah!" responded a handful of congressman.

"The yeahs have it," Futz rapped the gavel from his rostrum, "the funds for the Bontrager Bill are hereby terminated."

Eric clicked the television off. "Well I guess that pretty much puts a nail in our coffin."

"I don't get it," Kim was pacing the floor, "how can they cut off the funds overnight like that?"

"It's simple," Korf shrugged, heaving a discouraged sigh, "Congress can do anything it wants to."

"Well this isn't going to stop us," said Eric boldly, "we'll just have to seek funding elsewhere."

"Like where?" Kim asked with a disheartened look.

"I don't know, but I'm going to find out," Eric spoke with determination.

"Well what do we do in the meantime?" asked Kim.

"We continue to work on the project as we have been," encouraged Eric, "even if we have to scrape by for awhile. There's too much at stake to stop now.

We've been making good progress and we need to show Congress and any-one else who may try to throw up a roadblock that we will not be stopped."

"Bingo," Professor Felty who had been looking for Eric had just walked into the student center, "I couldn't have said it better myself Eric." the professor stepped toward Eric who stood amidst a group of students.

"Eric is right, we will find a way to fund this work and in the meantime we need to stick together and learn to overcome the problems that we are faced with. This is exactly why all of you are attending the university. To gain knowl-edge and experience that will better help you cope with the real world. Well, in the real world there are sometimes setbacks such as our loss of funds for the project. This means that we will have to become wiser in using the resources that we have and to overcome this obstacle in another way. Look at this as a learning experience and together we will succeed."

Woodcrest Drive
Dover, Delaware 19903

"It's going to be rough," Professor Felty took a sip of coffee as he sat at Karl's kitchen table. "We need funds to start building the new superconductive motor for the car, not to mention money for the car itself."

"What about a loan from the bank," asked Anne, "wouldn't they be inter-ested in funding such a project?"

"Probably not," Dan was pessimistic, "it's a high risk venture in their eyes."

"He's right," added the professor. "Despite our enthusiasm for the project and belief that it will be successful, the bank will probably feel otherwise."

"Hey!" interrupted Kim. "The reason funds were cutoff by congress in the first place was because we were first: trying to walk a fine line between a non-profit federally funded test project, and secondly: we were trying to give Vrod-kutsk an idea of what capitalism is. Well, why don't we stop walking that fine line and forget about being a non-profit test project? Why don't we just go ahead and incorporate SuperPower Automotive right here in Delaware? It has some of the easiest requirements in the nation for incorporating and we could sell stock in the venture to raise funds."

Although Delaware was the second smallest state in the nation, it carried a big stick in America's business sector. Delaware's low incorporation costs, accommodating corporate tax laws, liberal corporate officer and residency requirements, and separate court system solely dedicated to corporate law made it extremely attractive to businesses across the nation. In addition, it was a well known fact among Delawareans that over half of the Fortune 500 companies were incorporated in Delaware.

Kim's suggestion to incorporate in Delaware was a logical step for any new enterprise. In an effort to punish SuperPower Automotive, congress had simply cut out the middle bureaucracy or middle man to practicality and in the process done Bontrager's venture a favor.

Amused that he hadn't suggested such a logical remedy first, Karl responded enthusiastically. "That's not only a great idea; it's a viable solution, Kim." She's right, let's use our strengths and incorporate right here in Delaware."

"Won't you need a Chief Executive Officer? Dan asked.

"Well, Mr. Bontrager is the inspiration for the company, wouldn't he be the logical choice?" inquired Anne.

"Me, I don't have a business background," objected Karl with a stunned expression.

"We have all of the expertise that you'll need," insisted Professor Felty.

Karl neither sought, nor wanted the responsibility of such a position as CEO, "There is no way," he objected, "we need to get someone with a real business background to put into the driver's seat of SuperPower Automotive and I'm not it."

"Karl," Professor Felty looked at Karl as to convey that he had not lost his mind, now you're the reason why we're all here. *Bontrager* has become a brand name of sorts. If we are going to incorporate and expect to sell stock in this new corporation, we need the draw of your name, it's as simple as that."

Professor Felty could see that it would take some more convincing to get Karl on board as the CEO, but he felt that it was the only choice if they were going to generate enough excitement and revenue to fund such a venture.

Wilmington Stock Brokerage House
Wilmington, Delaware 19899

"Yes, this is the Wilmington Stock Brokerage House," Bonnie Brubacher answered the phone for the umpteenth time. "Yes we now carry SuperPower Automotive stocks…. Ten thousand shares, yes sir, feel free to stop in and we'll be happy to accommodate you."

Bonnie hung up the phone, "I'm telling you, Marie, I've never seen such short term demand for a new company."

"I know," answered Marie, "ever since they incorporated, people can't seem to get enough of that SuperPower stock. It's as if everyone in Delaware has opened their wallets to show support for Karl Bontrager and his group. People that I've never heard of before are calling, anyone from the little guy to the seasoned investor."

"That's it," said Bonnie as she reached for the phone to answer yet another call. "They're showing their pride in Delaware and getting a piece of the action at the same time. Hello, yes, this is the Wilmington Stock Brokerage House. Yes, I can purchase SuperPower Automotive stock…fifteen hundred shares…."

University of Delaware
Newark, Delaware 19716

"I just received a call from our new CEO, Eric," Professor Felty stepped to Eric's computer terminal.

"Oh," Eric's head turned on a swivel, "what did Mr. Bontrager have to say?"

"Things are looking up; I don't think that we'll be having any funding problems anymore."

"Fantastic!" he shouted, "then we can have the lab get started on the composites for the car?"

"It looks that way," smiled the professor. "How are the drawings coming?"

"Fine, Doktor Marchenko's been a big help."

"Good, keep up the good work," Professor Felty looked over the drawing that Eric had on the screen. "Hey, now that's innovative," The professor pointed to Eric's display.

"That was Karl's idea while Doktor Marchenko did the engineering. She gave me a freehand drawing of it; she said that it would capture some of the energy from the suspension and braking systems."

"Talk about brainstorming that's a great idea. By the way where is she?"

"She went to Middletown to meet Mr. Bontrager for lunch. I think she said it was a business luncheon," laughed Eric, "but I think that they've got a thing going."

"They have been seeing a lot of each other lately," smiled Professor Felty.

Vrodkutsk Nuclear Research Center
Commonwealth of Independent States

"How is the electron pump coming along, Viktor?" Direktor Gaslov startled the man who was leaning over the device.

"Oh, Direktor Gaslov," Engineer Belenko stood up to address his boss, "she's coming along well, just making some adjustments."

"Do you think it will be ready for Mr. Bontrager's arrival?"

"Yes sir, she's testing just fine with an optimal power output." Belenko took great pride in his work.

"Very good Viktor, after so many months of work it will be nice to see our dream finally realized." Gaslov patted the device as if it were a living and breathing thing.

"Yes, Direktor, the men are anxious to see the project come together, they've worked so hard."

"You know Viktor, I will retire soon and I plan to name you as my successor," Gaslov extended his hand and Viktor quickly reciprocated.

"Thank you, Direktor," Viktor was obviously pleased with the thought of a promotion, but at the same time saddened by the thought of his old friend's face being absent from the halls of the research center. "When that day comes we will miss you sir and I greatly appreciate your leadership in running this center."

"You've earned it, my friend," Direktor Gaslov turned to look throughout the laboratory. "This has been my home Viktor and I will miss being here and being with the people whom I've looked upon as family."

DC-3
Vrodkutskan Airspace

Despite federal funds being cutoff for Bontrager's group, Colonel Henry Macintyre had taken leave from the U.S. Air Force to guide Karl and his friends through former Soviet Union airspace to Vrodkutsk. There they would pick up the electron pump and Vrodkutskan engineers who would install it inside of the SuperCar back in Delaware.

Jeb Wheeler was at the controls of the DC-3 and Karl flew as copilot on the mission. Macintyre flew as the navigator; his experience in flying a multitude of C-5 Galaxy missions into Vrodkutsk was invaluable to the success of the mission. He not only knew the route, but the procedures for flying through the once hostile airspace, which Jeb and Karl were unfamiliar with.

They had flown from Jeb's airfield, up the east coast of the United States and Canada, then across stretches of the Atlantic, Greenland, Iceland, Norway, Sweden, and Finland before reaching the airspace of the Commonwealth of Independent States. The DC-3 lumbered along the air route at a cruise speed of 125 knots and an altitude of 12,000 feet. Flying this great distance in a World

War II vintage aircraft, the men grew to appreciate the heroics of aviators such as Lindbergh and Earhart.

"There's the airfield," Colonel Macintyre pointed to the horizon as he looked over Jeb's shoulder. "At least you have good spring weather. The last time I came in here with a Galaxy it was in the middle of a snow storm."

Jeb backed off on the throttle as he started his approach for landing.

Vrodkutsk International Airport
Commonwealth of Independent States

Karl Bontrager was the first of the three man crew to exit the DC-3 and the first to see Direktor Gaslov standing ready to greet him on the taxiway.

"Once again welcome Mr. Bontrager, we've been looking forward to your arrival."

Karl took a moment to stretch his weary legs, "It's nice to see you Direktor. Talk about a long trip and it's only half over."

"We have everything prepared for you. The electron pump is crated inside of the hangar and the engineers and I are looking forward to our flight to Delaware."

"Very good, that's what I like to hear." Karl waved for his friends to come over, "I believe you know Colonel Macintyre."

"Oh yes, the medivac flight, how can I forget," Gaslov shook MacIntyre's hand. "Once again, I'm deeply indebted to you Colonel."

"Direktor Gaslov," Macintyre patted the Direktor on the shoulder, "I wouldn't have missed this trip for the world."

"And this is our pilot," Jeb Wheeler exchanged hand shakes with Gaslov.

"The famous Red Tails," explained Gaslov excitedly. "Karl has told me very much about your aviation exploits of the Second World War, they are very impressive, Mr. Wheeler."

"Jeb, everyone calls me Jeb," smiled Wheeler.

"Very well, Jeb," complied Gaslov, "you can call me Dimitri."

"Sure thing Dimitri."

"Well, right this way gentlemen," Direktor Gaslov led the three men to the hangar. "Here it is," Gaslov pointed his cane toward a wooden crate at the doorway of the hangar. "With your permission Jeb, I'll have my men load it aboard your plane."

"No problem," said Jeb eyeing the four foot cube. "DC-3's carried cargo bigger than that over *the hump* during the Korean War. I'll get things ready inside," Jeb started to walk back toward the airplane.

"After we get the cargo loaded, I'll show you to your accommodations for this evening. I'm sure you all must be tired and hungry from such a long journey."

"That sounds like a good idea," said Macintyre.

"Likewise," agreed Karl, "and I know that Jeb could use a good rest before our flight back tomorrow morning."

Worldwide Oil Corporation
Houston, Texas 77002

"We'll have to resort to another method of dealing with Bontrager," Dennis Hollister had just read the business section of the Wall Street Journal. "As our stocks plummet, SuperPower Automotive's soar."

"The only way to turn the tables is to show that the SuperCar isn't what Bontrager's group makes it out to be." James Clark leaned on Hollister's desk, "I understand that they plan to test the car sometime this summer."

"What are you proposing, sabotage?" Hollister pretended shock.

"It's the only arrow left in our quiver." Clark looked Hollister straight in the eye, "We're tasked with ensuring the future of this company. Are we going to allow Bontrager to destroy it with his car or are we going to consider the interests of our stockholders?"

"I don't know James," Hollister scratched his head. "We've already gotten plenty of bad press from that tanker incident, we can't afford to have more."

"We can't afford not to," persisted Clark, "you've read the stock reports. Day by day, the losses are eating at this company's profits. First the oil spill, now this. We don't have the luxury of sitting on the fence. We need to take action now before the board removes you as head of this company."

"Blackmailing Oliver didn't work; what makes you think that this will be successful?" Hollister looked interested.

"It's all in the way that the public perceives it," answered Clark. "If they feel that the car is a dud from the outset, then it may break their perception of the feasibility of the car's technology. Anyhow, everything is perception, just look at television commercials. What's popular today is out tomorrow. And people tend to be very unforgiving when their money is at stake and under the right circumstances people will become disillusioned with the SuperCar."

"Do you think that you can get to the car?" Hollister inquired.

"Myself no, but I can find people who can," Clark came off as extremely cocky. "It just takes the right people, the kind of people who like money."

CHAPTER 21

Of Two Technologies

Summit Aviation
Middletown, Delaware 19709

"There they are!" shouted Korf spotting the DC-3 in the distance.

It was a bright spring day and the group of onlookers that stood next to the terminal had to shield their eyes from the sun as they watched the plane approach the airfield. As the tail dragger touched down, the growl of the *Pratt & Whitney* engines drowned out most conversation on the ground. The plane gradually slowed to a stop at the end of the strip where Jeb Wheeler and Karl could be seen at the controls. They taxied the airplane to a spot in front of the terminal.

The propellors were still slowing to a stop when the side door flung open and a smiling Colonel MacIntyre gave a thumbs-up. This was met with a unanimous cheer from the small crowd of students, faculty and well wishers.

"Anyone call Federal Express?" asked MacIntyre as he started down the ladder from the plane.

"Yes, commented Korf, "what about our overnight delivery? You guys have been gone for five days."

The crowd broke into laughter.

"We had to pick up some Chinese takeout in Hong Kong," joked MacIntyre. The colonel helped Direktor Gaslov and his associates as they moved down the ladder. Jeb and Karl were still doing their post flight checklist.

The White House
Washington, D.C. 20500

"I recommend an air strike, Mr. President," The Chairman of the Joint Chiefs of Staff, Admiral Glenn Walters got up from his chair and stepped to a map of Africa.

"One carrier should do it, here." The admiral pointed west of the island of Badasi. "We can assemble a strike force of A-6 Bombers and F-18 Hornets. Put a couple of Hawkeye's up to watch our back door and a patrol of F-14 Tomcats to intercept any Mig's that they may send our way."

From their reaction, most of the other men seated at the table seemed to be in favor of such an action.

"Sounds like a lot to get airborne Admiral," the president leaned back in his chair.

"Just taking precautions, Mr. President," the Admiral turned his back to the map. "We'll need to be ready if they attempt to launch a strike of their own."

"What if one of our pilots gets shot down over their airspace, is there any way to get him out?"

"It would be tough, Mr. President, but with a mission like this there will be risks."

"What about a SEAL team?" the president suggested as he checked the wall clock. "Do you think that they could get in and out without being detected? You know, make it look like a nuclear accident."

"Unless they placed the charges at key points around the containment building itself, the damage may indicate otherwise, Mr. President."

"Gentlemen, thank you for your time," the president stood up from his seat, "I have a meeting with the Speaker of the House now and I'll get back to you on this." All rose to their feet as the president made his way to the door.

College of Engineering, University of Delaware
Newark, Delaware 19716

"It's decided then," Professor Felty stood at a blackboard with chalk in hand, "Viktor Belenko will head the group to prepare the electron pump for installation. Doktor Marchenko and I will oversee the preparation of the electron pump and superconductive motor. Direktor Gaslov, Korf and Eric will supervise the construction of the car chassis, body and instrumentation, any questions?"

"When do we get started?" asked one of the students.

"We've got two hours until lunch," Professor Felty looked at his watch, "why don't we take that time to meet all of the members of our perspective groups. Then after lunch we'll get to work."

During the weeks that followed, student and professor, mechanic, engineer and layman, worked together to make the SuperCar a reality. Testing and adaptation took the electron pump, the superconductive motor, the graphite composite body and other components from being separate entities to becoming a conglomeration of technologies housed inside of one body, the aerodynamic body of the SuperCar.

The idea of using Delaware as a test bed for new ideas and cooperation, so eloquently spoken of by Karl Bontrager, those many months before at the Old Statehouse, had given birth to a revolutionary moment in history; a moment when post cold war superpowers set aside their differences and worked side-by-side for the first time on a project for their mutual benefit.

His vision had evolved to the point that these two great powers had hammered some of their *swords into plowshares* and had removed some of the animosity that each had possessed toward one another. Karl had been a catalyst for positive change and he was looked upon as a hero by the people.

Now it would soon be time to test the SuperCar, and despite its success or failure Karl's name was now destined to be synonymous with ideologue and visionary.

University of Delaware
Newark, Delaware 19716

Students, faculty, members of SuperPower Automotive Corporation, interested onlookers, reporters and invited guests stood in a half circle at the garage entrance. Doktor Marchenko stood beside Karl Bontrager as they waited for the garage door to open and the SuperCar to be rolled out on public display.

Slowly the garage door raised and applause began. The draped automobile was pushed out onto the asphalt by half a dozen men and the crowd grew more excited as they contemplated what they were about to see. The men brought the car to a stop halfway down the driveway.

Professor Felty stepped to the front of the car, "Before the unveiling, I would like to say a few words. During my career as a Professor of Engineering, I have never before worked on such a revolutionary project such as this. I have had the pleasure of meeting new people and learning of new technologies and I have enjoyed every minute of it. I'd like to give a special thanks to the Vrodkutskan delegation headed by Direktor Gaslov and Doktor Marchenko, who worked so hard on this project and brought vital knowledge and experience to it, not to mention the electron pump."

Gaslov nodded his head as if saying thanks and Petrova smiled broadly as the crowd applauded, "I would also like to thank the many students who took time from their studies to bring this project along with their endless hours of research and work." Once again the applause started.

"There are other people such as Mr. Jeb Wheeler and Colonel Macintyre who flew to Vrodkutsk to bring back the electron pump and numerous technical personnel," Professor Felty paused for more applause.

"But there is one man, and only one man, who had a vision. A man who had a vision that caught fire and sparked ideas, a man whom we've all come to look up to for inspiration, that man is Karl Bontrager, without his vision, we wouldn't be standing here right now."

Karl turned a bright shade of red as applause and cheers broke out in honor of him. "Karl Bontrager," began Professor Felty. "I'd be honored if you would step forward and christen this revolution of technology."

"Speech! Speech!" shouted several onloolers.

Karl slowly stepped forward and took a bottle from Professor Felty, noting the label. "How appropriate, vodka," the crowd laughed then Karl raised the bottle. "Before I christen this automobile, I will say a few words." The crowd grew silent.

"Many months ago my life consisted of little if any direction; but since that time a lot has happened and I have met several people who I now call friend, most of whom Professor Felty has mentioned but a couple that haven't as yet been recognized, "Kate Webster and Brock Mattingly." Karl looked at the two. "When I was *on the lamb*, Kate and Brock were my companions and the best friends a man could ask for. They know what the three of us went through and we stuck together through it all. I would like to ask them to come up here at this time and help me do the honors."

Kate and Brock stepped to the front of the crowd and Karl asked them to place their hands around the bottle along with his. He then hesitated for a moment, "Oh yes, there's one more person whom I'd like to participate, my new fiancée, Doktor Petrova Marchenko."

"Fiancée!" shouted Kimberly Bontrager. "Why didn't you tell me?" she ran up to her grandfather and gave him a kiss.

"I just did," laughed Karl as a smiling Petrova joined him in the midst of applause.

"Okay on the count of three," said Karl. "One! Two! Three!" The vodka bottle smashed across the left front wheel rim of the automobile while Professor Felty removed the cover that draped the car, "I christen thee, SuperCar."

The car was a piece of aerodynamic beauty, unlike most simpler and boxy attempts at electric cars. It was painted in blue and gold. It was a four passenger fastback with headlights that were flush with its front end. The dashboard contained all of the instrumentation necessary for monitoring the high tech components of the car.

"It's magnificent," exclaimed a reporter as he took some pictures. His observation was accompanied by adjectives such as, "Incredible, sleek, and bodacious."

"Where do you plan to test it?" asked an onlooker?

"We've got the perfect locale for that," answered Bontrager, without divulging anything.

University of Delaware
Newark, Delaware 19716

It was 2:00 AM and the two men went about their business as quietly as possible. One picked the lock of a side door while the other kept lookout. The first man slowly opened the door and motioned for the other to follow him inside the darkened garage. The second man closed the door gently behind him. At the center of the floor sat the SuperCar, draped with a cover.

"Remember," the first man spoke in hushed tones to the second, "we have to make it appear as an accident, so don't disturb anything." The second man nodded.

"Okay then, bring that handjack over here and when we're finished I want you to put it back right where you found it."

He placed the jack underneath the rear of the car and began pumping the handle.

"Who's there," came a loud voice from the shadows.

The two men were startled and began to run for the door. The first opened it and raced out of the garage; but the second man was tackled to the floor in mid flight; after which a short struggle ensued. Korf had knocked the smallish man unconscious with two blows of his fist.

A half hour later the Newark and campus police were at the crime scene.

"I came down late last night to do some work and must have fallen asleep in the back room," Korf told the authorities. "There were two men, one ran out the door and I couldn't stop him. This other guy," Korf pointed to the man who was now handcuffed, "was with him and they appeared to be getting ready to do something to the car. You know, we're supposed to test the car tomorrow."

One of the campus security guards held the man in place, while a city policeman read the man his rights.

"We'll take him to headquarters for questioning," a detective told Korf, "we'll get to the bottom of this."

The White House
Washington, D.C. 20500

"It's decided then," the president folded his hands on the table as he addressed his Security Counsel, "the event will take place tomorrow night."

"Perhaps we should reconsider, Mr. President," proposed one of the members voicing his concern.

"What's there to consider," responded the president. "According to our satellite surveillance they've already conducted an underground test. Should we wait until they take over the continent of Africa?"

Dover Downs
The Monster Mile
Dover, Delaware 19901

It was race day at Dover Downs and 80,000 NASCAR fans had packed into the grandstands and infield of the one mile oval known as *the Monster Mile*. The SuperCar was being prepared by Professor Felty, Direktor Gaslov and their students and engineers. As if two proud parents, Karl Bontrager and Doktor Marchenko stood off to the side while they watched the preparation.

"Well, whatever those two guys were up to they didn't get very far. The car checks out AOK," announced Korf.

"Great," Professor Felty slapped Korf on the back, "this will be a good gauge of how well our hard work has paid off."

"Where's Eric?" asked the professor.

"Here he comes," Kim pointed at the student walking toward her in racing overhauls. He carried a blue and gold helmet under his left arm.

Then the public address system suddenly came to life, "Race fans; prepare to witness automotive history today! As a special pre-race demonstration and test, the new revolutionary SuperCar will circle *the Monster Mile* for 25 laps."

"Remember not to overdo it Eric," Professor Felty told him, "this isn't a race car and it's not a race or a time trial, it's just a demonstration and test of the technology. Drive it at a comfortable speed and keep your eyes on the gauges. If you have any problems bring her back in immediately."

"I'll do my best," promised Eric as he entered the car and strapped himself into the seat.

"That's all we can ask," interjected Direktor Gaslov.

"Good luck Eric," sticking her head through the driver's side window, Kim gave Eric a kiss.

Unlike the 800-horsepower roar of the internal combustion engines found on the NASCAR racing circuit, the superconductive electric motor was virtually silent after Eric turned the ignition key. He placed the SuperCar in drive and pulled away from pit row to the cheering of race fans. Then staying on the steeply banked oval, he accelerated into turn one. The car disappeared from the sight of those standing in the infield, but by the exit of the second turn the SuperCar had moved high enough on the track that its blue and gold silhouette could be seen moving along the backstretch at about forty miles per hour.

It was considerably different driving on the high banked oval as opposed to the public roads that Eric was used to. If it hadn't been for the many practice laps that he had taken in a conventional race car, Eric wouldn't have believed that the car could operate at such a steep incline, but it did.

He had to feel his way around the turns and judge his speed accordingly. He checked the gauges and they all ran within specifications. The car was now moving along at sixty miles per hour as it came down the front straight away. Eric was too busy keeping the car under control to see the cheering fans in the grandstands or his colleagues standing along the infield.

For several laps Eric felt his way around the course, gradually gaining confidence in himself and the car. Unlike the sprint car racing he had done as a youngster at the dirt tracks of Blackbird and Harrington Raceways, he was alone on the track with all eyes watching him. Repeatedly, he steered the SuperCar in and out of each turn. Using caution, he pushed the speed higher and higher until deciding to limit the car's speed to seventy miles per hour. He knew that it had the power to go faster, but he would not chance destroying the car by trying to match the one hundred forty mile per hour speeds that were frequently registered by the professional drivers at the racetrack.

Then, he slowed the car to sixty miles per hour as he felt the fatigue of centrifugal force pulling at his arms, legs and head. As he approached the straightaway on his twenty-fifth lap, a man lowered a checkered flag in mock victory over the nose of the SuperCar and before a cheering crowd Eric had success-fully completed his test run.

Although it was only the first test of many that it would undergo, the Super-Car had shown real promise as a practical vehicle. The public stood on their feet amazed at the car of the near future. Eric stopped the car behind the infield wall.

"It was beautiful, Eric," screamed Kim.

"You proved that the SuperCar is viable," shouted Professor Felty.

"How did it handle?" asked Direktor Gaslov, trying to moderate his enthu-siasm.

Eric removed his helmet and shouted through the window, "She handled beautifully." Stepping out of the car Eric couldn't restrain himself, "She had plenty of power to go faster but I didn't want to push it."

"SuperPower Automotive is on its way," Karl stated emphatically.

"Yes, we're revolutionizing the automotive industry," agreed Doktor March-enko.

City of Dover Police Station
Dover, Delaware 19904

Ron Mathews stood on the steps of the City of Dover Police Station filing a report.

"This is Ron Mathews," the reporter started as he looked into the camera.

"Just minutes ago, Alan Bean, a press aide of Governor Oliver, had sub-jected himself to questioning by authorities in connection with a blackmail and cover-up conducted by Governor Oliver's office and Worldwide Oil Cor-poration. Bean has apparently stated that the governor, while still a congress-man, used his influence to steer the paths of highway construction projects across properties that he owned, in addition to an attempted smearing of Karl Bontrager. These and other accounts of wrongdoing by the governor led to Worldwide Oil Corporation and their attempted blackmail of the governor. The Texas based oil company pressured the governor to cut funding for the Bontrager Bill out of concern that the new SuperCar would be a threat to future oil revenues.

These claims seem to be supported by the questioning of a man who was apprehended just two days ago in a sabotage attempt on the SuperCar at the University of Delaware. It appears that the Federal Government will have to convene a grand jury since the claims seem to have been substantiated.

Governor Oliver and his press aide Gil Hickman have refused comment, but the investigation continues."

CHAPTER 22

To Endure the Endeavor

Southeastern Atlantic Ocean

"*Con...Radio* presently receiving flash traffic on the floating wire antenna," the announcement over the attack submarine's control room speaker caught the immediate attention of the entire watch station.

The duty quartermaster, fire control technician, planesmen, diving officer, and NavET looked at each other in intense curiosity, but stayed fast at their posts as they anxiously watched the *Officer of the Deck* lift the microphone for the 27MC communications circuit, "*Radio...Con* aye. *Radio*, bring that flash traffic to the *Control Room* as soon as it's onboard."

"*Con...Radio* aye," came the reply over the speaker.

"Messenger, have the captain lay to the control room immediately," the officer of the deck waited only a few moments before the after control room door opened and the radioman rushed in with the message board. A minute later Commander Richard Truxton arrived in the control room taking the message board from the young submariner. After reading the message, Commander Truxton scribbled his initials and time on the message. *Flash* traffic was the exception to the rule and in accordance with fleet operatives it was necessary for the commanding officer to see such communications immediately upon reception.

Commander Truxton noted the boat's heading, coarse, and speed on the ship's control panel, "Captain has the *Con!*" Truxton barked out.

"Captain has the *Con*," Repeated the *diving officer*.

"Ahead one third," was Truxton's first order, "make your depth one-five-zero feet."

The diving officer repeated the command; then instructed the two planesmen to bring the U.S.S. Endeavor to the desired depth and speed. "Five degree up bubble," the *diving officer* ordered the inboard planesman.

As the Endeavor began to nose upward, Truxton reached for the ship's communication's circuit, "Man battle stations," he ordered firmly.

Within minutes the control room was transformed into a busy nerve center. Crewmen took their places at the bank of weapons control consoles that lined the starboard side of the room, while the tracking party took up its position at the navigation table located at the aft end of the room.

Throughout the submarine, shipboard communications were being supplemented by crewmen who were donning sound powered telephone headsets. Reports flowed in from throughout the vessel, and the *Chief of the Watch* seated at the Ballast Control Panel kept track of each station as it reported in. "*Torpedo room* manned for battle stations, *sonar* manned for battle stations, *machinery room* manned for battle stations, *maneuvering* manned for battle stations."

After the last report came in, the *chief of the watch* addressed Commander Truxton, "Ship manned for battle stations, Captain."

"Very well, *Chief of the Watch*," Truxton responded.

Shortly thereafter; the submarine leveled off. "Depth one-five-zero feet, sir," the *diving officer* called out.

"Depth one-five-zero feet, aye," acknowledged Commander Truxton as he picked up the 27MC. "*Sonar…Con* report all contacts."

"*Con…Sonar*, aye." came the response over the speaker.

"*Con…Sonar*, presently hold three contacts: Sierra one bearing 130, sierra two bearing 215, and sierra three bearing 260, all classified as merchant ships."

"*Sonar…Con*, aye," confirmed Truxton, who was observing the tracks on the remote sonar display. After his study was complete, Truxton keyed the microphone once again, "*Torpedo Room…Con*, prepare for remote firing." At this command the torpedomen switched fire control from their station two deck levels below, to the one in the Control Room. As ordered in previous communications, the Tomahawks had already been loaded in tubes one-thru-four and the fire control technicians were feeding the main computer data about the submarines present location, speed and depth. This in turn was relayed to the guidance system of the four missiles through a series of umbilicals.

"Fire when ready," ordered Truxton.

Accompanied with the sound of high pressure air, one after another, the ejection pumps pushed each cruise missile from its torpedo tube. Then, as each broke the surface of the ocean its rocket motor fired sending it into a high speed low altitude flight path above the water to its target.

Within minutes of Commander Truxton's reading of the message, it was finished.

Vrodkutsk
Commonwealth of Independent States

Direktor Gaslov waved his cane at a stand of pine, spruce and birch that was in the distance, "The site stretches just beyond the tree line to the ravine that's off to your right."

Karl and Petrova Bontrager, and Direcktor Gaslov stood amidst a field of wild grass with a group of prospective investors that had traveled to Vrodkutsk from around the world. The group was visiting a proposed site for the new SuperPower Automotive plant. After the promising results from the testing of the SuperCar, the government of Vrodkutsk had decided to bank much of its future on the new automotive technology.

With the help of foreign investment Vrodkutsk would strive to become the first country in the world to introduce hydrogen powered vehicles in large numbers, a task that would even be a major financial, political and social challenge for an established Western democracy.

All involved realized that it would take many years, if not decades, to get the hydrogen infrastructure in place throughout Vrodkutsk to support such an endeavor. Processing plants would have to be built to produce the hydrogen gas, while conventional gas stations would have to be adapted to handle the hydrogen that would be used to fuel these revolutionary vehicles.

"During World War II Vrodkutsk was nothing more than an expendable buffer area between Nazi Germany and the Soviet Union," Gaslov turned to address the investors, "and upon this very site there was a sudden and violent tank battle."

Gaslov's mournful eyes and somber voice betrayed a soul that was etched with the experience of both personal and national tragedy, "For generations my family farmed this land in relative peace; then, after Hitler declared war on the Soviet Union we occasionally caught sight of German military aircraft, in the distance, flying sorties behind Soviet lines. It was different that morning though, because the peace was shattered by the high-pitched whine of Stukas diving on nearby Russian tanks. Startled in my second floor room, I leapt from my bed and raced to the window to see Soviet tanks advancing from the east toward German positions along the tree line. I heard my parents shouting in panic to alert my sister and brothers when I abruptly lost consciousness."

As Gaslov spoke of the battle, his impassioned demeanor transferred the reality of his hellish experience to the Bontragers and investors in ways that the most prolific books and films could not.

"I don't know how long it was before I awoke, but I was no longer on the second floor, rather, I was lying in a pile of rubble and my hearing was blunt as if my head was submerged in a pool of water. After a moment, I realized that I couldn't remember anything that had happened beyond standing at my bedroom window. My left leg was bleeding and in pain as I searched the debris and discovered that the explosion had taken my entire family," Gaslov's voice trailed off, the expression on his furrowed face offering more details than his words, "I was by myself. In shock, I stumbled along the perimeter of the chaotic battlefield and as if a great punishment had been placed upon me, I felt unfortunate to have survived."

The investors listened intently to Gaslov's chilling account.

"I felt guilty, growing angry and vengeful at those who had taken my family. During the days, weeks and years that followed, it ate at me so much that it preoccupied me to the point that it became difficult for me to function. I drank to curb my frustration with the endless tormenting tape that played repeatedly in my mind, but it was only a bandage that made matters worse."

Then, life seeped back into the Direktor's aging eyes and assuredness coupled with wisdom returned to his voice, "Remember this, it wasn't until I forgave those who had taken away that which was most important to me, that I could move forward with my life. It was selfishness on my part, but forgiveness was freedom for me. In a long awaited peace, I finally moved forward and began putting my life together. Now, on this soil in this moment of decision, I know why God almighty had spared me from the fate of my family, it was to fulfill his plan for my people.

Early on, when something could have been done to stop it, much of the world had stood by as the Nazi's manufactured their weaponry with immunity, then set out to rape Vrodkutsk, along with the rest of Europe. Then, after the defeat of the Germans, Vrodkutsk was subjected to the harsh and depraved reality of communism. As a result, the people of Vrodkutsk were subjected to the worst kinds of atrocities that anyone could have possibly imagined," Gaslov spoke to the investors in the only way that he knew how, from his heart. "Vrodkutsk is a fledgling country that needs to heal, forgiving the wrongs of the past so it can move forward and I am asking you to be the catalyst that gives these people hope for a better future."

Woodcrest Drive
Dover, Delaware 19904

Karl and Petrova sat on the couch after a visit from Kate Webster and Brock Mattingly.

"You can see that Amanda really likes Brock," said Petrova happily, "she's like a daughter to him."

"And Kate looks happier than I've seen her in some time," observed Karl. "I'm just glad that Brock took that position with SuperPower Automotive," Karl pressed the *on* button to the television remote, "I've been after him to join the company ever since they broke ground on the Vrodkutsk site."

Petrova was obviously pleased, "It looks like the company will provide them with a pretty secure future."

"What's this?" a picture of Governor Oliver prompted Karl to turn the volume up on the television.

"For the first time in Delaware history, a sitting governor is being arraigned on criminal charges." Ron Mathews was making yet another special report from the City of Dover Police Station. "Governor Oliver, his press aide Gil Hickman, Judge Reginald Stortz, Doktor Albert Hoffman, and the Worldwide Oil Corporation were a few of those implicated in the charges by Alan Bean, an aide to Governor Oliver.

If these charges stick there could be some lengthy prison sentences involved according to District Attorney Raymond Lewis and word has it that the District Attorney is building a very convincing case. Reportedly, when Mr. Bean was asked why he came forward at this time he said that his conscience, along with a broken promise, wouldn't allow him to cover-up for the governor any longer.

In yet other news, the U.S. government has just announced that at 2:00 PM Eastern Time a military strike was conducted against a nuclear facility on the island of Badasi. The nuclear plant was believed to be involved in nuclear weapon research and was targeted by cruise missiles that were launched from several attack submarines lying offshore of the island nation. Also, there has been speculation that Badasi's Jonathan Doe may have been killed during the air strike. Stay tuned for further reports."

Karl stood up from the couch, "Well, scratch another ruthless dictator," he said with approval.

"Yes, Jonathan Doe was obsessed with obtaining nuclear weapons," Petrova said turning off the TV. "He tried to get many technicians from Vrodkutsk to work on them. Karl, the world is an imperfect place and we can only try to make it a better place. That's what you have tried to do…make it a better place. If your ideas had not come to light, the nuclear technicians in Vrodkutsk would have been helping countries like Badasi develop their own nuclear weapons.

But since you caught the attention of the people in Vrodkutsk, they've started to become transformed by new ideas. I know these people. I grew up with them and I know that your ideas have helped them see the light and have started to change their economy and life for the better."

Karl looked at Petrova, "Nevertheless, I think that I've had enough excitement. This morning I went to the newsstand in Dover to get a coffee and paper when I happened to run into the assistant district attorney. He said that with everything that has come to light in the investigation, I might have a good case for getting my job back at the Old Statehouse."

Petrova had known that Karl neither sought after, nor needed, the attention that he had been receiving. "What are you going to do?" she asked supportively.

"Well, I'm seriously thinking about it," he said.

"That would allow me to have more time with you," Petrova said smiling, "but what about SuperPower Automotive? You're the Chief Executive Officer, who's going to run the company?"

"I'm a figurehead more than a CEO. I'm sure someone will pick up the reigns, maybe Kim, or Eric, or some hotshot kid with their MBA. All I know is that I've had my time in the spotlight and I'm satisfied with that. I'm ready to go back and become a normal citizen again. Who knows maybe I'll even write a book about what happened, how's *The Delaware Venture* sound to you Mrs. Bontrager? Karl smiled and thought about the events of the past year and Petrova pulled him close in her arms.

-Three months later-
The Old Statehouse,
Dover, Delaware 19903

Karl dressed in jacket and tie sat at his chair. Pictures of Petrova and Kim were positioned neatly beyond his desk calendar and he was searching for a pencil that he had misplaced when there was a knock at the door, "Yes, come in."

"Sorry to disturb you Mr. Bontrager, but I've finished the hallway," a little red faced man stood at the doorway in his olive drab work uniform. It was Lou Swetman. He was lucky to still have a job after word got out about his bowing to political pressure and firing Karl, but Karl insisted that Lou be kept on as a janitor until he had enough time to retire from the state.

"Good job Lou," said Karl appreciatively, "I'd appreciate it if you'd get Senator Fedders office next."

"Yes sir," said Lou obediently, then he began pushing his mop bucket from Karl's office door.

A few minutes later Karl picked up his suit jacket and began walking down the hall, pausing at the receptionist's desk for a moment, "Heather, if anyone calls for me I'm going to meet Mrs. Bontrager for lunch."

Karl was about to exit the building when an impulse urged him to stop and turn around. Standing there in reverence, he looked to the upper gallery of the Old Statehouse and paused; his mind revisiting the many positive experiences that he had as an outcome of the debate. To his satisfaction, he spotted an elementary school teacher touring the upper gallery with her class.

Then, as if preordained for that very moment, powerful beams of midday sunlight refracted about the rooftop cupola's panes of glass and Karl smiled broadly.

The End

978-0-595-38462-4
0-595-38462-5

Printed in the United States
70929LV00004B/354